CORPSE ON THE COB

AN ODELIA GREY MYSTERY

CORPSE ON THE COB

SUE ANN JAFFARIAN

THORNDIKE
CHIVERS

JAFFARIAN SUE ANN

This Large Print edition is published by Thorndike Press, Waterville, Maine, USA and by BBC Audiobooks Ltd, Bath, England.
Thorndike Press, a part of Gale, Cengage Learning.
Copyright © 2010 by Sue Ann Jaffarian.
The moral right of the author has been asserted.

The text of this Large Print edition is unabridged.
Other aspects of the book may vary from the original edition.
Set in 16 pt. Plantin.

LIBRARY OF CONGRESS CATALOGING-IN-PUBLICATION DATA

Jaffarian, Sue Ann, 1952–
    Corpse on the cob : an Odelia Grey mystery / by Sue Ann Jaffarian.
        p. cm. — (Thorndike Press large print mystery)
    ISBN-13: 978-1-4104-2506-5
    ISBN-10: 1-4104-2506-1
    1. Grey, Odelia (Fictitious character)—Fiction. 2. Legal assistants—California—Fiction. 3. Murder—Fiction. 4. Absentee mothers—Fiction. 5. Mothers and daughters—Fiction. 6. Massachusetts—Fiction. 7. Large type books. I. Title.
PS3610.A359C67 2010b
813'.6—dc22   2010005968

BRITISH LIBRARY CATALOGUING-IN-PUBLICATION DATA AVAILABLE
Published in 2010 in the U.S. by arrangement with Midnight Ink, an imprint of Llewellyn Publications, Woodbury, MN 55125–2989 USA, Inc.
Published in 2010 in the U.K. by arrangement with Llewellyn Worldwide Ltd.

U.K. Hardcover: 978 1 408 49136 2 (Chivers Large Print)
U.K. Softcover: 978 1 408 49137 9 (Camden Large Print)

Printed in the United States of America
1 2 3 4 5 6 7 14 13 12 11 10

For my niece Lindsay.
Thanks for introducing me to corn
mazes and for tracking through one by
my side for hours in the heat while I
did my research.

Love,
Aunt Sue

ACKNOWLEDGMENTS

As always, to Whitney Lee, my agent; Diana James, my manager; and to all the good folks at Llewellyn Worldwide/Midnight Ink, especially Bill Krause, Rebecca Zins, Marissa Pederson, and Ellen Dahl.

To the folks who allowed me to pick their talented and expert brains: attorney Mark Hardiman; Felicia Donovan, author of *Cyber Crime Fighters: Tales from the Trenches;* Lee Lofland, author of *Police Procedure & Investigation;* and Officer Brenda Tozloski of the Sunderland Police Department.

Special thanks to the many people I met while researching this book, especially the folks at Mike's Maze in Sunderland, Massachusetts (http://www.mikesmaze.com).

And last, but never least, to my dear friends and family, who are always by my side.

ONE

The dead guy on the ground did not look familiar. The woman crouched over the body did.

I tried to think of something to say to her, but what do you say to someone who walked out of your life thirty-four years ago without so much as a note, leaving worry and speculation of the worst kind in her wake? Not to mention shattering the already shaky self-esteem of an overweight, lonely teenage girl. And, honestly, a part of me always worried about what I would say to my mother, if given the chance. Would I be coldly polite? Weepy? Angry? Sentimental? Accusing? Or would I start off warm and fuzzy and morph into a stumpy Medusa, telling her to stick motherhood where the sun doesn't shine?

Dead body aside, I, Odelia Patience Grey, now had my big chance.

This whole misadventure started three weeks ago in Seal Beach, California, where

e with my paraplegic husband, Greg
ens; a golden retriever named Wainwright; a one-eyed, raggedy-eared cat
named Seamus; and a sweet, mischievous
cat called Muffin. By trade, I'm a corporate
paralegal at the Orange County law firm of
Wallace, Boer, Brown and Yates. It was
shortly after my fiftieth birthday. A pink
plastic pig was involved. In fact, I'm blam-
ing everything on that damn pig. And my
husband. And my father. And not necessarily in that order.

It was a Sunday afternoon. The pig had
just exploded before my eyes. I raised the
hammer in my right hand and delivered
another blow to its head, assuring that it
would never oink at me or anyone else
again. "Die, die, die," softly escaped my lips
as hot tears streamed down my flushed face.

"What in the hell are you doing?"

Ignoring the question, I raised the heavy
wood and rubber mallet and sent it crash-
ing down for a third time. I would have hit
the beast a fourth time, but as soon as I
raised the hammer above my head for the
next assault, it was snatched from my grip.

Whipping my head around, I faced Greg,
who now held the hammer in his hand.
"Give it back," I demanded.

His mouth hung open in undisguised

10

shock. "What in the hell are you doing?" he repeated.

"Killing my birthday present."

Seated on the floor of our kitchen, I was surrounded by carnage. Shards of pink plastic decorated the floor like ill-shaped confetti. Seamus and Muffin had taken refuge under the buffet when the slaughter began. Wainwright had come in with Greg. He was now busy sniffing through the damage, looking for life. He found none.

"What birthday present?" Greg put the hammer on a nearby counter and maneuvered his wheelchair closer to view the deceased. "I don't recall any gifts made of pink plastic."

He was right. The weekend before, our closest friends, Seth and Zee Washington, had thrown me a big fiftieth birthday bash at their home. The pink plastic pig had not been among the many gifts.

I got up from the floor. With much of my anger released, I was as limp and rubbery as a deflated balloon. I disappeared into our bathroom to splash cold water on my face.

"This morning, right after you left to play basketball, I got a call from Gigi," I explained when I returned, a wad of tissues at the ready in my hand.

"Uh-oh." Greg hung his head in frustration. He knew no call from Gigi, my step-mother, would be pleasant.

When I was thirteen, my mother had insisted on a divorce from my father, Horten Grey. Their marriage had been as rocky as the Maine seashore and just as cold and stormy, and I was caught in the middle. Both of my parents had their flaws. My father was sweet but extremely passive, allowing himself to be led around, first by my mother, later by his second wife and her disgusting family. I don't think my mother ever forgave him for not living up to her expectations. My mother, Grace Grey, was delusional, brow beating, and an alcoholic. Both were disappointed by the cards life had dealt them, yet neither seemed to realize they could discard and be dealt more, at least not until much later, when they finally divorced. A few years after the divorce, my mother discarded *me* and moved on to play in a new game.

I still remember the day I came home from high school to discover my mother had moved out — lock, stock, and vodka bottle. There was no note, no forwarding address, not even a prior clue that this might happen. That morning, I had left for school, as usual. She was getting ready for work, as usual. When my day was over, I returned to find her and all her personal items gone. I lived in our apartment alone for nearly a month, wondering if she'd return, half-hoping she wouldn't but not daring to call anyone. I even paid the rent out of my savings account to avoid having to call my dad. On the surface, I was sure she'd be back as soon as her bender was over. In my heart, I knew she wouldn't be. I wasn't a favorite handbag she'd simply forgotten. I was old baggage she didn't want to lug around anymore.

Eventually, of course, I had to call my dad, who was already married to Gigi, a hateful woman with two grown, just-as-hateful children. I went to live with them and moved out almost before the smoke had cleared from the candles on my eighteenth birthday cake.

Between my sixteenth and my fiftieth birthdays, I'd not heard one word from my mother. I didn't even know if she was still alive. My father never spoke of her and wouldn't allow me to discuss her. Until now, Grace Grey was the elephant in the corner of the room that is my life — the always-present yet never-acknowledged boogey-mom.

"And?" Greg encouraged me to continue.

I heaved my shoulders in an exaggerated

sigh. When I started to talk, my tears started again.

"Come here, sweetheart."

Greg rolled over to the sofa. Positioning his wheelchair and locking the wheels, he hoisted himself from the chair and onto our sofa with a strength and grace that always astounded me. Once he was settled, he indicated for me to join him. When I sat down next to him, he wrapped his protective arms around me and pulled me close. I burrowed into the solid warmth of my husband. We sat that way for several minutes — me crying softly, and Greg giving me time to get it out and collect myself.

"I'm sorry I'm so sweaty," he finally said, breaking the silence and referring to the fact that he'd just returned from playing basketball.

I looked up at him. "That's okay. I like you this way." I gave him a weak smile. He smiled back and kissed my forehead.

"So what's up with Gigi?"

"She called me to say she had a birthday present for me and a box of Dad's stuff she'd forgotten to give me the last time we were there." I blew my nose again. "So I went over to the house. She gave them to me. I left."

"Is what you just destroyed the gift?"

"It was a pink plastic pig."

"A piggy bank got you this upset?"

I shook my head from side to side. "No, it wasn't a piggy bank. It was this obnoxious plastic pig that you put in your fridge. Every time you open the door, the pig lets out this horrible snorting noise."

Greg pulled me closer. "Sweetheart, this isn't about an offensive gift, and you know it. You usually take Gigi's insults in stride."

He was right. At just over five feet tall and tipping the scales at two-hundred-plus pounds, I was used to barbs and insults from Gigi and her family about my weight. I had endured them for decades, from the moment my father married Gigi when I was a plump teenager.

"This is about your dad, isn't it?" Greg squeezed me tight, as if his arms could shut out the pain. "It's tough being orphaned, Odelia. Even at your age. Inevitable, but tough."

It was true; my father was gone. He had died almost four months ago. And even though he was elderly and his health was starting to break down, his death had devastated me. One morning, he simply got up and started scrambling himself a couple of eggs. Somewhere between the cooking and getting the plate to the kitchen table, he'd had a heart attack. The doctor told us it'd been fast, leaving no time for anyone to get help.

I pulled away just enough so I could look Greg full in the face.

"But that's just it, Greg. I'm *not* an orphan."

"Your mother is long gone, sweetheart." His voice was soft and gentle. "And she'd be in her late seventies, possibly her eighties."

"Seventy-seven, actually."

"Well, by now, it's quite possible she's dead also."

I shook my head and fought the tears starting to pool again. "She's not dead, Greg. She's alive. I called her today."

"You what?" He stared at me.

I pointed towards the dining room, drawing his attention to a small cardboard box sitting on the table.

"Gigi gave me that today. It contains some of my dad's stuff. Scraps and clippings and small mementos of his life." I took a deep breath. "I went through it when I got home and found an envelope addressed to Dad. It was from my mother. The postmark was more than twenty-five years ago."

"What did the letter say?"

"There was no letter, just the envelope."

I got up from the sofa and retrieved a business-size envelope, yellowed with age, from the box on the table and brought it to Greg. He held it as if it were a snake, disbelief radiating from his eyes like heat waves over asphalt.

"Grace Littlejohn," he read from the return address. Greg looked up. "I can't read the address — it's smudged. But it looks like New Hampshire."

"She's in Massachusetts now — a small town called Holmsbury. I ran a search on her using an online company."

"And you talked to her? What did she say?"

"Nothing but hello." When Greg shot me a curious look, I continued. "I called her. Someone answered the phone, a man. I asked for Grace Littlejohn. When she came on the line and I heard her voice, I knew it was my mother. But I couldn't say anything. I was completely tongue-tied. Can you believe it? So I hung up."

"After all this time, you just hung up?"

"What did you expect me to say, Greg?" My voice rose in frustration as I paced in front of him. " 'Hi, Mommy, can you bake me some cupcakes for school?' " I stopped pacing. "Not that she ever did that anyway."

"It would have been better than nothing,

don't you think?" Greg's voice was also increasing in volume.

We stared at each other, surprised at ourselves. We seldom raised our voices to each other. It told me how much his emotions were feeding off my already near-hysteria. Wainwright, sensing the disturbance between us, trotted over and nudged Greg, looking for reassurance that we were okay. He received a reassuring pat.

"Sweetheart, I'm sorry." Greg toned down his voice like the volume on a radio. "I know this must have been a shock to you today, but if you went to the trouble of looking her up, why not speak with her too?"

Tears rolled down my face again. I was turning into a regular waterworks. "Greg, she left me when I was sixteen, and not once did she try to get in touch with me. Why would she want to hear from me now?"

"Maybe she did try, Odelia. Maybe that's what was in that envelope. She might have written you a letter, and Horten didn't give it to you for some reason."

"The envelope was addressed to my father, not me." I pointed at the envelope in his hands. "Look at it."

He studied the address, then looked up at me. "Odelia, this letter was sent when you were about twenty-five years old and already out on your own. Maybe she wrote to your father asking about you — where you were, what you were doing. It stands to reason she would assume you wouldn't be living with Horten and Gigi at that age."

"If that's true, then why didn't Dad tell me or let me see it?"

Greg held out a hand to me. I took it and squeezed. This man wasn't just my lover and husband, he was my rock.

"I don't know why Horten didn't let you know about this letter. And unfortunately, you can't ask him about it."

No, I couldn't. It was a secret he took to his grave.

"I could always go to a séance and see what he has to say for himself."

Greg chuckled.

"Don't laugh. There's a woman at the office who goes to them regularly."

"Better yet, Odelia, why don't you make that call again. And this time, talk to the woman."

I eyed him as if he were crazy.

"I mean it, sweetheart. What do you have to lose?"

Silently, I ticked off three things inside my head: pride, nerve, sanity.

Two

"Can I come home now?"

"Did you meet your mother yet?"

I twitched my nose, hoping my husband could feel my annoyance through the phone. "No, but I'm in front of her house right now, and no one's home."

"Then you can't come home."

"I'm a grown woman, Greg. I'll come home if I damn well want too."

He laughed. "If that's so, then why are you asking my permission?"

"Smart-ass."

He laughed again, this time with more gusto.

I could picture Greg sitting in his wheelchair behind his big desk at Ocean Breeze Graphics in Huntington Beach — three thousand miles away. Wainwright would be hunkered down on the floor nearby. It was eight fifteen in the morning in California, three hours behind my current time. His pared-down Saturday staff would be there, and the place would be humming with activity and good-natured ribbing. Greg's employees love working for him, and no wonder. He treats them great and, thanks to an inheritance from his grandfather, even offers scholarship assistance for those who choose to attend college while working for him.

But I was still annoyed. After all, he's the one who insisted I travel to Massachusetts to meet my mother. He's the one who'd bought the ticket and used frequent flyer miles to upgrade it to first class. On top of that, he'd arranged for me to stay at a charming country bed-and-breakfast while here. And he'd talked my boss, Michael Steele, obnoxious attorney-at-law, into letting me have a last-minute mini-vacation.

All I had to do was get my fat ass on the plane and travel by rental car from Hartford, Connecticut, to Holmsbury, Massachusetts, the small town where my mother lived. Oh — and place a call to my mother beforehand to let her know I was coming. Which, by the way, I had failed to do. So now I was sitting in a rental car on the Saturday morning of Labor Day weekend on a lovely village road in front of a sweet house that supposedly belonged to my long-lost mother.

Just minutes before I called Greg, I had taken the long walk up the short path to the door of the house and rung the bell. When no one answered, I let out the breath I was holding and hightailed it back to the car, ready to catch a flight back to California.

"Did I tell you," I said into the phone, "that I rented a GPS with the car?"

"And what does this have to do with you facing your mother, Odelia?"

Ignoring his question, I continued down my own path of conversation. "According to this gizmo, the Ben & Jerry's factory is just a short three-hour drive north of here. If I left now, I might make it in time to take a tour."

"Uh-huh. You got a hankering to visit the promised land, do you? Wouldn't it be easier and more time-efficient to go to the grocery store to get your fix?"

"But it could be fun. More fun, though, if you were with me."

I had mixed feelings about Greg not coming with me. Even though he was swamped at work and short-handed while some of his key people were on vacation, he would have traveled with me had I asked him. On one hand, I thought it would be easier to deal with this meeting, or my inability to deal with it, without his cheerful encouragement and pushing. On the other hand, I missed him terribly, including his support and not-so-gentle nagging to just do it. Ever since waking up this morning alone in the big antique canopy bed, without Greg and without our furry four-legged children, I'd been out of sorts. And not just this morning. Ever since discovering my mother's whereabouts, I'd been crankier than usual — something Steele didn't hesitate to point out. Nor had Zee Washington, my best friend, minced words about how helpful and healthy it would be for me to get to the bottom of my mother's disappearance.

"Maybe," Greg suggested, "after you meet Grace, you can take a road trip to Vermont. Kind of like a reward."

A reward. I thought of Wainwright's beloved Snausages. Outside of verbal praise from us, our golden retriever considered Snausages the absolute gold standard in reward treats. When it came to Ben & Jerry's ice cream, I wasn't all that different. I wondered if they gave factory tours at the Del Monte plant where they made Snausages.

I was about to ask Greg about the animals when I noticed, and not for the first time, someone watching me from the house across the street. I could see a face peering out at me from behind frothy curtains framing a window.

"Greg, I'm being watched."

"What?"

"I'm being watched. Someone across the street is watching me from their window." I glanced over at the neighbor's house again, but the face had disappeared.

"Are you sure?"

"Yes, I'm sure. Maybe I should be moving along. I wouldn't want someone to think I was casing the joint for a robbery."

He laughed again.

"Why are you laughing? I wouldn't want them to call the police."

"Well, sweetheart, that wouldn't be a consideration if you'd called Grace first like I'd suggested."

"Are you giving me the old *I told you so* line?"

"I told you so."

"Uh-oh."

"What?" Greg's jocular mood turned serious in a flash.

"Someone just came out of that house and is walking towards me."

With Greg still on the phone, I watched as a white-haired woman left the house across the street and made her way down her driveway towards my car. She was wearing a white tee shirt and pink sweatpants with a gray stripe down each leg. Draped across her shoulders was a matching pink cardigan-style sweatshirt. On her feet were bright white sneakers. In one hand, she held a leash attached to a long-haired rat. As she got closer, I identified the rat as a long-haired miniature dachshund. The dog, its coat the color of stale baloney, marched in double-time at the end of the leash. When the woman got to the street, she picked up the dog.

"It's a little old lady in jogging clothes," I whispered into the phone. "What'll I do?"

"Is she toting a gun or a baseball bat?" I could hear him snickering.

"Just a wiener dog."

He snickered louder. "You're making this up."

"Afraid not. The woman's gotta be in her late seventies."

"Sweetheart, you've stared down the barrels of loaded guns and kept company with serial killers. I doubt if a septuagenarian and a dachshund are going to be much of a threat."

"How do you know? She could smother me with the dog. Did I say it was long-haired?"

As the woman approached my car, I gave

her as warm a smile as I could muster. The cell phone connection was still open — just in case.

"Hello," she said to me, her homey face displaying open curiosity. The dog let out a low growl.

"Hi," I answered, eyeing the animal with suspicion. "How are you today?"

She didn't respond to my question, but instead asked her own. "May I help you?"

"I'm sorry?"

"May I help you, dear?" she asked again. "I've noticed you sitting out here in your car for some time and wondered if you were lost."

If this were Southern California, no elderly woman in her right mind would saunter out to question a stranger hanging about her neighborhood, at least not without firepower or pepper spray. And a tiny dachshund is hardly a pit bull.

The woman was slightly built and would have been considered tall had she not been bent with age. Her face was lined and rosy, and she was wearing a lovely shade of pale pink lipstick. Her hair capped her head like the end of a fluffy white Q-tip. I had no doubt that her home across the street was just as perfectly groomed. Even the dog's coat glistened in the sun.

"Um, I stopped by to see Grace Little-john. But no one appears to be home."

She leaned forward and studied me through thick lenses with pale pink and silver frames. The dog growled more as it drifted closer. I leaned back in my seat. The woman broke into a big smile. "Why, you look just like Grace."

"I do?"

"Spitting image. You must be a relative. Are you a niece or something?"

I hesitated. In my tote bag was a photo of my mother taken when I was a child. She always hated having her picture taken, so I didn't have anything more recent. It was hard to tell from the photo if there was a strong resemblance.

"Yes, something like that." Then I added, "I'm just visiting, but it's a surprise, so I didn't call first."

If Greg was picking up the conversation via the microphone in my earpiece, I had no doubt he was rolling with laughter and mouthing *I told you so.*

"I'm Cynthia Rielley. I've lived across the street from Grace for over thirty years." She picked up one of the dog's paws and waved it at me. "And this is Coco." Coco growled again. "Shh, Coco," the woman commanded in a low voice before turning her attention back to me. "He's so protective of me." She smiled.

I smiled back. "Nice to meet you both. I'm Odelia Gre— Stevens. Mrs. Stevens." I glanced at the Littlejohn house. "I guess I could leave a note on the door and let them know where I'm staying."

"This is Labor Day weekend, dear. Grace won't be back home until very late tonight."

"Did she go out of town?" A hopeful tone crept into my voice.

"Oh, no. Labor Day weekend is when we have the Autumn Fair. Grace always works at the fair."

I remembered the owner of the B & B telling guests something about a local fair this morning over breakfast, but I hadn't been paying close attention. I had been too busy trying to swallow my nerves along with my blueberry pancakes.

"Is that like a county or state fair?"

"Yes, but on a smaller scale. Several of the small towns around here put it on to raise money for various local charities. It started more than ten years ago and grows every year." She straightened her shoulders in pride. "We now draw folks from as far away as Nashua and Boston. Why, there's even a corn maze."

"A corn maze?"

"Yes, every year Old Man Tyler plants a field of corn near the fair just for the maze and runs it every weekend for the whole month of September and most of October. It's very popular."

Awkwardness crept between us. I wasn't quite sure what to do or say. No matter what I'd just said to Mrs. Rielley, I had no intention of writing a note to leave on the door. But clearly she expected me to do something. The dog had stopped growling but was still keeping his big brown eyes fixed on me in case I tried to assault his mistress.

"I know," Mrs. Rielley said with a burst of excitement. "Why don't you drive on over to the fair and find Grace? She'll be so surprised."

You have no idea.

"I don't know. I wouldn't want to disturb her while she's working."

"Nonsense." Mrs. Rielley turned to face down the road in the direction my rental car was pointed. "You just go down this street a piece until you come to a small rotary. Take the second turn off the rotary; that's Old Mill Road. Go straight until Turner Junction. You can't miss it. There's a Dairy Queen and a Dunkin' Donuts on the corner. Turn left and keep going until you see the fair. There should be signs for it

29

along the way."

"Um . . . thank you very much, Mrs. Rielley."

She turned back towards me. "You're quite welcome, Mrs. Stevens. Just check the food booths. Grace is always in charge of things having to do with food."

Like mother, like daughter.

I started up the car, and Mrs. Rielley stepped back. Coco looked disappointed that I hadn't given him reason to sink his teeth into me.

"Maybe we'll see you there." She gave me a small wave goodbye. "My husband and I are going tonight. They always have country music on Saturday night, right after the fireworks."

"Did you hear that?" I said to Greg as soon as I was several blocks away from Mrs. Rielley.

Greg was laughing. "I even heard the dog growl. I hope you're heading to the fair."

"Are you nuts? I can't meet her in a public place. What if she makes a scene? What if she faints? Has a heart attack?"

"Which could have been avoided had you just made that call."

"Greg, are you going to nag me forever about this?"

"Nope, just until it stops being fun." He

30

paused. "I really do think you should go to the fair, sweetheart. Think about it. You could check your mother out from a distance before actually meeting her."

As if on autopilot, the car was following the directions given to me by Cynthia Rielley. I was about a mile beyond the rotary and could see the Dunkin' Donuts sign in the distance.

"I'm heading towards the fair now, honey. I'm not happy about it, but I can't seem to help myself."

"You're doing the right thing, Odelia, and I'm proud of you."

"Yeah, yeah, yeah."

He laughed.

"By the way, Greg, I need you to do me a favor."

"Anything, sweetheart."

"The next time you get the urge to buy me a first-class air ticket, could you make it to Bermuda or Hawaii?"

"I'll see what I can do." He laughed again.

I was glad he was so amused, because I wasn't. I was serious.

"I'll let you get back to your driving," he told me with enough reluctance in his voice to make me feel sad and tingly at the same time. "Call me in a few hours with a progress report. And please find out what a

31

corn maze is. I'm dying to know."

He gave me a sloppy kiss over the phone, and I returned it.

Well before I actually reached the fair, I started seeing cars parked along both sides of the road. I wondered if I should stop and park myself, but I didn't know how much farther the fairgrounds would be. I decided to keep driving, locate my destination, and then decide where best to park. A bit down the road, I saw a sign touting *AUTUMN FAIR PARKING $3*. Obviously, the folks parked alongside the road thought the hike was better than paying $3. They should see our parking back home, where lots charge $3-plus per fifteen-minute increments or $25 a day.

The parking lot for the fair was a huge, uneven section of field. I pulled in and paid my $3 to a pimply faced kid wearing an orange reflective vest over a tee shirt and scruffy jeans. Another kid, dressed the same, directed me to an open parking spot between a Ford pickup truck and a Dodge minivan.

At first glance, the Autumn Fair looked like any country fair. Not as large as a county or state fair, but much larger than I'd expected. Booths and the usual cheap carnival rides were set up across the street in the large adjoining parking lots of a farm machinery retailer, a country market, and a Veterans of Foreign Wars post.

The field used for parking seemed to be part of a large farm. There was a huge barn and matching house on the far edge of the field. The entire area was surrounded by fields occupied with various crops. A short dirt road led from the parking area away from the fair to another cleared spot surrounded by a low wooden fence. Beyond that fence was a large corn field. Within the fenced area were stacks of pumpkins, wagons and hay, a couple of concession booths, and picnic tables. Newly arrived visitors were heading in both directions, towards the fair and down towards the corn field, though most headed towards the fair. It didn't take a genius to know that this was the corn maze, especially since there was a painted sign on the edge of the field with CORN MAZE AND HAY RIDES emblazoned across it in red letters that were nearly four feet tall.

As I got out of the car, I was thankful I had dressed casually and worn good, sensible walking shoes. Back at the Maple Tree Bed and Breakfast, I'd tried on a couple of outfits this morning, not sure which I should wear when meeting my mother for the first time in over thirty years. I had only packed enough clothing for four or five days. Had I been home instead of on the road, I was sure half my closet would have been strewn across our bedroom. At first, I had opted for a cute summer dress and medium-heeled wedge sandals. The weather when I'd arrived yesterday had been nearly eighty degrees with high humidity, but the hostess of the B & B advised everyone this morning that they expected lower temperatures today with rain later. That tidbit of information caught my attention. So before leaving, I'd scooted back to my room to change into khaki pants, sneakers, and a light green, short-sleeved sweater. I also made sure I took along my lightweight hooded jacket. Looking at the drifting clouds above me and the uneven ground below me, I was glad I'd changed.

Screwing up my courage, I walked across the road and headed into the hubbub of the fair. It was crowded with people of all ages, including countless families towing several children and pushing strollers. I stood still a moment, surveying the layout. The rides were all clustered in an area of the farm machinery parking lot. That's where many of the young families appeared to be headed. Mrs. Rielley had said Grace Littlejohn worked with the food booths, so I immediately checked the ride area off my list.

Following my nose, I headed in the direction of the VFW lot, where I discovered the usual fair-type food booths, along with displays of homemade canned and baked goods for sale. Most of the booth food looked and smelled greasy — and delicious. Fair and carnival food should be in a category all by itself, like the sixth basic food group. It's not the type of stuff you'd eat in day-to-day life. I mean, fried dough, deep-fried Snickers, and corn dogs are hardly healthy eating, but it's fun to go to these events once in a while and eat the junk you'd normally eschew.

And I was getting hungry.

I am an emotional eater, meaning that when the going gets tough, the not-so-tough pick up a knife and fork. And considering that I was about to come face-to-face with my missing-link mother and all the emotions attendant to that, it was quite possible I could put this shindig into a food drought. But, I reasoned, perusing the food booths would also be a sly way of looking for her.

If Grace Littlejohn was in charge of the food booths, she could be working at any of them or flitting from one to another, making sure they were all running smoothly.

Trying to look like any casual Saturday fair-goer, I picked my way through the crowds at each booth and checked out the people cooking and serving at each one.

Most of the food booths were staffed by middle-aged and older women, with the occasional man or teen helping. Most of the women were dressed in slacks and short-sleeved or sleeveless shirts with colorful print aprons. None of them had name tags, which would have been helpful.

I tried to dig into my brain for my last mental image of my mother. As I recall, she was a bit taller than me and about sixty to seventy pounds lighter. Her hair was also similar to mine, a medium brown, but her eyes were different. I had green eyes, like my father. My mother's eyes were brown. But thirty years could have shortened her and added pounds. And hair color was always a wild card. It could be white, gray, or dyed any number of colors by now. I would just have to scrutinize all faces within a certain age group and hope Mrs. Rielley was right, that I *did* look like Grace Little-john. Surely I'd be able to recognize my own face in a crowd.

THREE

Later, when the police questioned all of us
who were in the maze, I felt like I was retell-
ing a dream. The whole thing was a hazy
occurrence stuck on replay in my brain. I
was in the maze, bumping through the
closely planted rows over a dirt path, looking for clues to the riddle that was part of
the maze's game. The clues were puzzle stations set up in many of the tiny clearings
and along larger aisles. If you solved the
puzzle, it gave you a clue to plug into the
riddle sheet they gave you when you entered
the maze. If you got them all correct, you
won a pumpkin. I didn't care about the
pumpkin, but I do like puzzles and was
enjoying the novelty of my first corn maze.
It also kept my brain from being trapped in
a neurotic spooling loop about my mother.

When I didn't locate Grace Littlejohn
among the food booths, I'd decided to
check out the maze before the clouds over-

head did more than threaten — and before I ate three or four more deep-fried Twinkies. One of the greasy, sweet, and yummy concoctions had been enough. Returning to my car, I stashed my bulky bag in the trunk and walked down to the corn maze. After taking in the maze, I figured I would do another turn through the food section, providing I hadn't successfully talked myself out of it.

When I first entered the maze, an attendant gave me the riddle sheet and a tall, skinny pole with a stiff numbered pennant attached to the top. The teenage girl who got me started explained that the flag helped control how many people were in the maze at one time and also served to locate folks who might get lost. If I got lost or tired and wanted someone to help me out of the maze, the pretty, freckle-faced girl advised with a toothy smile, all I had to do was raise the flag and start waving it above the corn. A spotter posted on a wooden tower just above the field would see it and send help. If the low number on my flag was any indication, the maze wasn't very busy yet.

As I explained to the police, I was stopped in a small cleared circle, trying to solve one of the puzzles, when I heard screams nearby.

As quickly as possible, I dashed through the maze, taking a zigzag path towards the noise. I wasn't the first to arrive. Ahead of me was a woman with a boy and a young couple. I'd met the couple at breakfast that morning at the B & B. Their names were Ollie and Abby. Like me, they were from California. The two of them were taking an uncharted road trip through New England.

Ollie was tall and slim. He wore wire-frame glasses, khaki shorts, and a *Heroes* tee shirt. Abby was shorter but just as slim. She was dressed in denim shorts and a bright blue tee shirt. On her head was a UCLA cap with her long brown hair pulled through the back. She was burrowed into Ollie's side, crying, as he put a call through to 911 on his cell phone.

The woman with the boy had been the one who'd screamed. And she was still screaming. The boy, who looked to be around twelve years old, resembled a startled meercat as he stood at attention and stared with wide eyes into a small patch of crushed cornstalks. It was here, among flattened cornstalks, that a body lay on its back with a woman hovering over it.

I turned the kid away from the macabre scene. "Here," I said, thrusting my flagpole into his hands, "lift this up and wave it around really fast. That will bring help." After a slight hesitation, he grabbed the pole and did as I asked, though he seemed listless about the task.

I turned to the woman. "This your son?" She was white as a sheet.

"Nephew. I have to get him out of here." Her voice rose with each word into a building shriek.

"Help should be here soon," I told her, trying to calm her down.

Indeed, people were heading towards us. The corn bordering the aisle gave way to the crush of a dozen looky-loos, all with their own flags. The stalks of corn bent with a loud rustling and cracking as the arteries of the maze filled with people pushing forward to get a gander at what was causing the fuss.

The maze had opened at noon. The girl at the entrance had said people usually visited the maze after they took in the fair, leaving the earlier hours less crowded. By late afternoon, she'd said, there would be people waiting for their turns through the field. Considering there was a corpse in the corn, I was very glad the maze was sparsely populated. I turned from the crowd and faced the problem at hand.

The murder weapon was obvious. A flag-pole, broken in half, had skewered the man like a hunk of shish kebob. A bright red flag bearing the number one was stuck into his chest and stood straight up as if heralding the first hole on a golf course. Kneeling beside the man was an elderly woman. It didn't take me long to place where I'd last seen her. As soon as recognition set in, my knees wobbled and the deep-fried Twinkie and corn dog in my gut did synchronized flip-flops.

I moved closer.

My eyes bugged out of my head as my dry mouth tried to wrap itself around my next word, a word as uncomfortable as chewing nails. "Mom?"

Even above the pandemonium, the woman heard my voice. She looked up. When she did, it was her turn to go bug-eyed and pale. She stared at me as if I were a ghost, totally forgetting that a dead man was stretched out in front of her, and his blood was on her hands. Forgetting, too, that we were sur-rounded by acres of tall, claustrophobic corn on a humid September day in rural Massachusetts. My long-lost mother looked at me as if I were something from another world — something fearful that had come to snatch her soul.

Maybe I was.

And maybe being a corpse magnet is genetic.

Ollie stepped forward with caution and checked the speared body for life. After placing his hand against the victim's neck, he shook his head slowly at the small crowd and returned to Abby's side. She leaned once again into his embrace and turned her head away from the scene.

Although she'd made no move towards Ollie as he checked the body, no one approached my mother. Unsure of whether or not she was the killer or just someone who had happened upon the body amongst the corn, everyone played it safe. Even I didn't move any closer than where I was at the front of the pack, but my inertia wasn't out of fear of harm, it was out of shock. I had planned on meeting my mother quietly, hoping to stem the surprise to both of us with some dignity.

Well, that ship had sailed.

I bit the inside of my lower lip. Greg was right: I should have called ahead.

A siren could be heard in the distance, its whine gaining in intensity like a hurricane hitting land as it got closer to the farm. Then it stopped short, like a voice cut off in mid-sentence. Soon authorities pushed through the crowd, ordering people to make room.

"Mom?"

This time, the word didn't come from me.

FOUR

"Greg, are you sitting down?"

"I'm *always* sitting down." He laughed.

I was back in my room at the Maple Tree Bed and Breakfast, sitting in a comfortable reading chair in a corner by an open window. There were two chairs, perfect for a little quiet time for a visiting couple.

From my second-story room, I had a lovely view of a meadow bisected by a meandering country road. Lining the road and dotting the landscape were beautiful trees, their green leaves tinged with red, orange, and gold. In a few weeks, they would be ablaze with full-blown fall colors. I had been sitting there quite a while, cell phone in hand, dreading making the call I knew I had to make. The sooner the better, I told myself. Like yanking a Band-Aid off a boo-boo, it would be unpleasant but unavoidable, so just get on with it.

It had been a few hours since I'd found

my mother perched over a dead body in the corn maze. Once the authorities arrived, we'd been herded out of the maze and into an area containing a half dozen or so picnic tables. As soon as other officers arrived, we were efficiently divided up and our statements taken. Because we were the first to stumble across the murder scene, they held me, along with the couple from California and the young woman and her nephew, the longest.

The picnic tables were under a tent, and good thing. Halfway through giving my statement for the second time, it started to rain. It wasn't a cool, refreshing rain, but a short shower that only succeeded in making everything wet and the air thicker and stickier. I wasn't used to this type of humidity. My clothing stuck to me, and my hair was limp and lifeless. Between the cloying air and the stress of seeing my mother, not to mention a dead man, I felt like I was breathing inside a balloon. The young officer taking my statement noticed my distress and brought me a cool drink.

Besides the body, Grace Littlejohn was the last one brought out of the maze. Guiding her was the man who'd called her Mom. He was tall, slim, and blond, probably in his mid-thirties. He wore a police uniform.

While in the maze, I'd looked him over and spotted a name tag that read Littlejohn.

My mother was thicker in build than I remembered. Her hair was white, worn short with a tight perm. She was dressed in navy blue slacks and a pale green tee shirt embroidered with small blue flowers. Blood stained the front of her shirt.

A couple of news trucks had appeared on the scene. Not a swarm like I was used to seeing in California, but enough to let me know that the murder was huge local news. Two reporters with microphones shouted questions at my mother and the cop as they passed. Officer Littlejohn whispered something into my mother's ear. She shifted her head down, away from the news cameras and reporters, as she was taken from the maze directly to a waiting police car. She was not handcuffed. Along the way, she passed those of us being questioned at the picnic tables. Only when she was near me did she look up. Her eyes latched onto my own and held, but she made no move to initiate further contact. I was sure she knew who I was, but circumstances were hardly conducive to a family reunion.

A few steps behind my mother was another cop escorting a young man. He was cuffed. He was tall and lanky and looked like he was in his late teens or early twenties. He wore the same shirts as the other kids who worked the maze — tee shirts printed with the farm name. His head lolled on his long neck and he displayed a goofy grin as he scuffled to another waiting police car. I didn't recall seeing him before, either in the maze or before I entered it. But being cuffed as he was made me think he was a suspect in the killing.

"What's up, sweetheart? Didn't the meeting go well?"

I struggled to find the right words to say. Greg was going to hit the roof when he found out I'd stumbled upon another body.

"Oh, don't tell me," he continued, his voice sounding disappointed. "Grace Littlejohn isn't your mother after all. The trip was just a wild goose chase."

I wish.

I cleared my throat. "No, Grace Littlejohn is definitely my mother. I recognized her right away."

"Did you speak with her?"

"Yes." One word constitutes speaking, doesn't it? I mean, he didn't ask me to quantify my speech.

When I paused again, Greg cut to the chase. "Just spill it, Odelia. I know you too well. Whenever you have something unsavory to say, you either babble uncontrollably about nothing or clam up. There's no middle of the road with you. Just tell me what happened."

"Okay, Greg, here's the thing."

I took a deep breath of humid New England air through the open window. It smelled fresh and earthy.

"I did find my mother. I did speak to her, and she saw and heard me. She even recognized me."

"And what did she say?"

"Um, nothing. It was an inconvenient time for her."

"Quit stalling, Odelia. You know it drives me nuts."

"Okay." I took another deep breath and shut my eyes tight, as if I were heading into a tunnel on a scary amusement ride. "At the time I found her, she was hovering over a . . . um . . . a . . ." I couldn't finish the sentence.

After a very long stretch of silence, Greg started to talk in a steady, firm voice — the voice he uses when he's desperately fighting to maintain control. "Odelia Grey Stevens, please tell me the next words you're about to say are not *dead body*."

I said nothing.

"Damn it, Odelia. If this is a joke, I am

not amused."

"It's no joke, Greg." He wasn't the only one getting hot under the collar. "And don't get mad at me. It's not like I arranged the whole situation just to annoy you. Believe me, if I'd known this was going to happen, I'd have stayed in California. In fact, it wasn't even my idea to come here in the first place, was it?" I took a deep breath. "And don't you even dare bring up the fact that I should've called first."

There was another long pause while the two of us retired to our respective emotional corners. Greg spoke first.

"Tell me what happened. And don't spare the details."

I brought Greg up to speed on everything, including the fact that someone else, one of the police officers, had called Grace Little-john *Mom.*

"Where are you now?"

"At the B & B."

"Why does this keep happening to you, Odelia?"

"Wish I knew. Maybe it's some curse we can have exorcised when I get home."

We fell into another uncomfortable silence, and once again Greg was the one to speak first.

"I want you on a plane home as soon as

possible, Odelia. I don't want you mixed up in anything where I can't protect you."

"I'm not mixed up in anything, Greg. But I do need to make sure my mother is all right. Now that I've found her, it hardly seems right to just dump everything and run home, especially since she knows I'm here."

"This morning you were begging to come home."

"This morning I hadn't seen my mother bent over a body with blood on her hands."

"Do you think she killed him?"

I was about to say I didn't know but upgraded it after a quick spin through my brain. "No, I don't. At least not on her own. Since I don't know my mother very well, I can't speak for her mindset, but I doubt an elderly woman could have overpowered and killed a man that way. He wasn't young, but he wasn't old either. It took strength to do that. Then there's also the guy they took away in cuffs. He seems to be the most likely candidate."

"So you think Grace just stumbled across the body? Hmm, maybe it's a family trait." His sarcasm was crystal clear.

"Maybe. Except one thing *is* bothering me. My mother was supposed to be managing the food booths across the street from

50

the corn field. It was lunchtime, and the food booths were busy. What was she doing wandering the maze when she was needed at the booths?"

"You're getting involved, Odelia. Just put your brain in park and get your backside on a plane home. Let your brother handle this."

My brother? Like a karate kick to my head, the implications of that officer calling Grace Littlejohn *Mom* hit me. If he was her son, then I had a brother — a brother I knew nothing about. Did he know about me?

"I can't, Greg. Not now. Please understand. What if it had been your mother?"

Greg let out a sharp bark of a laugh. "You really think my mother would even go into a corn field?"

Greg's mother, Renee Stevens, was the picture of gracious living. Lovely, relaxed, and always a lady, she never had a hair out of place, not even during harried holiday dinners. Greg's father, Ronald, doted on her, as did her three children. But she also had a core of steel and a generous heart that I'd seen in few others. Renee had been her son's biggest champion and strongest advocate following the tragic accident that had put him in a wheelchair when he was just thirteen. And it had been Renee who'd drummed into Greg's head that he could

51

do and be anything he wanted in life, wheelchair or no wheelchair.

Renee Stevens would never hike through a corn field or tackle a corn maze by choice, but put a loved one in trouble in the middle of it and she would take a machete to every stalk until she reached them. I loved my mother-in-law to pieces.

"Forget the corn maze, Greg. But if your mother were in trouble, wouldn't you want to help?"

"Of course I would, but when *you* help, you damn near get yourself killed." He paused long enough for me to almost hear the wheels grinding in that handsome head of his. "Okay, Odelia, if you won't come home, then I'm coming out there."

"There's no need, Greg. And you're so busy this weekend at the shop." Through the phone, I heard the clickety-clack of a keyboard being punched.

"There's a nonstop redeye into Boston. I can take care of work and then grab that."

"No, Greg. I'm fine." But he wasn't listening.

"Not as convenient as Hartford, but at least it's nonstop."

"Don't come, Greg."

"Could you find your way to Logan Airport?"

"I can find my way anywhere except out of this loopy conversation."

Silence on the other end.

"There is no need for you to come here, Greg. I'm going to see my mother, check in with my newfound brother, and see what's going on. I'll be back in California Monday night, as planned."

There were several deep sighs on the other end. I knew that sound. It was the sound of surrender. The sound of Greg understanding that I wasn't going to budge on the topic.

"Okay," he finally said, "stay if you like. Just be on that plane heading home on Monday and call me regularly. And let the police handle the murder investigation. Just meet and visit with your mother. Make sure she's okay, but that's it. And if you get the urge to come home early, give in to it. You understand?"

It was agreed that I would continue with my plan to meet my mother. Since I also wanted to meet Officer Littlejohn, I could kill two birds with one stone and also find out about her involvement in the murder. But, I assured Greg, that would be it. I'd always wanted a bigger family, body or no body gumming up the works. He understood that.

"You know, sweetheart," he said, just as we were saying goodbye, "I'm wishing right now you'd made that trek to the Ben & Jerry's factory."

I laughed. Greg didn't.

After the call, I took a quick shower and put on fresh clothes — jeans and a simple white camp shirt. My plan was to head over to the police station. It was late afternoon. By now, my mother would either be in a cell or released after being questioned. I was hoping to speak with Officer Littlejohn. I didn't care if he knew about me or not; I was going to make myself known.

The B & B kept a small guest pantry just off the kitchen. There they had hot coffee, as well as bottled water, cookies, and fresh fruit for their lodgers. It had been hours since I'd eaten that greasy fair food, and I needed something healthy. I grabbed a bottle of water and a banana to stave off my hunger until after my visit to the police. Just as I was leaving, I ran into the young couple from California as they were coming in. They stopped me.

"Wow," said Abby. "Can you believe this? I mean, in LA maybe, but here?" She removed her ball cap and shook out her long brown hair. Her face was pale with fatigue.

"We just came back from the police station," said Ollie. "By the way, I'm Oliver Grigsby, and this is my fiancée, Abigail Wong. I don't believe we were properly introduced at breakfast this morning." I gave them my name, and we shook hands.

"You've been there, at the police station, all this time?" I asked, surprised.

He shook his head. "Not all of it. Several news people were hounding us at the farm, so we just took off. We ended up driving around, finally stopping at this little diner for a late lunch."

"Not that we had much of an appetite," Abby added.

"That's for sure." Ollie put a protective arm around Abby. "We were on our way back here when the police called us on my cell and asked us to stop by the station. This time we were questioned by detectives from some state-level unit — Sea Pac or something like that. Pretty much the same questions we were asked back at the maze."

"You weren't asked anything new?"

Abby and Ollie looked at each other several moments before answering.

"Actually," Abby finally answered, looking like she'd rather skip the information, "right before we left, the chief of police asked to see us in private."

"In private? That's rather odd, isn't it, considering a state agency is now involved?"

Again, the couple exchanged glances before Abby continued. "Chief Littlejohn asked us specifically about you."

FIVE

Following the directions Ollie gave me, I found the police station that served the two tiny neighboring towns of Holmsbury and Saxton. It was located in a large two-story white house with green shutters, situated on a spacious lot bordered in the back by woods. In the front yard stood a majestic maple just starting to put on its colorful fall coat. A porch with several empty rocking chairs stretched across the front, with a wide set of steps leading up to the front door. Guarding the steps and each corner of the porch were thick, round columns. At one end of the porch, a handicap ramp had been added. Had it not been for the large sign at the end of the drive and scattered news personnel hovering about like vultures waiting for scraps, I would have thought it was the home of someone's elderly aunt. Much of the side yard had been paved over to create a large parking lot. Towards the back of the house, I spotted a couple of police vehicles parked near a back entrance. The original back door had been replaced with a wide commercial glass door.

Ollie and Abby had been questioned privately by Chief Littlejohn about me. He was no doubt the man I'd seen with my mother back at the maze, although he seemed young to be a chief of police. When they told him they'd just met me that morning, he'd been gruff and disbelieving, saying it was just too coincidental that the people who first stumbled upon the body in the maze were all from California and staying at the same bed-and-breakfast. He didn't buy their ignorance of me one bit. He'd also told them that he intended to question me thoroughly. My gut told me he knew who I was. Whether or not he knew before our mother was found crouching over a dead body was another matter, but dollars to donuts, he knew now.

Getting out of the car, I looked up at the big converted house and aimed a defiant chin in its direction. *Well, here I am, little brother. And you didn't even have to ask.*

As I walked up to the front entrance, a reporter stepped in front of me. It was a young woman, her blond hair styled in a half up-do. She introduced herself as being from a news station in Boston and flashed credentials at me. "I remember seeing you at the corn maze today," she said to me. "Can you tell us anything about the murder?"

The other news people crowded around, sensing a fresh tidbit.

When I said nothing, she continued. "Did you know the victim?"

"No, I didn't." I side-stepped to go around her and started up the steps.

"How about the suspect, Mrs. Littlejohn?"

I stopped dead in my tracks halfway up the steps but didn't turn around. In that split second, a million thoughts bombarded my brain like a meteor shower. I swallowed back the thought of my mother, long-lost or not, being a murder suspect and continued up the stairs, ignoring the reporter.

The interior of the large house had been renovated to suit the needs of a small and not-so-busy country police department. The front door opened onto a large foyer. To the left was a wide, curved staircase with a thick banister — the kind that made me wonder how many kids had traveled butt-first down it before this place became a police station. To the right of the staircase was a long hallway with a closed door at the end and a couple along the length of it. A large doorway stood immediately to the left of the entrance and was closed by two sliding wooden doors. To the right was a large opening leading to what was probably the original living room. The floors and staircase were covered with scuffed hardwood.

I stepped to my right into the large open area. The room had been transformed into a waiting room with a built-in counter, behind which sat a woman with long auburn hair held back from her face with a black plastic headband. She was of average size and shape and appeared to be fortyish. Her black-rimmed glasses were low on her nose, and she had a small mole on the chin of her plain face. She didn't wear a uniform, so I figured she was a civilian employee. A nameplate on the counter identified her as Joan Cummings.

There were several plastic chairs positioned around the room, along with a beat-up coffee table holding out-of-date magazines. No one was in the waiting area. From somewhere in the back, the hum of voices drifted into the waiting area, sprinkled every now and then with low laughter.

"Reporters have to remain outside," the woman said, glancing at me.

"I'm not a reporter." I stepped in front of

the counter. "I'd like to see Chief Little-john."

She gave me her attention. "The chief is quite busy at the moment. Perhaps someone else can help you. Is this an emergency?" Her tone was heavy and damp, like the weather.

"My name is Odelia Grey. I was at the corn maze earlier."

Placing an index finger on the bridge of her glasses, she scooted them up her nose and studied me with surprise. "That was fast."

"Excuse me?"

"I just left you a voice mail asking you to come in or call. Isn't that why you're here?"

Now it was my turn to be surprised. Before I said anything more, I dug around in my tote bag and retrieved my cell phone. It had fallen out of the pocket on the inside of the bag to the bottom, under all my junk. Sure enough, I had fresh voice mail.

"Sorry," I said to her, holding up my phone. "I never heard the ring. Did Chief Littlejohn want to see me?"

"Not that I know of. The detectives from CPAC asked me to call you to set up a time for you to come in. They're re-questioning some of the witnesses from today."

"What's CPAC?"

"Crime Prevention and Control Unit. It's part of the Massachusetts State Police."

"Oh."

"They handle major crimes like homicides."

"So it wasn't Chief Littlejohn who asked to see me?"

"No, Ms. Grey. The chief isn't involved with the case. CPAC is handling it."

"Oh."

I took a second to process the information. If Chief Littlejohn's mother was a suspect, it made sense for him not to be involved with the investigation — doubly so if the state police handled homicides as a rule. Yet Ollie and Abby had definitely said Littlejohn wanted to see me.

I gave the woman behind the counter a weak smile. "Well, I guess it doesn't matter who wants to see me. I'm here now."

"Unfortunately, the detectives were just called back to the farm. Why don't you take a seat? I'll see when they expect to return."

While I took a seat in one of the plastic chairs, Joan Cummings made a call. A minute later, she called me back to the counter.

"Looks like they're going to be a while. Could you come back tomorrow morning?"

"Sure. You have my cell number and, as I

told the police who questioned me earlier, I'm staying at the Maple Tree B & B in Saxton. I'm planning on being in the area until Monday."

"Fine, then. We'll call you about setting up a time. Keep your cell phone close."

"Why do they want to see me? I gave my statement twice today at the scene."

"I just make the calls, Ms. Grey. If they want to see you again, then they want to see you again. It is a murder investigation, after all."

Just as I was about to leave, I had a thought. I turned back to the counter. "Excuse me, but the old woman at the corn maze — the one who was found with the body — is she a suspect? Is she being held in custody?"

"It's not my place to tell you that, Ms. Grey."

Undeterred, I pressed. "What about the young man they took away? Is he the killer?"

"He most certainly is not!"

The ferocity of her reply made me take two steps back. Sensing her impropriety, she gathered herself back into her professional mode.

"The young man was a misunderstanding," she explained in a rigid but calmer voice. "He's been released."

"I'm sorry if I offended you. I was just curious."

"Only natural. You can ask the detectives any questions you have, Ms. Grey, when you see them. Or read about it in the newspaper. Have a good day."

Her words were as perfunctory and un-emotional as a canned voice mail recording from the IRS. Boy, nothing like being thoroughly dismissed. Problem was, I wasn't ready to be dismissed. I'd just come three thousand miles to surprise my missing mother, only to find her covered in the blood of a dead man. On top of that, I was starving. Right now was not the time for some bureaucrat to screw with me.

Instead of leaving, I stood in front of Joan Cummings until she was forced to look up at me. "Yes?"

"Chief Littlejohn — I really need to see him." If anyone knew where my mother was, it would be the chief.

Ms. Cummings gave off a deep sigh. "I told you, he's not here."

"Can you call him? It's rather urgent."

"What is it about?"

"His mother."

She gave me a weary look. "As I said, Chief Littlejohn is not handling the matter. Anything you need to say about the case

64

should be said to the CPAC detectives."

"May I leave him a message, then? Is that allowed?"

Another deep sigh. "Well, what is it?" She poised a pen over a phone message pad.

"Tell him his sister wants to speak with him. I believe you already have my number."

That got her attention. She stared open-mouthed at me, then shook it off and jotted down the message.

I left the station and waded through the small gathering of vigilant journalists to my car, not giving them so much as a cough along the way. Not being knowledgeable about the area, I decided to drive around and check things out. There had to be a central town district in either Holmsbury or Saxton where I could find a restaurant and get an early dinner. Then I remembered the GPS. Once it was powered up, I punched in a query for restaurants in the area. Several fast food chains came up, along with some local places, one of which was a seafood restaurant recommended by the people at the B & B. It was about eight miles away in yet another small town. I poked the go button on the gizmo and headed the rental car in that direction.

Driving in rural Massachusetts is nothing like driving in Southern California. Back home, cities blended one into the other with blurred boundaries, the houses, not unlike office cubicles, stacked side by side along miles of straight paved roads and sidewalks.

Here in the Holmsbury/Saxton area, most roads were two-lane and curved, following the flow of the natural landscape. Houses were far apart and often set back from the road, with groves of trees acting as natural fences. In the more populated areas, like where my mother lived, the houses were closer together but still distanced enough to maintain a sense of privacy and individuality.

I was driving along a road that hugged the bank of a small river when a car came up fast behind me. Traffic on this road had been very light, and right now there were only two cars to be seen — mine and this one. When it got near to me, it slowed down, falling into pace behind me. Glancing into my rear-view mirror, I noted just one person in the vehicle. While I continued driving, I pulled slightly to the right to allow room for the car to pass me on the narrow road. It made no move to go around. I sped up a bit to put distance between us. The other car stayed at the prior speed, allowing me to get farther ahead of it. I gave a sigh of relief. Just another driver going someplace on a Saturday afternoon. Still, I kept my cell phone handy.

I guided my vehicle around another bend in the road. Here the highway left the riverbank and cut through a grove of mature trees, their limbs of fall colors reaching out from either side to form a patchwork canopy. Lost in bucolic peace, I had almost forgotten about the car behind me — until a flashing colored light reminded me it was there.

I had no clue why I was being stopped, but I dutifully pulled over to the right, onto a flat patch of dirt. The other car pulled in behind me. It was a dark, nondescript sedan without a color bar on the roof, but the flashing light on the dashboard left no mistake in my mind that it was an official vehicle. Nor did the uniform on the man who got out of the car and headed my way. The officer in the uniform was of average height and a bit on the stocky side. He had graying hair and a full face. He appeared to be in his fifties. Maybe the detectives had tried to reach me again, but when I didn't respond, they had sent someone out to find me. I glanced down at my cell phone, but there had been no further missed calls. Maybe I was going too fast. I hadn't seen a posted speed limit for quite a while, and I'd heard about country speed traps.

"License and registration, please," the officer asked as soon as he reached my window.

I grabbed my wallet from my purse, pulled out my California driver's license, and handed it to him.

"The car's a rental, but I have the rental contract in the glove box if you'd like to see it."

"You're quite a ways from home, aren't you, Ms. Grey? What's the purpose of your visit here?"

"Just a long weekend to visit relatives."

"Like your mother, perhaps?"

The officer wasn't bent towards my window, so I couldn't see his face or badge. I leaned forward in my seat and stuck my head slightly out the window. He removed his sunglasses. We stared at each other, eyeball to eyeball, until my eyes wandered to the name tag over his pocket: *LITTLEJOHN*.

Okay, color me confused. The name tag said Littlejohn, but this was not the man I saw leading my mother out of the corn maze. He was much older than the other officer and thicker in build. Maybe this was Officer Littlejohn's father, which meant this could be my mother's husband — my stepfather. But that didn't make sense either. This man had to be about twenty years younger than my mother. That wouldn't be unheard of, exactly; after all, Greg is ten years younger than I am. But it seemed unlikely. My brain was on overload. I needed time and privacy to work it all out, to make sense of everything. Then again, maybe this was a cousin or uncle, or a relation like that. Slowly, one bit of information did make sense.

I stuck my right hand out the window towards the cop. "Chief Littlejohn, I presume?"

"You presume correct." Instead of shaking my hand, he handed me back my license. "We need to talk, Odelia. Where are you heading?"

I glanced at the GPS. "Um, to a place called the Blue Lobster."

"Good choice. Follow me, I know a short-cut." He turned to head back to his car.

In a slight panic, I called out my window, "You're coming to dinner with me?"

Chief Littlejohn turned back towards my car. This time he bent at the waist to get down closer to my level. He'd put his sunglasses back on and his mouth was a tight, thin line. "You got a problem with that?"

"Uh . . ."

After a long, tense moment, he broke into

a half smile. "Is there a law against a big brother taking his long-lost sister out to dinner?"

Six

The Blue Lobster was somewhere between a shack and a real restaurant. Located on a large corner lot seemingly out in the middle of nowhere, it shared a gravel parking lot with an old-fashioned ice cream stand. The restaurant itself was a weather-beaten blue building with three large eating areas — an inside area, a screened-in porch, and an outside deck. Judging from the way the building was laid out, it was clear that the Blue Lobster had started out as a simple and small take-out place, and over time evolved into what it was today. Each section looked like it had been added on in a different decade, with the open deck added last. The ice cream stand was a small, faded green building with a couple of windows in the front through which the treats were served. Its eating area consisted of about a half dozen picnic tables under a portable tent. Across the road was a large seasonable vegetable and fruit stand with its own parking lot. All of them were doing a brisk business.

On the way to the restaurant, I'd placed a call to Greg and gave him the latest update, especially about my dinner plans with Chief Littlejohn.

"I knew I should have gone with you," he'd told me.

"Don't worry, honey," I responded, trying to put his mind at ease. "I'll be fine."

"It's not just that, sweetheart. I'm sorry I'm missing this family reunion. It's turning into a regular soap opera. Each installment gets more bizarre. But chief of police or not, please be careful, and call me later."

Chief Littlejohn nodded to a few folks as we made our way into the restaurant and found a table near the edge of the screened-in porch. Many people stared and whispered as we walked by.

"Everyone's heard about this morning's events," he told me in a quiet voice. "And about my mother." He paused before correcting himself. "Our mother. Can't keep anything quiet in small towns like these."

"Well, there were news crews covering it."

"I'm sure it's much worse in California. The news media, I mean. Stuff like this rarely happens around here, so this is like throwing them a Grade A T-bone." He gave off a slight snort. "Although, even without the media, details of what happened would have made it as far north as Nashua, New Hampshire, by now, just through gossip."

"Chief Littlejohn," I began.

"Clark, please. We're family, after all." His tone was neither sarcastic nor warm.

I gave him a small smile of what I hoped would be reassurance of some kind, though for what I had no idea. "Okay, Clark."

He stopped me by holding up a hand in the halt position. "First things first." He handed me a greasy menu from a stack wedged between the napkin dispenser and condiments. "We can talk while we eat."

I was all for that. The air in the restaurant was blanketed with the smell of cooking oil and fish. My mouth watered, and my gut danced in joy. The menu consisted mostly of fried seafood, with a few steamed and grilled items tossed in as a salute to healthy eating. In spite of my desire to follow up the earlier fried Twinkie and corn dog with more grease, I settled for something grilled.

"My husband would love this place," I commented, trying to ease into some feeling of camaraderie. "He'd fry milk if he could."

"This place and the ice cream stand next

door are both owned by Gilchrist Dairy — family owned and operated. Been around forever. They make all their own ice cream, too, right up the road at the dairy farm. Flavor selection is limited, but it's the best you'll ever taste. Lots of family-operated businesses like this throughout the area. Like Buster's, the vegetable stand across the road. It's owned and operated by the Brown family farm. Has been for generations, even before there was a Buster Brown."

"Buster Brown?" I smiled with amusement.

"Yep." Clark grinned back at me. "Buster's real name is Boniface. He has a brother named Clement. Their crazy mother thought naming her boys after popes would assure them a place in heaven, but why she didn't pick the names John or Paul is anyone's guess. Clement goes by Clem."

"You're making this up."

"Not at all. Ask anyone. Thing is, instead of being saintly, those names made fighters out of those boys. Meanest sonsabitches to walk this earth. Run a nice farm though."

Clark put down his menu and looked at me. "So, what would you like? Here, we go up and order, and they bring it to us when it's ready."

"I'll take the grilled halibut."

"Like hell you will. This place is famous for its fried food. You order anything grilled and I'll be the laughing stock of three counties. After what went down today at that damn corn maze, don't add insult to injury."

Although he'd removed his sunglasses, I couldn't tell if Clark was serious or joking. His face remained blank, his voice even.

"Tell you what, California girl, I'll order for us both." He got up to go to the order window. "You allergic to anything, like shellfish?"

I shook my head.

"Beer, coke, lemonade?"

"Iced tea, if they have it."

After he left our table, I stopped a middle-aged waitress with a low-cut top who'd just delivered a tray to a table near ours. I inquired about the ladies' room. When I returned, Clark was back at our table, on which was the largest plastic glass of iced tea I'd ever seen, along with utensils. Clark was drinking coffee.

While we took sips of our drinks, Clark Littlejohn and I studied each other. He seemed to be scrutinizing my face, taking in every line, pore, and nuance. He also seemed to be looking past facial characteristics, as if he could penetrate skin and bone and study my brain simply because he wanted to. It was easy to see he wasn't going to be an easy nut to crack. I, on the other hand, would probably crumble in his hands like a toasted French baguette.

"You look like Mom," he finally said.

"So I'm told. And you have her eyes and mouth, which puzzles me."

"How so?"

"You said you're my big brother, indicating you're older than I am. When you first said that, I assumed you were the son of my mother's husband, not her blood son. But you definitely look like Mom. My mother left California thirty-four years ago, and, please excuse me for this, but you are way over thirty-four years old. However, the Officer Littlejohn I saw at the maze today is about that age, yet he looks less like me than you do. What gives?"

"You're very observant. I like that." He took a big gulp of coffee. "I am your mother's son and your half brother, and so is Grady — Grady Littlejohn, the other Littlejohn cop. It's a long, complex story."

"I've got time, and this is pretty much what I came here to find out. The murder was a bonus."

"I see you have the family trait of sarcasm. Mom's the queen pin of cynicism and mockery. It totally bypassed Grady."

"Is that good or bad for Grady?"

Clark didn't respond but looked away, focusing instead on a small crowd of teens who'd just piled out of a truck in front of the ice cream stand.

I threw out another question. "Have you always known about me?"

He turned back to face me. "No. Mom finally told me, actually told both of us, after my father died. Until then, she'd never said a word about you or where she'd been after she came back."

"She left me for you?"

"She left me first, Odelia."

Our food came. The waitress unloaded it from a large tray onto our table. I'd never seen so much fried food for two people. Outside of the fries and coleslaw, I wasn't even sure what most of it was, although it all smelled divine.

"We expecting company?" I asked once the waitress took her leave.

"I used to smoke and drink," Clark explained as he arranged the paper containers. "Now I eat when I'm stressed. Looks like that's another family trait we share."

Was he calling me fat? I started to get my feathers ruffled but quickly calmed down. Who was I kidding? I am fat. It's not like I can hide my two-hundred-something pounds with a little foundation and a few vertical stripes, so I owned up to it.

Although hardly thin, Clark was just a little thick and paunchy. "But it only shows a little on you," I said. "On me, this stuff will kick off its shoes and make itself at home."

The comment produced a slight chuckle. "Don't kid yourself, Sis. I have to work out almost every day to keep my girlish figure. Imagine what I'd look like if I didn't."

He pushed a small cup of chowder in front of me. "Start with this. Best clam chowder in all New England." He pronounced it *chowda.* Next, he moved a plate containing a long toasted bun filled with something mixed with mayonnaise. "This is a lobster roll." It came out *lobsta.* "Just lobster meat, mayo, celery, a little lettuce and onion."

Clark picked up his own lobster roll and took a bite that lobbed off a third of the bun. While he chewed, he pointed to the other items. "Fried clams, fried scallops, coleslaw, and fries," he said with a partially full mouth. He swallowed. "The fries came with the other stuff or I would have skipped them. There's tartar sauce in that dish and cocktail sauce in that squeeze bottle next to the salt and pepper." He punctuated his food commentary by taking another bite of his lobster roll.

Not to be left behind, I picked up a spoon and dug into the clam chowder. Although the other stuff was new to me, I'd had chowder before, but Clark was right — this was the best I'd ever tasted. After a few spoonfuls, I took a small bite of the lobster roll, followed by a fried clam and a scallop. It was all heavenly and made me wish I could take some home for Greg. But good food or not, I was also hungry for information. After a couple more bites, I tried to get us back on topic.

"Where do you want to start, Clark? With our sketchy family or with the murder?" When he kept eating, I continued. "Is Mom a suspect? Where is she now? Who's the dead guy? And who's the kid they took away in cuffs?" I had more questions but thought those were enough for now. No sense going into overload at our first meeting.

Clark regarded me while he continued eating. Having polished off his lobster roll, he was now doing damage to the clams and scallops, rotating between dipping them into tartar sauce and cocktail sauce. I couldn't tell if he was avoiding my questions altogether or wondering how much to tell me.

After one final bite of coleslaw, I pushed my plate back and wiped my hands with one of the packaged towelettes delivered with the meal. I pulled my iced tea glass closer and fixed my eyes on him.

"Well?"

"I'm trying to decide what's mine to tell."

In silence, he polished off the last fried clam, licked his fingers, then tore open and cleaned up with his own moist disposable towel.

"Want more tea?" he asked, getting up from the table. As soon as I shook my head, he left to replenish his coffee mug from a nearby beverage refill station. Now I knew how Greg felt. Clark's procrastination was driving me nuts, just as my stalling drove Greg crazy.

When Clark returned to the table, I prodded with more oomph. "What do you mean by 'yours to tell'? I came all this way to find out about my mother. Now she's involved in a murder. Whatever you know, spill it." I leaned back in my chair and crossed my arms across my chest.

A slow smile crept across Clark's face, then scurried away. "As far as the murder goes, I'm not really supposed to be involved. CPAC is handling it, and since my mother is a suspect, at least for now, I wouldn't be investigating the case, even if they weren't."

"But surely they'll tell you what they

suspect or what they find out? I mean, at least as a professional courtesy?"

He shrugged with his face, his eyebrows raised, his mouth twisted to the side. His shoulders remained still. "Maybe, maybe not. But at this point, they haven't learned anything concrete. Just that Mom was found at the scene of the crime with the victim's blood on her hands. But that part you already know. As for the victim, his name was Frankie McKenna."

"Did Mom know him?"

"Highly doubtful. He was from the Boston area. Not sure why he was here."

"The fair?"

Clark scoffed again. "Also doubtful."

He took a long drink of coffee and stared out the window. The teens had long since gotten their ice cream and left, and others had arrived to stand at the windows for their own cones and cups. The parking lot was filling up, but as time passed, most of the new arrivals were making their way to the Blue Lobster for dinner. Around us, the place was starting to hum. It looked like we'd gotten there just before the Saturday night dinner rush.

"The kid in cuffs had nothing to do with the murder. It was a drug bust that happened to go down at the same time. Just a kid smoking pot. We dragged him in and questioned him about the murder, then gave him a slap on the wrist and let him go."

"I'm sure you had bigger things to worry about today than a little weed."

"For sure."

He lightly tapped his fingers on the table. "As far as the family history goes, I think that's something Mom should tell you herself. It's her story, we're just bit players. But I will tell you that you, Grady, and I all had different fathers. My father, Leland Littlejohn, adopted and raised Grady as his own."

"My father died a few months ago." As I said it, my heart lurched a bit. "We were very close."

"Sorry to hear that. Leland died about eight years ago, shortly after I came back to Holmsbury."

"What about Grady's father?"

Clark turned back. "Don't know. Grady was only about two when Mom returned to Holmsbury. Not sure he even remembers his dad, if he ever even met him. Always had a difficult time accepting Leland, even though Leland loved him and provided for him. He tried to find his father once, but Mom wouldn't help him. He doesn't even know his name."

"It's not on his birth certificate?"

"Says *father unknown.* Until Leland adopted him, his last name was Grey, like yours."

My mother, for whatever reason, had wreaked havoc on all three of her children's lives. Did she not even care? Was she really that selfish and callous?

"Mom was a big drinker last I saw her." I had uncrossed my arms and was leaning forward, toying with the straw in my tea. "One day, I came home from school, and she was gone. Never heard from her again. I was sixteen at the time."

Clark shook his head in what I took to be empathy. "She's been sober close to twenty-five years. She tried to stop drinking off and on, but finally Leland put his foot down, said if she didn't get help and stop once and for all, he'd kick her out for good. Seeing she had no place to go, she cleaned up." He snorted softly. "Being sober didn't change her disposition none, though. She's pretty cantankerous. People either love her or hate her. There's no middle of the road with Grace Littlejohn."

"What about you?"

The question brought Clark Littlejohn up short for a moment, but he recovered quickly. "She's my mother. I love her, but I don't have to like her."

"Can't get much more honest than that."
I took another drink of tea. "What about
your family, Clark? You married? Have
kids?"

"Divorced." He paused to think. "About
six years now. Linda and I were separated a
few years before that. Have two daughters
— Marie, who lives in Arlington, Virginia,
with her husband and daughter. My other
daughter, Lorraine, is in grad school in
Wisconsin. She's single but has been living
with the same guy for a long time."

Wow, I thought. *I'm not only a sister, but an
aunt and great-aunt.* It boggled my mind. "I
hope I get to meet your family one day."

Clark offered a small, short smile. "I hope
you do, too. Though I've never mentioned
you to them, so it would be quite a shock."

I paused to think about what I wanted to
ask next. "Do you think she killed that man?
Mom, I mean? Give me your professional
opinion."

"Professionally speaking, it looks bad —
but professionally, I also know things are
usually never how they appear."

"What does she have to say about it?"

Clark raised his face to the ceiling and
blew out air. I could see the muscles in his
thick neck go taut. After a few seconds, he

looked back at me.

"Mom's giving everyone the silent treatment about the murder. Won't say a word about why she was there, if she knew McKenna, nothing. Not even to the lawyer I got for her. Only thing she said was to Grady, back at the farm. Kept telling him over and over that his sister was in the maze, that she saw you."

"He never spoke to me at the farm."

"Grady thought Mom had slipped a cog. You know, in shock over the murder. When he told me, I went through the witness list, and there you were — Odelia Grey — up front and center for the spectacle."

"But Grady knew I existed?"

Clark paused, measuring his words carefully, like salt added to a delicate dish. "The way Mom put it when she told us, we sort of assumed you were a child who had died years before."

Ouch. Not only was I abandoned, I was left for dead and buried. Inside, I felt raw and bloody, like fresh hamburger, as if I'd just been discarded all over again. I felt my hands start to shake and grasped my iced tea glass to still them. Surprisingly, my eyes were dry. I knew I had to keep moving forward, no matter how much it hurt.

I gave Clark a quick rundown of how I

had found the envelope and traced my mother to Holmsbury, including how Cynthia Rielley had encouraged me to go to the fair.

"Mrs. Rielley's a nice lady. Nosy, though — better than having a private security company patrolling the neighborhood."

"Nasty little dog she has there."

He smiled slightly. "Yeah, Coco thinks he's a rottweiler. Back in high school, I dated Mrs. Rielley's daughter, Darlene. Darlene's a college professor now, living in Nebraska."

There was something both soothing and scary about living in a place where everyone knows everyone else. Seal Beach, where Greg and I live, is a small, densely populated beach community covering only about twelve square miles, but except for the people on our short block and maybe a few people on other streets, we didn't know many other folks in the area, at least not well. Here, people knew everyone for miles in every direction. And they knew their families for generations.

"Where's Mom now?"

"At the hospital." He must have read alarm on my face, because he added, "Not to worry. They're keeping her for observation because of the shock and her age. She'll

be out tomorrow or the next day. After tha
it will depend on what the detectives find
out and her cooperation. Even if she's
charged, she'll probably be released on bail
because of her age. She's hardly a flight
risk."

A few weeks ago, I didn't have a mother.
Now I had a mother facing a possible
murder charge *and* leading people to believe
I was dead. Not for the first time, I wished
I'd never seen that envelope.

SEVEN

While I was contemplating the ups and downs of having a new family, especially one with a murder in the midst of it, a woman with dark red, curly hair worn in a ponytail walked over to our table. Her curvy figure was dressed in denim shorts and a red, white, and blue striped tee shirt. In her hands were two large beverage to-go cups, each with a lid and straw. She looked me up and down with curiosity bordering on rudeness before turning to Clark.

"This the fabled dead sister?" She jerked her head in my direction.

"Fabled," Clark said, "but hardly dead, as you can see."

"Does everyone in town know about me?" I asked.

"Not yet, but give it time." Clark indicated the woman. "This is Cathy Morgan, Grady's live-in."

"Fiancée," Cathy corrected.

I extended a hand to her. "Odelia Grey. Nice to meet you, Cathy."

Cathy Morgan put down one of the drinks and took my offered hand, shaking it quickly. It was damp and cold from holding the cup. "At least, Clark, *she* has some manners. Maybe she can teach you some while she's here."

"Don't you have green beans or corn or some such shit to sell?"

"Just came in for a Coke, asshole."

The two sneered at each other before Cathy turned to me. "I should probably thank you."

"Me? What for?"

"That boy in the corn maze was my son, Troy. He was with my dipshit sister-in-law. Troy told me how his Aunt Tara fell to pieces and some lady stepped in and calmed her down. Said you had him waving a flag for help. That's the way to handle kids, keep them busy. You must have some of your own."

I shook my head. "No, no kids. It just seemed like the thing to do."

"Troy remembers the flag waving and helping more than seeing a dead body. As a mother, I can't tell you how much I appreciate that." She gave Clark the evil eye. "Of course, the police are doing their damnedest to encourage him to remember every-thing in detail."

Clark sighed. "Questioning witnesses is part of the process, Cathy. You know that."

She kept her narrowed eyes on Clark. "So what's up with the old lady? I always thought Grace was capable of killing."

Clark glared back at her. "I'm pretty sure my mother had nothing to do with the murder. Just like your boy, she was in the maze having fun."

"Who are you kidding, Clark Littlejohn? That old bat never had any fun in her life — and she resents anyone who does."

Just as Cathy was about to say something more, a burly man dressed in dirty jeans and a sweaty tee shirt entered the porch area and headed straight for our table. His face was lined and burnished by the sun, and topped off by a mop of thick reddish brown hair. He seemed oblivious to the stares he received from the other patrons.

"What in the hell are you doing?" he asked, though I wasn't sure at first who he was addressing until Cathy turned on him.

"I'm just getting a couple of Cokes, Clem. Simmer down."

Clem. Must be Clement Brown, I thought, unless Clem was a common name in these parts.

"You can't leave that boy to attend the stand by himself, Cathy, especially today with all those news bastards hanging around. Where's your head?"

"It was just for a few minutes. He'll be fine."

"Don't you think he's been through enough today?"

It was then that Clem turned his attention to us. "Chief," he said by way of greeting to Clark.

"Hey, Clem. This is Odelia Grey." Clark indicated me by raising his coffee cup in my direction. "She's my and Grady's half sister."

"Half sister?"

Cathy nudged the farmer with her shoulder. "I'll tell you about it back at the stand."

As the two started to take their leave, Cathy turned back around. "Gee, Clark, too bad there's no death penalty in Massachusetts. I'd love to see Grace's saggy old ass fry. *Zzzzzzzzzzt!*"

"Don't mind her," Clark said to me after Cathy and Clem left. "She and Mom don't get along very well. Mom doesn't think she's good enough for Grady."

"Didn't seem like you like her any better."

"I don't. Cathy's the only sister of the Brown boys. That was Clem. Tara, who you met in the corn maze, is his wife. Cathy runs the vegetable stand for the family. She's just as mean and hateful as her brothers."

"At least she was given a normal name."

Clark laughed. "Her real name's Chastity. She changed it to Catherine as soon as she was old enough to file the papers. Her own chastity had been long gone by then. Was married to a guy from south Boston named Les Morgan. Came back here with her boy when Les disappeared with a waitress from Atlantic City." Clark stopped long enough to slurp some coffee. "Been tied up with Grady almost a year now. 'Course, she shacked up with a couple of others first, but Grady says he doesn't care. Says he's in love. Trust me, he's not the smart one in the family."

Greg was right, it *was* like a soap opera.

Clark's cell phone rang. It had rung twice before during our conversation. Both times he had told the caller he'd call them back. This time when he glanced at the display, he excused himself and went over to a corner of the porch where no one was seated. A few minutes later, he came back to our table.

"Someone wants to talk to you," he said, holding the phone out to me.

"Me?" Immediately, I thought it must be

my mother. I steeled myself for the co   s
sation I'd dreaded for thirty-four years

"Hello," I said, trying to keep my
steady and firm.

"Damn it, Odelia, what in the hell have
you gotten yourself into now?"

"Dev?"

Detective Devin Frye of the Newport
Beach Police was on the phone. And not
my phone, but the phone of Police Chief
Clark Littlejohn, my surprise big brother.
Dev Frye is a close friend of mine and
Greg's. The three of us met during the
investigation of the murder of my friend
Sophie London several years ago, and, for a
while, both Dev and Greg vied for my heart.
Dev also seems to think it's his job to
protect me, and it drives him nuts that I
stumble upon murders and murderers from
time to time. Greg doesn't like it any better,
but he's learning to roll with it, so to speak.
And since we've been married, Greg's been
known to stick his nose where it doesn't
belong, right along with mine. This drives
Dev doubly nuts, yet he's been unable to
stop it.

"How did you find me, Dev? And what
are you doing, calling me on this phone?"

"I didn't call *you,* Odelia. I was returning
a call to Chief Littlejohn. Imagine my

urprise when I find out it's about you and a murder in Massachusetts. Taking your nosiness national now, are you?"

Clark threw a couple of bucks on the table as a tip and motioned for me to follow him outside. The Blue Lobster was getting crowded, and the whole world did not need to hear this conversation.

"You know," Dev continued, "right before I called the chief back, Greg called me. He's worried sick. Wanted me to check out Littlejohn, see if he's a good guy or not. Then, on the other hand, I have this Chief Littlejohn calling me from Massachusetts, checking up on you and asking about all those investigations you've been involved with."

I twitched my nose as I stood between my rental car and Clark's car. "How would he know about those? Am I in some police database or something like that?"

"No, Odelia, you're not. According to him, he Googled you and read up on news reports involving you and those crimes."

I looked over at Clark. "He *Googled* me?" Clark turned away and pretended to check out a small child juggling a double-dip cone. "I'm on Google?"

"Jesus, Odelia, are you the only person in the world who has never Googled yourself? Of course you're on Google. Every time a newspaper or news agency wrote something about those murders and mentioned you, it ended up somewhere on Google." Dev took a deep breath. "The chief called the station here to ask about you. Of course, they turned the call over to me, since everyone knows I'm your cop o' choice."

Dev hadn't raised his voice to me. He didn't need to. The sarcasm, highlighted by his naturally deep and rocky tone, was enough to let me know he was frustrated.

Just as he was about to say more, and I dreaded him saying more, the call waiting on Clark's phone chimed.

"Dev, there's another call coming in on Clark's phone. Gotta go."

Before I handed the phone to Clark, I heard Dev cram in, "I'll call you on yours in fifteen minutes. Be there." It was definitely an order.

Clark took his phone and answered the call. "What's going on?" he said without saying hello. While he listened to his caller, I fished around in my tote bag for my own phone. After asking a few more questions, Clark finished his call and came to my side.

"You have plans for later on?"

"Not really. I came here to see my mother. It was the only thing on my agenda."

"Then meet me in front of Three Rivers

Community Hospital around eight thirty, and you might get your chance."

"Tonight? Is that such a good idea, after everything that's happened today?"

"That was Grady on the phone. He's at the hospital now. They gave Mom a sedative earlier, but she's starting to come out of it. I'm calling her lawyer and going over there now. The CPAC folks will be anxious to question her again and see if resting loosened her tongue any." He holstered his phone and got out his car keys. "I think it best we test the waters before springing you on her, but why don't you plan on being there at half past eight? If I think it's not a good idea or if morning would be best, I'll call you."

"Three Rivers Community Hospital, right?"

"Yes, just ask someone, or plug it into your GPS."

He started to head for the driver's side of his vehicle. Halfway there, he turned and came back. He held out his right hand to me. "For whatever it's worth, Odelia, I'm glad we finally met."

I took his hand. I didn't shake it but gave it a warm squeeze, accompanied by a smile. "By the way, what did Dev Frye tell you about me?"

"He said, should I get the urge to lock you up, I shouldn't hesitate."

Dev Frye's call came in a bit later than he said it would. I had just pulled into the driveway of the bed-and-breakfast and was turning off the engine.

"Hi," I said into the earpiece.

"You still with Chief Littlejohn?"

"No, but I'm supposed to meet him later tonight at the hospital. That's where my mother is right now."

"Greg said he's your brother. That true?"

After getting out of the car and locking it, I headed towards the back yard of the B & B, where there was a lovely sitting area for guests under the shade of a large tree. While I settled myself into a comfortable cushioned chair, I filled Dev in on what had happened since this morning.

"So Greg asked you to check out the chief? What did you find out?"

"That's why it took me a bit longer to call you back. Found out Clark Littlejohn used to be in the Boston PD. An old buddy of mine retired from the force there and went to live in Las Cruces, New Mexico. I put in a call to him."

"And?"

"Hard to say. Littlejohn received a couple

of commendations during his years in Boston, but his last few years were pretty rocky."

"He was a dirty cop?"

"Some rumors, but nothing charged or proven. Mostly, he was a drunk, made some bad decisions. According to my buddy, Littlejohn's marriage went on the rocks at the same time. He said Littlejohn was well liked by his fellow officers and was overall a very good cop. Made detective right before it all started falling apart for him."

"He mentioned something at dinner that he used to smoke and drink, but he didn't specify that the drinking was anything more than casual. My mother was an alcoholic. Clark said she's been sober now for about twenty-five years."

"It's not unusual for alcoholism to run in a family."

"Hard to tell over one meal, but Clark struck me as basically a decent guy. A bit gruff and melancholy, but then his mother was just found crouching over a dead man. Not good for the chief of police."

"Your mother, too."

"Thanks for reminding me. And don't you even think of making a crack about it being genetic."

"Who, me? I'd never say something like

that." Dev's deep chuckle resonated over the phone line like a low growl from a friendly dog.

"Bullshit."

Dev laughed louder.

"Should I be concerned about Clark?"

"From what I've learned, he sounds like a good guy with some former bad habits. But play it safe and keep your guard up, and get your ass on the first plane home tomorrow."

"I'm staying until Monday. It's just two days away, Dev. I want to spend some time with my mother just in case they send her to prison." The sound of Cathy's cheerful *Zzzzzzzzzt!* filled my audio memory like an annoying glitch on a soundtrack. I shuddered.

"Just let those CPAC guys do their job and stay out of their way. You can wait on the sidelines with the Littlejohns."

My nose twitched like Peter Rabbit's. "Did you tell Clark to lock me up if he got the urge?"

"No, I told him you were a pain in the ass. That he should lock you up now and save himself grief later."

After ending my call with Dev, I called Greg and brought him up to date. Greg underlined Dev's advice to lay low and get the hell out of Dodge as soon as possible.

Before giving him a wet phone kiss, I promised to call after my visit to the hospital.

I had a bit of time to kill before I made my way to the hospital, so I stayed under the tree and pulled a paperback book from my tote. But evening was setting in and so were the bugs, forcing me to head inside and settle in a comfy chair in the parlor.

One of the reasons I carry such a big bag is because I lug so much junk around with me — things like a small bottle of water and a book. Recently, the firm assigned me a BlackBerry. Mike Steele had been trying to saddle me with one for two years, but until now I had successfully fended him off. I never thought I needed one. After all, I always have my cell phone with me. It was Greg who finally convinced me to say yes to the BlackBerry, touting its convenience. So now, besides all the other stuff in my bag, I had a new thingamabob to carry. I spotted the BlackBerry, pulled it out, and turned it on. It promptly loaded up both my work and personal e-mails. Putting the book aside, I dutifully read the work-related e-mails I'd received since I was last in the office on Thursday. Most of them were from Steele, asking questions and giving me tasks to do when I returned to work on Tuesday.

I answered a couple of the questions and received a reply back almost immediately. Steele must be working, either from home or at the office. Or maybe he was just checking his e-mail at the same time I was. It didn't surprise me. He's one of the people for whom the term *CrackBerry* fits.

Steele's e-mail asked if I was still out of town and had I met my mother yet. I replied: *Yes and Yes.*

Fast back was the question: *Happy or disappointed?* Mike Steele could type faster with his thumbs than anyone I knew.

I wondered what to tell Steele. Finally, I punched in: *It's kind of complicated.*

This time I didn't get a reply. This time the BlackBerry in my hand rang. I thought about leaving it on the chair under a pillow and going upstairs to my room. I could also shut off the contraption and not turn it on again until I reached California. The problem with that was he'd just call my cell phone, and that I did need to keep on in case Greg or Clark called. With a big sigh, I answered the BlackBerry.

"Okay, Grey, what's up?" my boss in California said as soon as I answered.

"Nothing's up, Steele."

"Whenever you say something's complicated, it's usually code for *disaster on the*

101

horizon."

"It is not," I snapped. "It's just that my mother was shocked to see me."

"Did you call first?"

"No, I did not." My voice strained to hold back the building annoyance. "I wanted to surprise her."

"Is that a smart thing to do with a woman that age?"

I paused just long enough to decide what to say and how to phrase it to keep him off my back. "Here's the thing, Steele."

"Uh-oh. There's another one of your catastrophe-lurking catch phrases."

"It is not."

"Tell me what's going on, or I'll call Greg and find out from him."

"I'm not a five-year-old, Steele."

"Then stop acting like one, and tell me what's happening. You've pretty much given away all your tells."

"Tells?"

"You know, Grey, as in poker. You couldn't bluff your way out of a Burger King."

I sighed. "Well, in my defense, it wasn't my fault."

"Oh, shit!" he yelled. "Don't tell me someone's dead!"

EIGHT

By the time I filled Steele in and worked my way through his hysterics and demands that I get my big behind on a plane back to California ASAP, I was exhausted, mentally and physically, and the heavy, greasy food I'd consumed earlier wasn't helping any. The last thing I wanted to do was to go to that hospital and face my mother. I just wasn't up to it. I also wasn't up to another call from California. All that was missing was a call from Zee and Seth Washington, but, thankfully, there was a good chance that they didn't know about my latest crime calamity. They'd left California Thursday for an Alaskan cruise.

What I really wanted was to crawl in bed.

While I was contemplating calling Clark and begging off from meeting him at the hospital tonight, Ollie and Abby came down the stairs. They appeared to be arguing, but as they got closer I realized it was teasing. I waved to them. They waved back and bounced over to where I sat like a couple of energetic puppies.

"We took this great hike today," Abby said. After today's events, it was good to see her full of excitement. "Felt good to do something so physical after this morning. Now we're off to get some dinner. Want to join us?"

Ollie was fiddling with his phone but added, "Sure, come with us. It'll be fun."

"Ollie, would you put that thing down," Abby chided. "I swear, tonight when you're sleeping, I'm going to erase those photos."

Abby turned to me. "He took photos of the crime scene today. How morbid is that?"

My ears went on alert. "Photos from the corn maze?"

"Yes, he's always shooting things with that phone camera. Sometimes it's fun, but usually it drives me nuts. Like today." She made a swipe with her hand for the phone, but Ollie, being a foot taller, easily managed to keep it from her grasp.

"Did you tell the police about the photos?"

Ollie and Abby looked at each other in such a way I knew they hadn't. Ollie finally answered, "I was afraid they'd confiscate my iPhone. I need it for work."

"The police really should have those

photos. You never know what they might reveal."

"That's what I told him," Abby added. "But I have to agree with his fear that they would take the phone and not return it, even if we offered to download or e-mail the photos to them. We're leaving tomorrow morning and didn't want to be held up."

I looked down at the BlackBerry still clutched in my hand. "Tell you what, why don't you e-mail them to me? I can save them to my BlackBerry and let the police know I have them if they want them. The folks from CPAC are supposed to call me to set up a time to meet."

Ollie said, "You sure?"

"Positive. It's no big deal if they take the BlackBerry — I'll still have my regular cell phone. I'm meeting Chief Littlejohn later, I can tell him, too."

The young couple discussed it silently through looks and shrugs.

"Okay," Ollie announced. "What's your e-mail address?"

Since I could access both my personal and work e-mail on the device, I rattled off my personal e-mail address.

After sending Ollie and Abby on their way to dinner, with a recommendation for the Blue Lobster, I retired to my room to clean up and relax before going to the hospital. E-mails containing photos from the corn maze were coming in from Ollie at a steady pace. Probably either he or Abby were shooting them off to me while the other drove. I also took this time to plug my cell phone into its charger. It was getting low on juice and this was not the time to let it die, one of my bad habits back home.

Since I hadn't made the call to Clark to beg off meeting Mom, I decided I might as well get ready. I was fast wishing I'd brought more clothes as I prepared to make my fourth change of the day. Deciding I didn't want to meet my mother in casual pants, I pulled out the dress and sandals I'd originally put on this morning. I was getting ready to slip into the dress when my cell phone rang. It was Clark.

"Hold off on coming to the hospital," he told me.

"Is Mom okay?"

"The CPAC guys just left, and she's exhausted."

"Did she finally talk about what happened in the maze?"

"Nope. Very frustrating for everyone. Grady and I are meeting with her lawyer in a few minutes. He's not too happy, seeing that she won't even talk to him."

I hesitated before speaking, knowing I was hardly the main priority here. "Um, Clark, did she say anything about me?"

Now it was his turn to hesitate.

"She doesn't want to see me, does she?"

"It's complicated."

I treated myself to a sad little chuckle. Steele was right, that phrase does smack of bad news and impending doom.

"I told Grady about you," Clark continued. "He was relieved to know Mom wasn't rambling about nothing or hallucinating, though he's a bit confused and surprised, considering what Mom led us to believe. Then I told the guys from CPAC. I had to, Odelia, you know that."

"Yes, of course. I would have told them when they interviewed me anyway."

"Tomorrow morning, Odelia. They want to see you at nine tomorrow morning at the station. I told them I'd pass that along to you. Plan on spending a few hours with them."

"And what about Mom? Did you speak to her about meeting me?"

"Yes, I did, just now." He fell silent.

I held my breath and waited for him to continue, unsure of what I wanted him to say.

"Mom wants to see you, Odelia, she really

does. But she's also dreading it. I'm sure you can understand."

"Yes, I do, Clark. I feel the same way."

I was about to tell Clark abut Ollie's photos when an upside to this postponement occurred to me. If I told Clark about the photos, I had no doubt he'd want to see them immediately and would tell CPAC about them. They might even want to take my BlackBerry tonight. That would give me no time to review the photos and make my own copies, which I definitely wanted to do.

"I'm sorry, Clark, but I didn't hear that." I was so busy plotting my next move with the photos, I hadn't heard his last comment.

"I said, let's see how she is tomorrow after your meeting at the station. A good night's sleep might ease the way for both of you."

"Good idea. I'm pretty tired myself. I think I'll settle in with a book."

As soon as Clark said good night, I called Greg. He'd just gotten home from the gym.

"Hi, it's me. I need a favor."

"A plane ticket out of Murderland for tomorrow morning?"

"Very funny, but no. This is something techie-related — right up your alley. In a nutshell, I need you to be my eyes."

I explained about the photos and told Greg I was going to e-mail them to him. I asked him to open each one, enlarge it, and scrutinize it for any minute detail that might be important. My hubs has an eye for detail, especially on the computer. I really wanted to view the photos with him but couldn't under the circumstances, with the Black-Berry being so limited in size.

"You're getting involved, Odelia. Exactly what I asked you *not* to do."

"We're just looking at photos of the crime scene, Greg. If we find anything tonight, I can point it out to the police tomorrow. I'm not snooping around or anything like that."

"Looking at these photos is snooping, Odelia."

There was silence, then I heard him say in the background, "Your mommy's nuts. I hope you guys know that." A smile crossed my face, and my heart ached to be home. Wainwright and the two cats must have been circling around Greg while he was speaking with me.

Finally, he spoke to me again. "Okay, I'll check out the photos, but don't e-mail them to me. Instead, give me your password, and I'll access them directly. I don't want the police to know that you've sent those photos off somewhere."

My password? In the short time Greg and I have been married, it never occurred to me to share my e-mail password with him. It's not that I don't trust him, I do. And I certainly don't have anything in my e-mails, sent or received, that I wouldn't want him to see or that might upset him. Most of my online correspondence was with friends and former coworkers that I'd met over the years and a few college friends that I still kept in touch with. It was pretty tame stuff, but it still rattled me as much as if he were snooping in my diary, providing I kept one. I was being silly, and I knew it. Besides, I told myself, if it continued to bother me, I could always change it when I got home.

As if he'd read my mind, Greg laughed and said, "Don't worry, Odelia, I won't read any of your juicy e-mails, just the ones you write to men in prison."

"I don't write to anyone in prison, Greg Stevens, and you know it."

He laughed harder. "Okay, then, when you get home, I'll give you my password. Seems only fair."

"Don't be a smart-ass. It's no big deal."

Laughter aside, I went back to the topic of the photos. "Greg, you don't think Clark Littlejohn is involved, do you? In the murder, I mean."

"After talking with Dev, probably not, but you never know. Wouldn't be the first time a cop did something underhanded. But just to be on the safe side, I'd rather everyone think you were just passing them along like a good citizen. I don't want anyone even getting a whiff that you might be involved. Just make sure the police get those photos in the morning."

"I will. Oh, and by the way, Greg, calling Dev was really unnecessary, but I love you for looking out for me."

"That's my job, sweetheart. Ocean Breeze Graphics is just a sideline." His words made me even more homesick.

It was close to ten when I made my way downstairs in my nightie and robe to the guest pantry to make myself a cup of herbal tea. I had tried to read while I waited for any news from Greg on the enlargements, but I couldn't keep my mind on my book, so instead I scratched out the skeleton of my new family tree on some note paper I'd found in the writing desk in my room. Three kids, three different fathers, one mother in common. Suddenly, my Christmas card list, like this situation, had become complicated.

In the corridor, I bumped into Mrs. Friar, the owner of the B & B. The Friars lived in a cute little house next to the Maple Tree Bed and Breakfast. The B & B itself had only four guest rooms, three upstairs and one down, all with private bathrooms. The one downstairs was perfect for the elderly and disabled and had its own private entrance. There was also a kitchen, dining room, and parlor downstairs. Right now, only the couple from California and I occupied the upstairs. An older couple occupied the room downstairs.

"You're working late," I said to Mrs. Friar, a short, energetic woman in her late sixties.

"We have a guest arriving tonight. Very last minute. Usually we don't accept guests after eight o'clock, but the Carroltons left today after hearing about the murder at the Tyler farm, and tomorrow that nice young couple is leaving. So any chance we have to fill a vacancy, we'll take it, late or not."

"I would think with this being Labor Day weekend that your inn would be full."

"Next weekend it will be, and every weekend right through foliage season, but Labor Day is still a bit early for the leaves. People are still thinking about going to the Cape over Labor Day. The new guest specifically asked about the availability of a ground-floor room, so since the Carroltons vacated, it worked out nicely. I just had to give it a quick clean-up. He said he'd be here around ten."

"A single man?"

"Apparently so. Said he decided at the last minute to come into town and surprise a family member."

As we chatted, a dark SUV pulled into the driveway. A man got out. All I could make out in the poorly lit parking area was that he was on the short side and slight, wore a baseball cap pulled down low, and carried a small duffel bag and briefcase.

"That must be Mr. Carter now."

While Mrs. Friar bustled out to greet the new arrival, I closed my robe tighter and continued making my tea, taking my time with it. I could make Mr. Carter's acquaintance over breakfast the next morning, but I didn't want to leave Mrs. Friar on her own to greet a stranger. I'm sure she did it all the time and this certainly wasn't a high crime area, but after the death in the corn maze, I wasn't leaving anything to chance.

"Here, Mr. Carter, let me show you to your room," I heard Mrs. Friar say. "Everything's ready for you."

The two of them made their way from the back door down the corridor towards me.

"This is our guest pantry. There are thermoses of coffee and hot water for tea 24/7 for guests, along with treats like cookies and fruit, including a small fridge to store your own drinks. Feel free to help yourself."

As Mrs. Friar passed by me, she made a brief introduction. "And this is Ms. Grey, one of our current guests. Ms. Grey, this is William Carter."

Mr. Carter stopped and held out his hand to me. I took it and shook politely, but he didn't let go. Noting that Mrs. Friar was already several steps ahead, he raised his head so I could see under the cap.

Mr. Carter winked at me and whispered, "Hello, little mama."

NINE

"Willie!"

"So much for being incognito."

Mrs. Friar turned to us. "You two know each other?"

"Ms. Grey — actually it's Mrs. Stevens — is the family member I came to surprise." Willie, never one to be slow on his feet, added, "I'm her husband's cousin."

Mrs. Friar clapped her hands in delight and beamed at our little reunion.

Willie, still clutching my hand, said to me, but for Mrs. Friar's benefit, "Greg told me you were here on family business, so when I finished up my meetings, I decided to scoot over and say hello. No sense you being alone on a holiday weekend."

"What a surprise indeed." I gave him a quick hug, again for Mrs. Friar's benefit. "I spoke to Greg not too long ago, and he didn't say a word about you."

"I asked him not to just in case I couldn't

make it."

Because I was waiting for a call from Greg about the photos, I had brought my cell phone downstairs with me. It chose that minute to ring. The ring identified Greg as the caller.

"Speak of the devil." I answered the call with Mrs. Friar and Willie watching. "Hi, honey. Guess who's here? That's right, your *cousin* Willie. What a big surprise. You really *should* have told me."

I handed the phone to Willie. "He wants to say hello."

Willie took the phone eagerly, as if he talked to Greg every day. Dollars to donuts, there was something going on that I didn't know about.

"Hey, cousin. I made it."

Had Mrs. Friar not been watching with a face full of hearts and flowers, I would have insisted on using the speaker feature so I could hear what Greg was saying.

"Sure, no problem," Willie continued, "I'll keep your lady out of mischief. Not to worry." Willie winked at me, and Mrs. Friar giggled. I twitched my nose. Whatever Greg said next made Willie laugh.

"Here, talk to lover boy." Willie handed the phone back to me. "I don't want to keep Mrs. Friar waiting any longer."

As the two of them continued on to Willie's room, I returned to my conversation with Greg. "What's this all about, Greg?"

"I called to let you know those photos are going to take a bit longer to download and review, sweetheart. Lots of cornstalks to scrutinize. It's like trying to find Waldo."

"That's not what I'm talking about, and you know it." I lowered my voice. "What gives with Willie? How do you two even know each other?"

"We're sharing passwords now, why not criminal friends?"

I was about to say something snotty when Mrs. Friar came back down the hall and headed for the back door. She smiled and told me to have a pleasant evening before she left. I smiled back.

When I didn't answer right away, Greg continued. "Willie contacted me shortly after you almost died in that fire in El Segundo. We met, had a few beers, and he gave me his contact info. Said to call on him if you ever got into a situation I couldn't handle."

"I'm not in any *situation,* Greg; and if I were, I'd handle it."

"Well, here's the crazy thing about this. I didn't call Willie and ask him to look in on you. He called me to find out where you were. He already knew you were up to your pretty neck in a murder when he called."

"But who would have told him?"

"Beats me, but I'm glad whoever it was did, because I was about to call him myself. And I'm glad Willie was already on the East Coast. He got there in record time. Maybe he can keep you from getting into a *situation*."

Greg told me to go to bed so I'd be fresh to meet the detectives in the morning. He said he would continue looking at photos and would leave me a voice mail if he found anything worth telling the cops about. After hanging up, I freshened my tea and filled another cup with coffee. With both hot mugs in my hands, I headed to Willie's door and tapped on it with my elbow. After opening the door, he took the offered coffee and waved me inside.

Willie's room was much larger than mine and contained twin beds. It had a small sitting area by a bay window with two chairs, a reading lamp, and small, low, tile-top table. Since this room had been outfitted to accommodate guests with disabilities, it was uncluttered with fussy antiques and there was plenty of space between the pieces of furniture. The bathroom and its doorway had been enlarged and the private entrance led to a wheelchair ramp. But even with these adjustments, the overall décor was just as charming as the rooms upstairs.

"Twin beds? Is Enrique joining you?"

Enrique, a young, handsome Latino, was Willie's right-hand man and sometimes-bodyguard.

"I'm solo this time, little mama. Since he finished his education, Enrique mostly works in-house handling my international businesses. Besides, he's on his honeymoon. Got married last weekend."

The news brought a warm smile to my face.

I put my mug on the table, plopped myself down into one of the upholstered chairs, and got down to business. "So, why are you here?"

"First, tell me who else is in the house?"

Willie was always aware of his surroundings — one of the side effects of being on the lam. "Just a young couple from California. Their room is upstairs across from mine, and I heard them come in just before you arrived. They're leaving tomorrow morning."

Satisfied with my response, Willie sat in the other chair and sipped his coffee before answering. "As to your question, what can I say?" He grinned. "I'm like Batman. Shine a distress signal into the sky, and I leap into action."

"So who turned on the signal? I sure didn't."

In response, Willie shrugged and took another sip of coffee.

"Greg just confessed that you two have become quite chummy."

"I like your hubby, Odelia. Great guy. Saw it right off. And he's smart, too. Not that I would expect you to marry dumb." He winked at me. "In spite of everything Greg can do, he understands and accepts what he can't do. After hearing about your last escapade — you know, the one with the serial killer and big-ass blaze — I approached Greg and offered up my services if ever he needed them. He appreciated the gesture, even paid for the beers and pizza."

"But it wasn't Greg who snapped on the distress signal, was it?"

"No, it wasn't." Willie crossed one leg over the other and settled back in his chair comfortably. You would have thought we really were family catching up on old times.

"So? Who was it?" I started running down in my head the list of people in my life who knew about Willie: Greg, Dev, Steele, Seth, and Zee. But Seth and Zee were on a cruise.

"What did you do, leave your con information with all my friends?"

Willie laughed. "Actually, I only left it with Greg. But some of your friends do know how to get word to the criminal element all on their own."

I gave that some thought. "It had to be Dev, then."

"Ah, yes, the good Detective Devin Frye. But you don't think he'd call me, do you? After all, he's one of Newport Beach's finest." Willie said this with a smirk, accompanied by another wink, which confirmed my guess. "Dev put out the word to an acquaintance of his to tell an acquaintance of mine to tell me to give Greg a jingle. It's almost faster than e-mail."

He took a big gulp of coffee. "And what's this I hear, that you have a half brother who's chief of police in this burg?"

"Actually, it seems I have two half brothers, and both are police officers. Speaking of which, aren't you worried someone will spot you and turn you in?"

Willie's real name was William Proctor. At one time, he'd been the founder and CEO of a huge online investment company called Investanet. At least he was — until he cleaned out the company and disappeared with every dime belonging to his investors.

We'd met when I was investigating the death of one of the firm's clients, a prominent businessman and lunch box collector.

From the twinkle in his eye, Willie obviously found my question amusing. "I've pretty much fallen off the radar, little mama. With all those Wall Street clowns walking away from failed companies with billions, my theft is like a misdemeanor. Only thing is, I did it quietly, while they're committing their crimes on prime-time news and getting away scot-free." He shook his head. "Annoying, isn't it?"

I stared at him — the forerunner of today's corporate criminals being disgusted by current headlines. Go figure. Willie may be my friend, but in no way do I condone what he did, and he knows that.

"Also, a lot of people still believe William Proctor is dead. Even so, I intend to be careful while I'm here. My mission is quite simple, little mama. I'm to make sure your plump, perky ass is on a plane back to California on Monday, even if I have to stuff you in a crate and ship you air freight."

He put down his coffee cup and leaned forward. Pulling a gun out from under his shirt in the back, he put it on the table. His face took on a serious demeanor, like storm clouds blown in by a sudden gust of wind.

"Fill me in and don't spare the details."

For the next hour or so, I told Willie the entire story — from finding the envelope, to finding my mother in the maze with a body, to dinner with Clark Littlejohn, even the photos and my appointment the next morning to speak with the people from CPAC. Through the whole thing, Willie remained impassive, moving only to adjust his comfort level in the chair from time to time. Occasionally, he asked a question for clarification.

At the end of my saga, Willie leaned back with his hands clasped behind his head and stared at the ceiling. I sat quietly, watching his Adam's apple move up and down his thin neck like an air bubble caught in a plastic tube. Since I'd last seen him, Willie had trimmed up his beard. It was short and styled and seeded with gray strands. His hair had thinned more, and what he had left was cropped short. Designer wire frames had replaced his thick, black-rimmed glasses and didn't hide the lines around his eyes, which had deepened like cracks in an aging sidewalk.

When I first met Willie, he was grieving for his wife, a death for which he blamed himself. He also relished his criminal status, and while he was never impetuous, it was obvious he enjoyed playing outlaw. The man before me was still a fugitive, but with less flourish, like a bad boy who'd grown up and turned his childhood hobby into a full-time, responsible career. Although I didn't know exactly what Willie was involved with these days, I did know that he'd taken much of his stolen funds and invested in many businesses. It was also my gut feeling that although Willie still walked on the wrong side of justice, many of his current endeavors were probably legitimate, even if funded by illegitimate means.

After a short while, Willie leaned towards me, his hands on his thighs. "Little mama, the murder aside, what are you going to do if your mother refuses to see you? That's what you came here for, isn't it?"

That possibility had occurred to me when Clark called earlier. What would I do? I had come all this way to see her, possibly even confront her for all the pain she'd caused. What if my trip was for nothing? Could I return to playing the part of the dead, forgotten child?

"I guess I'd have to go home with my questions unanswered."

Getting out of my chair, I paced the room while I churned things over in my mind. My steps were short and static, as they started and stopped with my brain activity.

"Given the murder, she might want to see me, but just not at this time. In that case, Clark — that's my chief of police half brother — has my information. The ball will be in her court at that point."

"Can you live with that?"

"I honestly don't know, Willie, but I may have to. I've lived with it this long."

"And what about the murder?"

"What about it?"

"Do you have it in that squirrelly little head of yours to get involved?"

I stopped pacing long enough to shrug. "I don't think she did it, and I think the police will determine that as well." I took a few more steps and stopped again. "She's old, Willie, and certainly not strong enough to have stabbed the guy in that manner. The victim was skewered with a broken pole, for gawd's sake." The thought of it made my spine feel like curling ribbon run across scissors. "But I also don't think she just happened to have stumbled on the body. She was supposed to be working the food booths at the fair. What was she doing in the maze to begin with? I definitely think she knows something about the killing, maybe even who did it."

Willie chuckled. It sounded like dice being shaken in a Yahtzee cup. "So, you *are* planning on getting involved."

"She's my mother, Willie. Bad mother or not, she's still my mother."

"Let your brothers deal with it, Odelia."

"That's exactly what Greg said."

He chuckled again. "Greg's a very wise man. Wise enough to know you won't do that." Getting up, Willie stretched. "That's why they sent me. Greg can't follow you around except in a limited capacity, and Dev . . . well, let's just say Dev won't cross certain lines of professionalism. Me, I have no such scruples."

"So they sent you to do their dirty work?"

Willie came over to where I stood and faced me, placing a hand on each of my shoulders. "Little mama, this isn't dirty work. Running around after you while you play Sherlock Holmes — to me, this is a day at Disneyland riding all the best attractions."

"But I thought your job was to get me on a plane home on Monday."

"It is, so whatever you end up doing, do it quick. Greg told me your plane leaves about four thirty in the afternoon."

When I started to say something, Willie stopped me by placing an index finger against my lips.

126

"Don't make me measure you for that crate."

I stepped back and fixed him with my best challenging look. "I wear a size 20 dress, Willie. Do the math."

TEN

Clark was waiting for me when I finished my interview with the two detectives from CPAC. One had been African-American, the other white. Both looked like they had been booked from central casting for a second-rate TV cop show. For starters, they went over the same questions the officers had asked when I was first interviewed at the farm. They followed that up with new ones, like was I really Grace Littlejohn's daughter? Why had I chosen this weekend, after all the time that had passed, to come to Massachusetts? Was I connected to Frankie McKenna, the victim, in any way? Was this a plan to set up my mother in an act of revenge? Did I know any of the other witnesses?

As for the photos, I decided to keep them to myself. Last night, Willie had advised me not to give them up, saying I had no legal obligation to hand them over. I must admit,

I'd wondered that myself. Seeing they were on my BlackBerry, had the police taken the device, they would have had access to my work e-mails — e-mails that contained confidential client information. In the end, I placed a call to Steele. I wasn't surprised when I didn't reach him right off. It was Saturday night, and he was probably on a date. I left both a voice mail and an e-mail saying I needed to talk to him before eight thirty the next morning, Eastern time. He returned the call about twenty minutes later.

"What's up, Grey? You in jail?" I could hear the sounds of light music and voices in the background.

"No, I'm not in jail. Geez."

"Pity. Safest place for you, considering."

A smart-ass remark was on the tip of my tongue, but I shelved it to get to the problem at hand. "Sorry to disturb you, Steele, but I need some advice before I meet with the state police tomorrow morning at nine."

"No problem. I got dragged to some boring black-tie party on a yacht. Anything you're doing is a hundred times more exciting, believe me."

"Steele, a friend is with me. I'm going to put you on speaker."

I gave Steele a run-down on the photo situation and asked whether or not I had to turn them and/or the BlackBerry over to the police.

"You have no obligation to turn those photos over to anyone," Steele advised me. "And I certainly do not want that Black-Berry in the hands of the police. It's the firm's property."

"See," Willie said, "just as I told you."

"Who is that?" asked Steele.

"Name's William Carter — I'm Greg's cousin."

There was a moment of silence on Steele's end. "I don't remember Greg having a cousin named William Carter."

"Come on, Steele, how would you know Greg's cousins?"

"I met them at your wedding, Grey. As I recall, he only has two male cousins, and neither of them are named William."

Willie and I looked at each other. "He's good," Willie said.

"Oh . . . my . . . god! I know who you are. You're Grey's felon-in-waiting, William Proc — ."

"William Carter, Mr. Steele," Willie said, cutting him off. "Greg's cousin from the other side of the family. I'm afraid I couldn't make the wedding."

"Jesus, Grey, next time, *you* sail on the S.S. *Comatose*, and I'll hang out with

Greg's . . . cousin."

As Clark had predicted, the questioning lasted a couple of hours. I was beat and cranky when I left, and eager to step out into the sunshine. Had I been a criminal, I would have cracked after fifteen minutes.

While I was asleep, Greg had left a voice mail saying he hadn't found anything special in the photos but was still working on it. He said he was taking them into his office, where he had newer and more sophisticated computer equipment.

Willie, meanwhile, was staying clear of the police station for obvious reasons. Even though he'd crowed that he was old news and even considered dead by most, he was taking no chances. He said he was going to go digging around the Tyler farm and talk to some folks, as well as stay in touch with Greg about the photos. He'd brought a laptop with him and offered to press it into service so we could view the photos along with Greg. After I was done with the CPAC crew, I was to call him on the disposable cell phone he'd purchased for the trip so we could meet up. I was about to call Willie when I saw Clark.

"How'd it go in there, Odelia?"

Clark was leaning against one of the thick,

round porch columns when I came out of the station house. Standing next to him, in a less relaxed pose, was the other Officer Littlejohn.

"Oh, by the way, this here is our little brother, Grady." Clark cocked a thumb in Grady's direction. "Grady, this is Odelia Grey Stevens, Mom's other kid, the one sandwiched between us and, obviously, not deceased."

Time-wise, I may have been sandwiched between Clark and Grady in the gene pool, but looking at Grady, it appeared that Mom had restocked it with fresh DNA. While Clark and I looked somewhat alike in both build and face, and both of us definitely looked like our mother, Grady looked like neither of us. He was much more fair in both his complexion and hair, and his build was tall and slim — the type who could eat at the Blue Lobster all he wanted without worrying about gaining weight. He was a good-looking man, too, leaning towards Brad Pitt but not quite making it, like a third-runner-up in a lookalike contest.

I held out my right hand, but Grady regarded it with as much interest as if I were handing him a turd. I had received a much warmer welcome from his girlfriend, Cathy Morgan, and that had been cool, at best.

Grady mumbled something before turning to stare off in the direction of the street beyond the driveway. He was obviously not thrilled to have a new big sister. Maybe it had something to do with the age gap. Clark and I were much closer in age, but sixteen years divided me and Grady. Not being the shy, retiring type, I studied him as much as his brother had scrutinized me the day before, stopping just short of checking his shirt tag for size. I couldn't quite tell if he was shy or rude, or maybe it was arrogance that kept him from acknowledging my presence while Clark and I spoke about the questioning. But, I reminded myself, his reserve could also be the outcome of concern for our mother.

Clark continued to press me about every detail of my interview with CPAC until I was about to run screaming from the porch. Between his intensity and the negative vibes coming from Grady, I was glad I had kept my mouth shut about the photographs. If they knew I had such things, no doubt they'd be all over me and not in the interest of helping CPAC.

While I was being interrogated by Clark with Grady as his backup, Joan Cummings came out of the police station and walked past us. Clark stopped talking as soon as he saw her. Grady looked away.

"Hey, Joan," Clark said, giving her a small, stiff smile. "Heading to lunch?"

The clerk took in the three of us with an eagle eye. "Yes, Chief, hope you don't mind."

"Who's covering the desk?"

"Bobby. He'll also be covering for me tomorrow and Tuesday while I'm off." Her words were delivered in the same dull tone she'd used on me both yesterday and earlier today when I'd arrived. The woman seemed to have only one speed and one frequency.

"Good. Enjoy your lunch."

As soon as Joan left, Clark went back to questioning me about my CPAC interview.

I was confused. Clark was behaving a lot differently towards me today than he had yesterday. Not quite hostile, but not nearly as chummy. Had something happened? Or was it Grady's presence that altered his attitude? Together, they seemed as solid as a brick wall — a wall with barbed wire strung across the top. And unlike yesterday, today in Clark's presence my antennae were buzzing with caution, telling me to watch my words and body language.

Listening to my trusty senses, I plastered on my yes-I'm-a-dummy fake smile. "I'm sure the detectives will let you know anything they find out as soon as they can."

Grady rolled his eyes before he looked away. Clark openly studied me. From the concentration in his eyes, I wished he'd follow his brother's lead and just ignore me. It was one of those times I really wouldn't have minded it.

"By the way, Clark, any progress with Mom this morning? Is she talking about what happened?"

"All she's saying now is that she stumbled upon McKenna in the maze and tried to help him."

"Do you believe her?" I noted that this question caused Grady to look in my direction.

"Why wouldn't I?"

"More importantly," I pressed, "does CPAC believe her?"

He ignored my question. "About anything else, Mom's staying tighter than her girdle."

"May I see her today?"

Grady spun around. "Why don't you just go home? No one wants you here, especially our mother."

Whoa!

Clark snapped at his brother. "Stop it, Grady."

Grady sullenly turned a back to us both.

Clark studied the back of Grady's head

before returning his attention to me. "Hard to say about Mom. We'll see how she's doing and let you know." He looked at Grady again, then back at me. "But don't get your hopes up."

They would let me know, huh? Looking first at Clark, then Grady, I seriously doubted that. Yesterday, Clark seemed perfectly fine with letting me see my mother. Today, he was throwing down strips of nails in the roadway. Something told me that unless I got into the hospital under my own steam, I'd be heading home without seeing Grace Littlejohn. And while I wanted to be sensitive to what she'd just gone through, I also didn't want to go home without some satisfaction. Last night, when Willie had asked me if I could go home without seeing her, I'd said I might have to and learn to live with it. Well, this morning I wasn't so sure.

My bullshit detectors continued to work overtime as I stood on the porch of the Holmsbury-Saxton police station talking to my half brothers. Something was rotten in the state of Denmark — or, in this case, western Massachusetts. I'd bet my plane ticket home on it.

ELEVEN

"I hear this place called the Blue Lobster is pretty good." Willie glanced over at me. "Want to try it?"

We were in Willie's SUV. We'd just left the B & B and were heading out to get some lunch and to discuss our morning activities. I'd just gotten off the phone with Greg. Considering the three-hour time difference, he'd gone into his office very early this morning to get a jump on the photos. He'd downloaded several already, enlarged them to show detail, and e-mailed them back to my personal account. After I returned from the police station, Willie and I spent almost two hours viewing them on the laptop, but with no luck. My eyes felt scratchy from all the strain.

Dev had also called this morning. When I asked him about Willie, he'd been cagey about it.

"I don't know what you're talking about,

Odelia," he'd said to me.

I was about to press the point when it struck me that Dev Frye would never be able to confess to knowing the whereabouts of William Proctor. He did, however, give me some advice.

"If Greg's *cousin* has to disappear suddenly, don't take it personally, and don't follow him."

Dev was currently working a double homicide but asked me to keep in touch. Seeing that he was a cop, I didn't tell him about the photos. I knew he'd insist I turn them over immediately, and I wasn't quite sure that was the best route to take — at least not yet.

It seemed many of the men in my life were working hard to keep me safe, even if there was no reason to worry about my safety. It felt wonderful and annoying at the same time, like biting into a warm chocolate chip cookie only to hit a piece of nutshell.

"So," Willie pressed, "the Blue Lobster, or someplace else?"

"I ate at the Blue Lobster yesterday."

"Then someplace else. Any ideas?"

I gave thought to another restaurant, then changed my mind. "No, let's go to the Blue Lobster. I ate there yesterday with Clark, so chances are slim that we'll bump into him there today."

"Good thinking, but are you sure you don't mind?"

"The food's delicious, but almost all of it is deep fried or made with mayo. That sound good to you?"

"Like heaven. My cholesterol's kind of sketchy. Can't remember when I last ate something fried."

"For dessert, we can walk next door and pick up a couple of scoops of homemade ice cream, the kind made with thick cream." I laughed. "That will throw your system into real shock."

Willie grinned. "Stop it, you're exciting me."

The Blue Lobster was bustling with activity. Most people were in casual attire but some were in dressier clothing. Those folks had probably just come from church. We claimed a table on the outside deck, not far from where we parked the car. Willie sat facing the road. I noticed his eyes were always moving, continually scanning his surroundings, making sure of all possible exits and escape routes, and all possible danger. Even when he seemed relaxed, it was obvious it was only on the surface, like a smooth, cool iceberg with its sharp, jagged edges just beneath the water.

We made our food choices, and Willie went inside to place our order. He returned with three cold bottles of beer in hand. I could easily see him and Greg bonding over beer and pizza and smiled. *Mi felon es su felon.*

Neither of us spoke about the murder or my mother. Instead, we sat enjoying the warm, humid day, surrounded by trees and fields. People came and went from the restaurant and the ice cream stand. Across the street, Buster's vegetable stand was open and just as busy.

"I love rural areas like this," Willie said, breaking the silence. "Nice, slow pace; good people; fresh air." He had polished off his first beer quickly and started on his second, taking it slower, while I nursed my one. "I prefer living in more metropolitan areas, but I always loved the country."

"Where did you grow up?"

"Would you believe Butte, Montana?"

"Not in a million years."

"It's true. Left to go to college in California and never returned. While I was at school, my dad got a job in New Jersey, and the family moved there. I adopted New Jersey as my home state after that."

"Your family still there?"

"My mother is — and my sister, who's

divorced with no kids. Father's been dead a number of years. That's where I was before I dashed up to rescue you."

"I don't need rescuing, Willie."

"It's early yet, little mama." He took a pull off his beer. "Give it time."

"I'm sorry this took you away from your family."

"Don't be — I was going to leave today anyway. I can take just so much family togetherness, especially since they frown on my unlawful status." He took another long, thoughtful draft from his beer. "Of course, they don't fuss when the substantial support money rolls in each month."

For a fleeting moment, I saw beneath the iceberg and viewed its prickly underbelly. I wondered if Willie was happy with the path he'd chosen. It seemed like a lonely life. Once, before Greg and I were married, Willie had asked me to leave everything and follow him underground. I was having my own emotional issues at the time, and for a few seconds the idea had intrigued me, although I knew I'd never be happy living the life I only imagined Willie leading.

"Speaking of family, I was very sorry to hear about your dad, Odelia. I know you two were close."

"Thanks, Willie. Dad wasn't the sharpest tool in the shed, but I never doubted that he loved me. Not for a moment." I started tearing up and internally ordered myself to knock it off.

Willie raised his bottle in my direction. "To Horten Grey. He raised one hell of a daughter."

I blushed and clinked bottles with him, winning the battle with my tears, but just barely. "To Horten Grey."

Our food came, and Willie groaned with open delight as he surveyed the plates being put in front of us. Foregoing grease today in favor of mayonnaise and butter, I'd ordered a cup of chowder and another lobster roll with coleslaw. Willie had ordered a combo plate overflowing with fried clams, scallops, fish filets, and fries, with a side of slaw.

I took my first bite of creamy chowder. "Tonight for dinner, I've *got* to find a salad."

"You and me both, little mama. But for now, we dine like pigs at the trough." He winked and licked the grease from his fingers.

While we ate, I told Willie about my time spent with the CPAC detectives and about my conversation with the Littlejohn brothers. While I was at the police station, Willie was going to have his people check out

Francis McKenna. So far, he'd heard nothing.

"I agree with you, little mama, sounds like your brothers don't want you to meet your mother. Something changed the chief's mind. Would be interesting to find out what it was, especially with the alteration in his attitude just since yesterday. He knows about your sleuthing, doesn't he?"

"Yes, I believe so."

"Maybe he's concerned you'll learn something from good ol' Mom before he does. Just because he's not on the case officially doesn't mean he's not investigating on his own."

It was the same thought that had crossed my mind. Clark had asked Dev specifically about the murders I'd been involved with. He knew I had a problem keeping my nose out of things.

"But if he knows about some of my past activities, wouldn't you think he'd *want* me involved — you know, to help?"

Willie shook his head. "First of all, little mama, cops do not like it when civilians get involved. You should know that from your dealings with Dev Frye. Secondly, it's possible the chief might not want you uncovering something he doesn't want uncovered. He might have his own ideas about the murder or its motive — ideas he doesn't want public. And you never know, either he or his brother could be involved somehow or connected in some unsavory way to the victim."

"Certainly something to consider." I took a bite of sandwich and rolled that thought around in my head while I chewed. After parking it in a compartment of my brain for later consideration, I changed the subject. "Did you find out anything at the farm?"

"Not much. People are rather shocked about the whole thing. Titillated, too. It's definitely feeding the gossip mills. A lot of curious folks were hanging around the corn maze, snapping photos of it from behind the yellow tape." He ate a fat, juicy clam and washed it down with beer. "I pretended I was a reporter and started asking questions."

I nodded. "You know, when I first entered the maze, they gave me a numbered flagpole and made a note that I was alone. They were quite diligent in telling me the procedure. That was how they controlled the number of people in the maze at any one time. I wonder if Frankie McKenna was given the flag with number one. And how did my mother get into the maze without a flag? Or was she given the first one? And if neither were, who had it? All the others were accounted for when the police rounded us up for questioning. I had number six."

I finished my beer while I gave it some thought. "I'm sure the police have notes on it, but I'm also sure they wouldn't share any of that with me."

"I managed to find someone who was working the maze that day and asked her about the first pole. She said she had noticed it missing when the maze opened for business but didn't think anything about it. She said sometimes they get misplaced or mixed up."

"You know, I forgot about something that might be important." I looked at Willie with wide eyes as a tidbit of information surfaced from the depths of my memory. "The girl at the maze also told me that someone is always posted in a watchtower above the maze. That's the person who keeps an eye out for waving flags and sends help. I wonder who was in the tower during the murder and if they saw anything?"

Willie went on alert. "That's definitely information worth pursuing. I'll go back to the farm and see who was in the tower that morning."

"Was the fair across the street open today?"

"Yep. Probably had a better turnout because of the murder. People came to gawk at the corn maze and stayed to visit the fair." He drained his bottle, then pushed back his plate. "I made the rounds of the food booths, too. Like you said, Grace was supposed to have been working the booths. The folks I spoke to had no idea what she was doing in the maze."

"People actually talked to you about it?"

Willie smiled. "Of course, little mama. I can be quite persuasive, especially when I'm hinting that their names might end up in the *New York Times.*"

"That's shameful."

"Never said my services came wrapped with integrity." His intelligent eyes measured me, deciding what to say next.

"What?" I asked. "You have more to tell me?"

"It's just that I asked around about Grace Littlejohn." He paused a long time, making me want to eat his cold, leftover fries in frustration.

"And?"

"It's just that I got the impression she wasn't a sweet little old lady."

"She wasn't a sweet middle-aged lady either." It was my turn to pause, wondering how much I wanted to know. Finally, I

146

asked the dreaded question. "What did people say about her?"

"Nothing horrible, just that she has a temper and can be stubborn and opinionated."

"Sound like anyone you know?"

He laughed. "In part, yes, but have you ever assaulted anyone?"

"You're forgetting that I shot and killed a person a few years back. You were there, remember?"

"Indeed, but you did it to save someone's life. Seems your mother has a reputation of causing scenes, even slapping people every now and then."

"She never touched me that I can remember. But then she hardly spoke to me. It was like living with a ghost."

Then I remembered Cynthia Rielley. She didn't seem to have a problem with my mother, or maybe she was just being nice. On the other hand, Cathy Morgan openly despised Grace Littlejohn. Willie interrupted my thoughts.

"People did say, though, that these incidents happened in years past, not recently. But the general consensus is that she lost her temper and did the poor schmuck in."

"I still don't buy that a seventy-seven-year-old woman had the strength to overcome and spear Frankie McKenna to death like that. You saw the photos."

"People can do amazing things when adrenaline kicks in." Willie started to get up. "I am going to get some coffee. Want anything else?"

"Some iced tea would be great. This humidity is making me sweat worse than a hundred hot flashes."

While Willie was gone, I cleaned up our table, gathering the various paper plates and plastic utensils and dumping them into a nearby trash bin. Using a couple of the little wipes, I cleaned the table top, then myself, all the time thinking about my mother's alleged temper. Actually, the cleaning was an attempt to keep busy and *not* think about my mother. It wasn't working. There weren't enough disposable moist towelettes or dirty tabletops in the world to prevent my mind from bubbling and brewing like a witch's cauldron. Then again, maybe if I started cleaning other tables, I could earn a few tips.

My mother may not have ever hurt me physically, but, if I was honest with myself, I'd have to acknowledge her white-hot temper. She and my dad went at it pretty good, especially right before they split up, with most of the violence stemming from my mother, especially when she'd been drinking. While not a common occurrence, on more than one occasion I had seen her strike him and throw objects. It had been like living in a war zone.

When Willie returned with our beverages, he had his disposable cell phone sandwiched in the crook of his neck, held there by his raised shoulder. He was speaking in Spanish. After putting the cups down on the table, he held the phone tight to his ear and continued the conversation. Mostly he listened, interjecting a few words every so often.

"According to my sources," Willie said to me after ending the conversation, "Frankie McKenna was definitely a lowlife from Boston. He worked for a drug dealer."

"A drug dealer?"

He nodded. "Yep. It was his job to act as liaison between retailers and the home office."

"Meaning?"

"McKenna probably distributed product to and picked up money from local pushers."

"Drugs? Here?"

"Wake up, little mama, drugs are everywhere. Although that doesn't necessarily mean he was in town doing business. But he did have a possible local connection." He took a sip of his coffee. I chewed the end of my straw. "I took the liberty of having my people also check into your brothers. I hope you don't mind."

"Mind? I'm actually embarrassed that I didn't think of it first." When Willie didn't offer up the information immediately, I added, "So?"

"Nothing much on Grady. He's had a string of dead-end jobs until he became a cop here, thanks to his big brother. But Clark is a different story."

After making sure no one was listening, I leaned forward. "Dev told me Clark was a good cop and even made detective, until his life and career started falling apart, mostly because of his drinking."

Again, Willie nodded. "The scuttlebutt is that Clark Littlejohn was a hotshot cop with a major drinking and whoring problem in his day. He left the force when a drug investigation went bad and several people were killed, including his partner. He killed one of the alleged dealers but was exonerated. It was determined a clean shoot."

"Dev didn't provide me with those gory details, just that Clark had a drinking problem and had screwed up his career with some bad decisions."

"And that's pretty much what happened. But it still opens the door to suspicion about his current behavior. You see, it was rumored that Clark had done some private business with the guy he shot — that he shot him to hide their relationship."

I picked my jaw up off the clean table. "You think my mother knows about that?"

"Not sure. But remember, it's just a rumor." Willie did a visual scan of our surroundings. "But it could be that McKenna is a guy from Clark's past. Maybe he was threatening to make noise, and she killed him to protect Clark."

"Or maybe Clark's involved with something illegal now. Maybe *he* did the killing, and my mother saw it and is trying to cover for him. He and Grady might even be involved in something together."

I tried to take a drink of tea but found my straw chewed beyond use. Yanking it out of the way, I brought the big glass to my lips and drank half the iced tea down in one long gulping action, much like a wet/dry shop vac. I drank until I coughed.

"Slow down," Willie cautioned. "You're going to drown in that stuff, and I don't know CPR."

I wiped my mouth with the back of my hand. "All I wanted was to find my mother, chat with her, have a good cry, maybe even scream and yell a little. After thirty-four years, I think I'm entitled. The last thing I wanted was to end up in the middle of a drug-related murder — or *any* murder. Especially one involving family."

Willie reached across the table and gently took one of my shaking hands in his. "What do you want to do?"

"I don't know."

"Do you want to go home? Just give me the word, and you're on a plane tonight back to Mr. Hot Wheels."

"Tonight? But my ticket is for tomorrow!"

"No worries, little mama. You want to go home today, we'll just swing back to the inn so you can pick up your things, then head to the airport. You can even leave the rental car. An associate of mine will turn it in for you."

Boy, it was tempting.

"You're really eager to get me on a plane back to California, aren't you?"

Willie leaned back in his chair and sipped his coffee a couple of times before answering. "I'm eager to make sure you don't get involved in something dangerous. If I get you home tonight, Greg and Dev will crown me a hero. Maybe next time, Greg will even spring for extra cheese on the pizza."

My head was starting to hurt. The pros and cons of leaving ran through it like floodwater through a gully. Who needed a mother? I had Greg's mother, a woman who loved and cared about me. I even had a crazy, bitchy stepmother. And who needed brothers? Not counting Gigi's jerk of a son, I already had two back in California. Seth Washington was the best surrogate brother anyone could have, along with Greg's older brother. I was fine without my crazy lineage.

Still, my blood ran through the veins of these people — these strangers. The old adage *blood is thicker than water* ran through my brain like an old vinyl record with a skip. But this wasn't about water, this was about drugs, murder, and people who knew about my existence but chose to pretend they didn't, or even led others to believe I was dead.

More importantly, this was about dealing with my abandonment issues and the stuff that had screwed me up for so long.

Plucking a napkin from the dispenser on the table, I dabbed at my eyes and blew my nose.

"Brothers or no brothers, Willie, let's go to the hospital. I'll give you my answer after I meet my mother. That's what I came here for, and no one, not even a bad-ass chief of police, is going to stand in the way of me doing that."

TWELVE

We didn't head straight for the hospital. After some discussion, we agreed it was best to pursue the watchtower lead while the fair was still going on. Willie had said that even though the corn maze was closed, the Tyler farm was still operating the hay rides and the concessions, with the maze now being a destination of curiosity. He also wanted to do some reconnaissance at the hospital first, to see how difficult it would be for me to see my mother before we barged on in.

I didn't feel like going back to the scene of the crime, at least not yet. So I begged off, saying I wanted to stay at the inn, maybe even take a nap. The stress of everything was getting to me, wearing me down like the rough side of a cheese grater until my nerves were raw. Before taking off, Willie kissed my cheek and told me to stay out of trouble. How much trouble could I get into taking a nap?

After Willie took off for the farm, I tried my best to settle down, but I couldn't. At the thought of finally coming face to face with my mother, my emotions were close to the surface of my skin and fairly hummed with worry. I tried to shake it off but was unsucessful. Finally, I started doodling with my earlier notes on my new extended family. To the rough outline I added an offshoot from Grady and wrote in Cathy Morgan's name. From her, it expanded to include her brothers, Buster and Clem. Under Cathy's name, I wrote *Troy.* Under Clem Brown, I jotted his wife's name. I didn't know about the rest of the Brown family, but at this point I didn't care. Tara and Troy had been the first ones to reach the murder scene. It made me wonder if they had noticed anything peculiar before Tara began screaming. Cathy had said that the police had questioned Troy, but she hadn't said if it had jarred anything loose.

In another column, I wrote down *Ollie and Abby,* with a huge question mark. Were they the sweet young couple from California they seemed to be, or were they clever murderers? Saxton did seem an odd place for such an active, vibrant couple to stop for a holiday weekend. But, I reminded myself, they did send me the photos of the crime scene. I doubted seriously if a murderer would do that, knowing or believing that the pictures would end up in the hands of the police. They'd left that morning while I was at the police station, but I couldn't recall if they said where they were heading next. Maybe they weren't even from California. Maybe they were assassins who'd set up a meeting in the maze with McKenna for the purpose of ambushing him. Ollie would have been strong enough to drive the spear through McKenna's body. And, then again, maybe they saw something they'd sooner forget, and that's why they took off so soon after the incident.

My mind was in overdrive thinking about the possibilities. I had to get out of my room before I went mad and started peeling the quaint wallpaper off the walls. Maybe I should join Willie at the corn maze. I might remember something that could be helpful.

Grabbing my car keys and bag, I trotted down the stairs and headed for the parking lot. Mrs. Friar was in the kitchen tidying up and restocking the staples for her delicious breakfasts. She was humming while she worked. Seeing her, I stopped in my tracks.

"Mrs. Friar," I said, interrupting her work. "That young couple from California, Ollie and Abby — do you know where they were heading from here? I so enjoyed meeting them."

Mrs. Friar wiped her hands on her apron and looked up. "Why, yes, I do. They went to the Cape for a few days. Staying at a B & B a friend of mine runs." Mrs. Friar stood up and took a drink from a tall glass filled with ice and pink liquid.

"Where were they before they came here? Although it's lovely here, it doesn't seem lively enough for a young couple like them."

"So true. We mostly get middle-aged and older couples. They were in Maine before coming here, at an inn run by an acquaintance of mine just outside of Portland." Mrs. Friar laughed lightly. "Most of us who operate B & B's in New England know each other, and sometimes that can be very useful. The young people wanted to go to Cape Cod from there, but it being Labor Day weekend, there were no decent vacancies and they hadn't made reservations ahead of time. Mrs. Howard — that's the innkeeper in Maine — suggested they come here and see the lovely countryside and wait for the crowds to thin out at the shore. While they were here, I made a few calls and was able to get them in starting tonight at my friend's place. It's just a few blocks from the beach."

"It's nice that you all refer to each other's

inns." It seemed clear to me that Ollie and Abby were exactly what they seemed to be. I mentally scratched them off my suspects list.

"Yes, we try to do that. And I'm sure my friend will give them some references for their next stop, if she can." She took another drink from her glass. "Oh, where are my manners? Would you like some pink lemonade, Ms. Grey?"

"No, but thank you. I'm going out for a bit."

"Where's Mr. Carter today?"

"He's off doing his own thing for a while."

Mrs. Friar suddenly turned serious. Looking around, she made sure we were alone before she spoke again. When she did, her voice was barely above a whisper. "Ms. Grey, I don't want to seem as nosy as a mouse in the pantry, but I heard today at church that you're related to that Littlejohn woman. You know, the woman who killed that man in the corn maze. Is that true?"

Well, slap me silly; what do I say to that? I scanned my brain for something, anything, to tell her, finally deciding on the truth. Anything else would just fuel the gossip flames more.

"Yes, Mrs. Friar, I am related to Mrs. Littlejohn. I came here to visit her. But I don't believe the police have determined her to be the killer."

Mrs. Friar came closer. "Well, Mrs. Brown told me that her grandson Troy got quite an eyeful. Seems he's the one who stumbled upon Mrs. Littlejohn doing the deed."

"Troy?"

She nodded. "That's what Mrs. Brown said. Troy was running through the maze like a wild man from Borneo, not minding his Aunt Tara one bit, when he ran smack into Mrs. Littlejohn and the body."

"But did he see her actually kill him?"

"Mrs. Brown didn't say — just said Troy hasn't been the same since. Had a bad nightmare last night."

After saying goodbye to Mrs. Friar, I scooted out the door to my rental car, my plans changed. I had a new destination — Buster Brown's vegetable stand.

When I got to the produce stand, there were several customers wandering the orderly displays of fresh fruit and vegetables. The stand consisted of a very large rectangular shed with a roll-up front door — like a garage but wider and more shallow. Vegetables and fruit were neatly separated, each to their own area, and displayed on high wooden tables set at a slight slant to show off the goods. Some of the produce, like apples and pears, was displayed in bushel baskets. Cards with neatly printed prices were attached to stakes and mounted above each item for sale. To the far left was a cash register and a table on which home-baked goods, jams, canned goods, and jugs of cider were offered for sale. The floor was covered with scattered hay. It was a nice and orderly setup that smelled earthy and fresh. Sniffing the air, I could identify almost every distinct item, including the particles of dirt still clinging to the skins of the vegetables. So unlike but more enjoyable than a regular supermarket.

Cathy Morgan seemed to be the only one working the stand. She was surprised to see me but friendly enough, considering I was Grace Littlejohn's daughter and Clark's half sister. I guess I hadn't done anything yet to rile her up, but with my track record, it was just a matter of time.

In between the usual customers who brought bags of produce up to the counter to be weighed and purchased, the stand also appeared to have a casual drive-up feature. While I was there, several vehicles pulled in and called to Cathy for either a dozen or half-dozen ears of fresh corn. Some just honked. She grabbed some pre-packaged bags from near the counter and trotted them out to the waiting vehicles, explaining to me that these were regular customers who'd called ahead.

"I was driving around the area and thought I'd stop by and say hello," I told her between customers. "And I wanted to see how Troy was doing. Something like this could be so traumatic, especially for a kid."

"That's nice of you, but he's fine." Her conversation was cut short by a black, late-model pickup truck that rolled into the parking area and honked two times. Cathy reached behind the counter and dashed out with two bags of corn.

When she returned, I looked wistfully at the bountiful, neatly stacked produce. "Makes me wish I could cook some up for tonight. I've eaten two days in a row at the Blue Lobster." I nodded my head in the direction of the busy restaurant across the street. "I'm in desperate need of veggies."

Cathy gave me a small smile — the first she'd granted me. "Know what you mean. Working here, I tend to go to the Lobster way too often for meals."

"Speaking of which, can you recommend a restaurant for dinner tonight? Someplace that serves good salads?"

Before dashing off to serve another drive-through customer, Cathy gave me the name of a place in a mall on the outskirts of Holmsbury, just off the interstate. It was a national chain restaurant. When she returned, I prodded further about Troy.

"I really don't mean to interfere," I told her. Who the hell was I kidding? Of course, I meant to interfere. Interfering, to me, was like nail-biting for others — a bad habit I couldn't break. "But it's just that I heard that Troy had a bad nightmare last night."

Cathy shot me a cloudy look. "Who in the hell would tell you that?" Before I could answer, she shook her head roughly, like a dog, and continued. "Argh. That damn Grady. He must've told Clark, and Clark told you, right?"

"Actually, I heard it from Mrs. Friar, the woman who runs the B & B where I'm staying."

"Bonnie Friar? Over in Saxton?"

I nodded.

"Jesus, does the whole world need to know our business?" Cathy expelled an angry gust of air. "My damn mother must've been yakking about it at church this morning. It's a wonder she ever shuts up long enough to take communion."

"So it's true? He did have a nightmare last night?"

"Kids have nightmares all the time."

"I also heard he was the first to come upon the murder scene. Is that true?"

Before she could answer, another car drove in and honked twice. Like a trained seal, Cathy grabbed two sacks of corn from behind the counter and ran out. It was then I noticed that when she came back in, she didn't put the cash for the sale into the cash register, as she had done with the other customer purchases. In fact, she didn't put it anywhere. It just seemed to disappear from the vehicle to the counter. Either she was giving the bagged corn away, or she was pocketing the money. But why? It was a family business. And why only that product? Was she stealing from her own family?

Before we could continue our conversation, a large, older woman walked up to the counter with a bag of apples and some pears, peaches, and several zucchini. Cathy carefully weighed the produce and told the woman the total price. The woman paid her. Cathy put the money into the register and gave the customer her change. Before the customer left the counter, a red coupe pulled into the drive and honked once. Cathy excused herself and delivered a single bag of corn to the driver of the coupe. Upon returning to the stand, Cathy did not put any money into the register. Before it pulled out, I checked the plates on the coupe. The vehicle was from New Hampshire.

Alone again, Cathy picked up our conversation without answering my last question. "Don't worry about Troy. He'll be fine in time — at least he will be if the police leave him alone. He's been questioned twice by those jerks from CPAC, on top of the interrogation he went through at the farm. They won't leave him alone. I'm just short of filing harassment charges."

"They called me back into the station today for more questioning," I said sympathetically.

"Every time they question him, Troy gets so nervous, he gets headaches. They're scaring the shit out of him."

"Maybe you should take him to a counselor so he can talk about how he feels about what he saw."

Cathy Morgan looked at me like I was a dunce. "Isn't that what he's doing with the cops, talking about it? I think what he needs to do is stop thinking about it altogether." She rearranged the jars of jams. They were already as neat as a regiment of soldiers lined up for inspection. "What they need to do is arrest that old bag. It's obvious she killed McKenna."

"Grace? You really think my mother killed

that man?"

Cathy leaned towards me until she was so close, I could smell the shampoo she'd used that morning on her hair. "If she were my mother, I'd run — run like hell, all the way back to California. *Today.*"

She certainly didn't try to hide her hatred for Grace Littlejohn, not even from me.

"I get the feeling you two don't get along."

"Oh, please. No one who's ever dated Grady has been good enough for him. Even back in high school." Cathy laughed. "The only time she had anything nice to say about Linda — that's Clark's ex — was after they divorced. The old woman's a piece of work." While she talked, she moved over to a display and busied herself rearranging a few plump tomatoes that had the audacity to break rank.

"Once you and Grady are married, you'll be faced with dealing with Grace for a long time."

"Hopefully not too long. The bitch can't live forever."

Geez, even though my mother and I weren't close, that comment was way over the line in lack of taste and sensitivity. Cathy seemed oblivious to the fact she'd just told me she hoped my mother wouldn't live much longer. In fact, she appeared rather gleeful over the notion.

"And what about Clark?" I asked. "There didn't seem to be any love lost between the two of you either."

"Clark's an asshole." Cathy took a deep breath and looked out towards the Blue Lobster. "Don't like him, never did." A hot blush streaked her cheeks. She was either lying or had come down with a sudden fever.

"Clark seems like an okay guy to me. A bit gruff, maybe."

"Told you, he's an asshole." She marched away to attend a newly arrived customer — one who had walked in, not honked like some ill-mannered date.

Cathy Morgan used very colorful descriptions in discussing the people in my family. I wondered what my assigned word would end up being and how long it would be before I was tagged with it, much as a freeway overpass is tagged by miscreants wielding spray paint.

After cashing up the customer and taking care of another drive-through, Cathy came back to where I stood. "Tell me, was Grace such an evil bitch when she was younger?"

I thought about the question before answering, comparing Grace Grey to Grace Littlejohn. "Yes and no. She could be very difficult, but she was quieter about it. She was drinking then, so she was out of it a lot of the time. She didn't so much interfere with as much as neglect the people around her."

"I wish she'd go back to drinking and neglecting. Be a whole lot easier on Grady and me, that's for sure."

"How does Troy get along with Grace?"

"She doesn't pick on him like she does the women around her. In fact, she rather favors him. I think he reminds her of Grady, even though he's not Grady's natural son."

A white sedan pulled in and honked. Before trotting out to the waiting car, Cathy grabbed not only a bag of corn but another smaller bag that appeared to hold several yellow and green squash. This time, though, Cathy didn't come right back in. Instead, heated words could be heard between her and the driver of the vehicle. No one else was in the stand at the moment. Picking up a small handheld shopping basket, I moved to the outside edge of the building, closer to the parking lot, and considered some pears while tuning my ears to the conversation. The gist of it seemed to be that the driver owed Cathy money, and she wasn't giving him the merchandise until he paid up. The amount of six hundred dollars was tossed about a few times. Finally, the car took off, peeling out of the drive, sending gravel like shrapnel in its wake. Cathy returned to the stand, still holding the bags of vegetables.

After tossing in a couple of different kinds of apples, I took my basket to the counter. I nodded at the bag of corn in her hand. "Change his mind?"

"Damn loser. Running a tab and won't pay. I made it clear, no cash, no produce."

"A tab for fruit and vegetables?"

Cathy glanced up at me, then looked away. "Sure, for a few locals. People are always stopping by for stuff on their way home and don't have cash on them. We trust them. Generally, they drop the money off the next day. But that guy," she jerked a chin towards the road. "He stiffs us all the time. You don't think of vegetables as being expensive, but it adds up."

She was about to say more when a battered truck rolled into the side parking area. On the side was stenciled *Brown Bros.* Clem hopped out of the cab, followed by a German shepherd. He grabbed a box of produce from the back of the truck and headed in our direction. "Got nothing better to do than beat your gums?" he said to Cathy when he reached us.

"Don't worry, Clem," Cathy responded, a hand on her hip. "I'm working. This place is neat as a pin, and the customers are happy."

Clem Brown turned to me and furrowed his brow until his forehead looked like the fields he planted. The dog stood at attention by his side. "This isn't a coffee klatch. If you're going to buy the stuff in your basket, then do it and be gone. Cathy's got work to do."

Pretty sure Clem had killed my discussion with Cathy, I bought my fruit and said goodbye. As I was leaving, I glanced back in my rear-view mirror. Clem was staring at me, watching me leave. Or was that making sure I was leaving?

THIRTEEN

At home in California, I walk almost every day for exercise, with Wainwright as my companion. It had only been a couple of days, but I missed my morning walk. It wasn't merely good exercise; it also helped me to think clearly. Many a problem, big and small, had been dissected and brought to resolution while pounding the pavement and the sand around Seal Beach. Most of the time when I travel, I toss exercise clothes into my luggage just in case I feel the need to move my joints and clear my head. This trip, although only a couple days, was no different. Back at the B & B, I changed into some black, stretchy exercise capris and a long purple tee shirt with a sunburst on the front. Instead of taking my iPod, which is usually plugged into my ears during my walks, I tucked my cell phone in the pocket of my pants in case either Willie or Greg called.

I headed south on the winding road in front of the inn. There were no sidewalks, just dirt and gravel shoulders on each side of the narrow road, with lush vegetation beyond that. Along the left side was a low, irregular stone fence, uneven and jagged in spots, that had probably been there since the time of the minutemen. Overhead, the trees, slender birch and sturdy maples, whispered in the humid breeze as a chorus to the gentle hum of insects and call of birds. The air was sweet and heavy. I filled my lungs with it, sucking it deep into every chamber. The road wasn't well traveled. Just the odd car or truck went by while I plodded along. In the distance, I heard the call of a child, followed by the bark of a dog. Houses were sparse, and the ones I saw were well maintained, with large yards and gardens. As I passed one house, I smelled charcoal being fired up in an outdoor grill.

With the steady slap of my sneakers as the metronome for my thoughts, the details of the last two days marched through my brain in chronological order. I inspected each one for clues and details. Then I started mentally rearranging them, hoping to make some sense of the chaos.

My mother was found hovering over a dead body, with blood on her hands. *Check.*

My mother seemed too old to have stabbed McKenna with the broken flagpole. *Check.* Troy Morgan may have been the first one to stumble upon the scene. *Check.* McKenna was known to be involved with drugs. *Check.* Clark was involved with a drug-related shooting in Boston years ago. *Check.* Cathy was lying about her feelings about Clark. *Maybe.* Something funny was going on at Buster's. *Double check.*

Pulling out my phone, I called Willie. "Where are you?" I asked, as soon as he answered.

"The question, little mama, is where are *you?* You're huffing and puffing like the little engine that could."

"I'm in the middle of a power walk to burn off stress and some of that fattening food."

"Me, I'm at the hospital. I have an idea how you can get a little one-on-one time with your mother."

"Great. And the watchtower?" I talked while walking, keeping my eyes on the road in front of me while my brain concentrated on the call. The exercise and humidity caused sweat to flow down my forehead and back like champagne at New Year's. I wiped my brow with my free hand and wished I'd brought a bottle of water.

"I have the name of the kid manning it during the time of the murder. He wasn't there today, so I couldn't talk to him, but he's local, so it shouldn't be too difficult to find him."

"What's his name?"

"Marty Cummings."

"Cummings? A Joan Cummings works at the police station. Wonder if she's any relation."

"That's his mother. When I asked around about the kid, someone told me his mother worked at the PD."

"Are you lying to people again, Willie, telling them they might get their names in the paper?"

"Hey, if something works for me, I stick with it. But here's the interesting thing. One of the other kids working at Tyler's told me Marty wasn't in the tower that morning like he was supposed to be."

"So he wasn't the one who spotted the flags and called for help."

"No, someone on the ground saw them and heard the screams."

My feet stopped moving. Paused in the road, I concentrated on remembering the configuration of the maze and the area around it. "So where was this Marty kid if he wasn't at his post?"

Willie laughed. "They found him in the port-a-john, stoned out of his mind."

"Potted in the potty?" It struck me as funny and would have been funnier had someone not died that morning.

"There's more. The other kid told me Marty had a nice, plump bag of weed on him when he was found, but out of deference to his mother and her position, the cops ignored that little fact and just questioned him. Farmer Tyler, on the other hand, fired the little sucker."

Drugs again. And now the puzzle of Joan Cummings' outburst made sense. It was her son who had been nabbed for drugs and handcuffed in front of everyone. No wonder she was on the verge of going postal that morning. I put my feet back to work, using the rhythm to keep my thoughts focused.

"Willie, I paid a visit to the produce stand this afternoon, and something funny is going on down there. My gut tells me it's drugs."

"Why not? It's organic."

"I'm serious, Willie." I filled him in on my observations about the drive-through customers who received special corn in special bags and how none of that money appeared to be going into the general till. I also told him about Cathy's fight with the driver of the white sedan and my not-so-cordial greeting by Clem Brown.

"Certainly sounds fishy. Why don't I drive over there and check it out?"

"You going to pose as a customer?"

"Not exactly. Most likely, she has a specific client base. A stranger wandering in and asking for a little something special immediately would make her think 'undercover cop.' But don't worry, I'll come up with something."

I glanced at my watch. "Do you want to meet up at the inn later? Or should I go straight to the hospital instead?"

"Let's meet at the hospital in about two and a half hours. That will be right about dinnertime for most folks. My contact says there are few visitors at that time. Most come earlier in the day or after their dinner. The patients themselves eat pretty early."

"You have a contact at the local hospital?" It boggled my mind.

"I do now." I could hear his smirk through the phone.

After hanging up from Willie, I repocketed my cell and threw myself into my walking, pumping my arms and pushing my chunky legs like steady pistons. I kept it up for another ten minutes, then crossed the street and started back, keeping up the same steady pace. Pushing my body harder, I tried not to think about meeting my mother in a few hours.

Not very far from the inn, I saw a car approach. As the distance between us closed, I noted that it was a dark blue, late-model Honda. It slowed down. As soon as it passed, the car made a U-turn and pulled up next to me. I glanced over to see the driver was the reporter from outside the police department yesterday morning, the young blond.

"Mrs. Stevens, may I have a word with you?" she called from her vehicle.

I kept walking, wondering how she got my name. The car kept pace with me. "I gave my report to the police. I have nothing to say to you."

"Mrs. Stevens, as I told you yesterday, my name is Brenda Bixby. I'm a journalist."

"I remember." In spite of being tired, I moved my legs a little faster. "Still have nothing to say."

"I'm working on a special story involving yesterday's murder, and I need your help."

I ignored her.

"You see, I don't think the murder is the real story. I think the real story is *you*."

I stopped in my tracks and stared at her. The car pulled ahead a few feet before it also stopped. Brenda Bixby stepped out of the car but didn't move towards me. She was dressed in slim, snug-fitting jeans and a tight green sweater, both showing her figure off to its best advantage. Her long blond hair was loose around her pretty face. Studying her now, I could see she was much younger than I had thought the day before, perhaps only in her mid-twenties.

"I know you're Grace Littlejohn's daughter, Mrs. Stevens. And I know you haven't seen your mother in a very long time." She ran a hand through her hair, pushing it behind an ear on one side. "Tell me how it feels to finally come face to face with her over a corpse."

"Is this some kind of sick joke?"

"It's no joke, Mrs. Stevens. Our viewers will eat this up. Mother goes missing. Years later, daughter finds her — but when she does, Mommy is covered in a dead man's blood. It's sensational."

I shook my head in disbelief. "How could you know all this?"

Brenda Bixby shot me a smug look. "I have my sources." She took a small step towards me. "Since yesterday, I've done quite a bit of digging on you, Odelia Grey Stevens. Married to a paraplegic. Reside in Seal Beach, California. Paralegal at the same law firm for many years. Why, you're even a notary." She took another step in my direction. "More importantly, you have a nose for murder."

"Cripes." I stomped my right foot in frustration. "Has the whole freaking world Googled me this week?"

She laughed. "I didn't Google you. I'm a journalist. I have information sources most people don't."

Geez, now she was sounding like Willie.

"What do you want, Ms. Bixby? I have to get back and get ready for an appointment."

"You going to see your mother?"

"Not unless Chief Littlejohn says she's up to meeting me, which doesn't seem likely."

"Give me your story, Odelia. I'll make it worth your while."

"That's Mrs. Stevens to you."

At first, Brenda looked surprised by my snappish comment, then her facial features melted back into her former smug demeanor. "I can always write it without you, based on the information I've already dug up."

I started walking away. "Be my guest," I shot over my right shoulder. "Just be careful of slander. I have my sources, too. Legal ones."

"Maybe I'll even throw in a few hints that

you and mommy weren't so estranged after all. Maybe the two of you did Frankie Mc-Kenna in, and you're letting Grace Little-john take the fall."

I stopped short, my anger bubbling inside like a pressure cooker with a faulty valve.

"Seems awfully strange that you'd find her on exactly the day she chose to kill someone, doesn't it?" Brenda's tone was haughty and taunting, grating on my nerves, bringing up awful memories of being teased and bullied when I was in elementary school, an age when kids made fun of you to your face, before they learned to hide it in giggles produced from behind cupped hands, then graduated to blindsiding you on rural roads.

No, Odelia, I told myself. *Don't rise to her bait. Keep walking.* I continued to put one foot in front of the other, putting distance between me and Brenda Bixby with each step of my size 9 sneakers. Up ahead, I could see the Maple Tree Bed and Breakfast. I was almost up to a jog.

"Whatever it is you and your mother are hiding, Odelia," Brenda called from behind me, "I'll find it. Trust me — I have a nose for a red-hot story."

FOURTEEN

Three Rivers Community Hospital was located on the banks of a river just outside of Holmsbury. It was a tidy, modern, two-story facility that served the general needs of the communities around it. It was also small — so small that it could have fit into the parking lot of Hoag Hospital back in Newport Beach. Its size, and the fact that the local people all seemed to know one another, was going to make it difficult to get in to see my mother without rousing curiosity.

Just as I pulled into the hospital parking lot, my cell phone rang. It was Willie. I tapped the button on my earpiece to answer.

"Where in the hell are you?" he asked. "You're late. Did you get cold feet?"

"I'll explain later. I'm pulling into the parking lot right now."

It had taken me forever to drive from the inn to the hospital because I was paranoid that the journalist from hell was following me. I drove up and down country roads, got on the interstate, got off the interstate — I even drove to a mall and had a cup of coffee before finally making my way to the hospital through the magic of the GPS. Brenda Bixby swore she'd get to the bottom of whatever I was hiding. Well, I wasn't hiding anything, unless you counted Willie. The last thing I wanted was for her to do her gold-star digging on him.

I spotted Willie's SUV parked between two pickups on the far side of the building. I started to head for it, but he stopped me.

"Don't park near me," he warned. "But don't park close to the entrance either — that's where the chief would park. I was told he's already been here today, but you never know. Do you see his vehicle anywhere?"

I scanned the parking lot for Clark's car but didn't see it. There weren't any other official vehicles in evidence either.

"Nope. No police cars either."

"Good."

After parking, Willie gave me further instructions. "Your mother is in a room on the second floor in the back. There doesn't appear to be any special watch on her, which makes me think the cops don't link her to the actual killing of McKenna.

Otherwise, there would be a guard."

"So I can just saunter in?" It seemed too easy, but I'd take easy over difficult any day.

"Not so fast, slick. I'm sure the nurses are keeping an eye out for reporters and will question anyone not instantly recognized as a family member. Clark might even have them keeping an eye out for you specifically."

I was keeping my eyes peeled for reporters, too. "So what can we do?"

"Don't worry, I have it all set up."

As Willie directed, I parked my car and walked into the hospital like I knew what I was doing. Once there, I was to hang a left and walk to the end of the corridor. I followed his instructions and found myself in the hospital chapel. Up front, a woman knelt in prayer. The chapel was small and dimly lit, the only sound being the woman crying through her mumbled supplication. I sat in a pew near the back and off to the side and waited.

It wasn't long before the doors to the chapel opened, and there she was — my mother. She was being pushed in a wheelchair by a young African-American man in an orderly uniform. When he spotted me, he directed the chair in my direction. My mother's head was slightly down and her eyes appeared closed. She was dressed in a hospital gown and thin cotton robe. Across her lap was a light blanket. Her short, permed hair had been brushed away from her face, and her glasses rested low on her nose. She looked old and shrunken. She didn't look up until her chair stopped in front of me. When she did, she didn't look surprised at all.

The young man nodded to me and told my mother he'd be back in fifteen minutes to get her. Then he went over to the woman praying. "Mrs. Collins, Mr. Collins is awake now, if you'd like to see him."

The woman looked up, her wet, swollen face full of hope. After crossing herself in front of the altar, she followed the orderly out.

The first words spoken to me by my mother in over thirty-four years were, "I knew you'd come."

"Really? How could you know that, especially since you hardly know me at all." I kept my voice low out of respect for my surroundings. My tone, however, was another story, as I struggled with the emotional rumblings inside me.

"I know you, Odelia, better than you think." She gave me a short nod and a half wink. "Clark told me you'd changed your mind, but I didn't believe him. You never were the type to give up easily. I knew once you'd found me, you wouldn't leave without saying what you'd come to say."

Okay, so she does know me. And obviously Clark doesn't or he never would have lied. What's more, why would he tell her that unless he was confident he could keep us apart? He must think I'm a docile fool — that I would go along with whatever he and Grady cooked up to tell me. It only made me more determined to get to the bottom of things.

We stared at each other, my mother and I, neither speaking. I felt the weight of time ticking away. How could I say what I had to say to this woman in under fifteen minutes?

"Aren't you going to ask me if I killed Frankie McKenna? Everyone else has."

"Of all the questions I do have for you, Mom, that isn't one of them."

"No?"

"I've never thought you killed him. And I don't think the police think you're the killer either. If they did, there would be no way they'd let you out of your room without a police escort. You'd be under constant surveillance."

She looked at me with greater interest. "That's right, you're some sort of modern

Miss Marple, aren't you? I read about you on the Internet."

"You Googled me?" I raised my hands in surrender.

"Every year on your birthday since I got my own computer. At first there was nothing, then some interesting things started showing up."

A doozy of a headache was forming behind my left eye, giving me a lopsided squint.

Grace Littlejohn scanned me up and down. "I see you never lost your baby fat."

"No, Mom. As much as I tried to duck it, it just kept finding its way back."

She chuckled softly. "I remember how you used to love those mint Girl Scout cookies. Me, I always liked the shortbread, but every year you'd beg me to buy the mint ones. If I didn't watch you, you'd eat the whole box. You still eat those things?"

"Every chance I get." I said the words with defiance and a jaw set in concrete. "You don't happen to have any on you now, do you, Mom?"

My sarcasm went right over her head. "It's September, Odelia." She shook her head as if I'd just declared a belief in purple-spotted aliens. "Who in the world would have Girl Scout cookies this time of year?"

"Geez, how about me? I have at least six

boxes in my home freezer and two in my desk drawer at the office."

She laughed again, then stopped short like someone pulled her plug from a wall socket. "You're serious, aren't you? No wonder you're still as big as a house."

The headache marched to my other eye, advancing on it without mercy.

"A girl's got to find comfort where she can, Mom. You found the bottle. I found cookies." I watched the meaning of my words seep into her skull like ink on a blotter, but she gave no indication of its impact.

"You must be fifty years old by now. You married? Got any kids?"

She was trying to steer the conversation towards common pleasantries. Okay, I'd play her game, at least for a few minutes, but old woman or not, I wasn't going to let her off that easy. As she said, I came to say what I had to say.

"Wasn't that on Google?" When she didn't respond to my sass, I answered her questions. "I've been married almost two years. No children."

"Married kind of late, didn't you?" When I didn't reply, she studied me again. "How did you find me, Odelia? Did Horten finally tell you? He still married to that lunatic?"

I swallowed hard. "Dad's dead. He died just a few months ago."

"I'm —" she started, then hesitated before continuing. "I'm sorry." The words squeaked out of her like air squeezed from a rubber ducky, and the emotion seemed genuine. "Though I'm not surprised. I have one foot in the grave myself, and he was older than me by several years."

"Gigi gave me a box of his things. There was an envelope inside the box with your name and an address in New Hampshire."

She nodded. "Yes, I remember. Wrote it while I was in that hospital up north. I was there a few months drying out. That was the first time I wrote him, and the last. He made it clear I wasn't welcome."

"Welcome? Were you coming back?"

She gave off a sad little laugh. "No, I wasn't coming back. It was part of the process, asking people's forgiveness."

I scanned my memory bank for information. Clark had said Mom had been sober for nearly twenty-five years, and the letter had been sent about that long ago.

"You mean the twelve-step program?"

She nodded without looking at me. "Yes, step nine, as I recall." She turned to look directly at me. There was a glimmer of pride in her eyes. "I've been sober a very long time, Odelia. I want you to know that."

"Clark told me. I'm glad, Mom. Really, I am." *Still pissed,* I said to myself, *but glad.*

"I wrote to your father. I asked him to forgive me for disappearing and leaving you like I did."

My headache increased. My brain exploded into shards like dishes smashed at a Greek party.

"And what about *me,* Mom? I don't recall receiving a letter." My voice rose a notch, jabbing the air like an ice pick. When she didn't answer, I added with lower volume, "Wouldn't Dad give you my address?"

The little old lady with the frizzy hair and doughy body retreated into herself. For a moment, I feared she was going to up and die, simply expire on the spot, leaving me with the same unanswered questions and yet another dead body. This was my mother; the woman who gave me life. While I didn't want to throw my arms around her neck and weep, neither did I want to kick her over the side of a building. After all these years, I still wasn't sure what I wanted from her. Answers, yes, but what else? I rubbed my temples and waited. After a bit, she came out of herself, much like a turtle from its shell. She looked at me and braced herself, as if readying for a slap she was sure would come.

"I never asked Horten for your address. I only asked his forgiveness."

It was an honest response and to the point, and so was my reply, which came back at her like a corresponding left jab. "I repeat, what about me? Didn't *I* deserve an apology? Or wasn't abandoning a sensitive, insecure teenage girl a worthy enough transgression?"

Grace Littlejohn looked around the empty chapel. I couldn't tell if she was stalling for time or looking for an escape. Without looking at me, she said, "Step nine is about making amends to people we've injured." She turned her face back to me. "Except when such amends might hurt the other person." She looked down at her hands, which I noticed for the first time were shaking. She clutched them together in an effort to control them. "I felt it would do you more harm to have me back in your life than to stay away."

Standing up from the pew, I positioned myself directly in front of her. I stared down at her. She looked up, recoiling slightly, but kept her eyes pinned to mine.

"So you thought it best for me to remain in the dark? To keep wondering for thirty-four years what it was I did that drove you away? Never knowing if you were alive or dead?"

"Your father could have told you I was alive."

"My father obviously thought it best to keep you away from me. Right or wrong, he was doing his job — protecting me." I took a few steps back, afraid of the raw emotion spouting from me like bile. "Did Dad know why you left?"

She shook her head slowly back and forth. "I never told him."

I turned away from Grace Littlejohn and inhaled deeply, blowing it out in one big gush of air like a punctured tire. I repeated the process a few times and felt my headache subside a little. A part of me wanted to leave. *It would be easy,* I told myself. *Just go back to the inn, grab my things, and let Willie drive me to whichever airport offered the next flight back to California.* Isn't that why I came to the hospital — to determine if I was going to take a flight today or wait until my scheduled flight tomorrow? Although at this minute, I couldn't see what good staying one more day would do.

I took another deep breath. *Go ahead, Odelia,* I told myself, *ask her the question you've been wanting to ask since you were sixteen years old. Do it now, and get it over with. Shit or get off the pot.*

Turning back around, I said, "So, Mom, the fifty-million-dollar question: why *did* you leave?"

FIFTEEN

"No, Odelia, absolutely not."

Willie and I were seated in a booth at the restaurant Cathy had recommended. In front of us were large, empty salad bowls. I'd had a mixed vegetable chopped salad with chicken, and Willie had devoured a Cobb salad. We were settling in with mugs of decaf coffee and discussing the day.

"Yes, Willie, it's what I have to do."

"You're going back to the inn and packing your stuff," he ordered. "If you don't, I'll pack it for you."

I could tell he was serious.

"I have to do this, Willie."

"No, you don't. You don't owe that woman anything, Odelia. Not a damn thing. And I'm sure your husband would agree with me on this. Not to mention Dev Frye."

"It's not about owing anyone anything." I struggled to keep my voice down. "It's about doing what's right in my gut. And my gut is saying to stay and help her."

"Did she ask you for help?"

I looked away. "No, she didn't."

"Did she ask you to stay?"

My eyes were bulging like strained levees, fighting to hold back the tears. "No, she didn't." I felt a chill and covered my shoulders with my sweater.

"Did she at least tell you why she left all those years ago? Did she have any sort of explanation for her behavior?"

"Yes." My voice was small, as if coming from someone else — a stranger whispering to me from the other side of a closed window.

When I'd asked my mother why she'd left thirty-four years ago, she answered me without a single hesitation.

"I was pregnant and ran off with the baby's father." Her words were clipped and sharp, like cut fingernails that still needed filing.

"Pregnant? With Grady?"

Without confirmation, she'd moved forward with her story. "I didn't want to bring shame on you, Odelia." My mother straightened herself in the wheelchair and pulled the lap blanket closer. "What young woman needs a drunk mother with an illegitimate baby?"

"You cold, Mom?" I started to tuck her blanket up a little higher across her chest.

With a trembling hand, she waved me off and continued. "I thought you'd be better off without me. And a long, teary goodbye wouldn't have helped either of us. I thought it best to simply disappear."

"Best for whom?"

She gave me a hard look. "Best for all, Odelia. And I still feel that way, so don't go trying to make me feel sorrier than I already am. I'm not the nurturing, guilt-ridden, motherly type. Never was."

I gave her my own steely stare. "And don't I know it."

Clark had said that Grady's birth certificate didn't name a father, that Grace had given him the surname of Grey until Leland Littlejohn adopted him.

"What happened to the guy, Mom? Did you love him?"

"Thought I did." Her voice retreated until it became small and shaky. "For a while, I thought I might be able to start fresh, but he dumped me in Missouri. I knew I couldn't go back to California, so I came here to Leland. I knew he'd at least take Grady in, though I wasn't sure he'd do the same for me."

"But he did. Clark's father took you

back, right?"

My mother nodded. "Yes, seems he . . . well, he had a purpose for me. And he fell in love with Grady at first sight. We remarried."

"One big happy family, huh? And what about Clark? According to him, you left him behind when he was not much more than a toddler. Bet he has some resentment he's never worked out. Seems to be a pattern here, don't you think?"

"That was different, Odelia. Leland didn't want me, he only wanted Clark. I was a baby machine and housekeeper to him, nothing more."

"Excuse me?"

Her voice changed from that of an old woman with regrets to one of defense. "Leland Littlejohn was a homosexual living in the closet. They had to back then. He was an engineer with a large company and didn't want to jeopardize his career. He also wanted children, plain and simple. We had a deal. He'd marry me. I'd have a baby for him. After, I was free to divorce him, as long as I gave custody of the child to him. In return, he'd provide me with a settlement that would give me a new start."

I reeled back, never expecting this. Growing up, my mother had never told me anything about her past, and questions about it were met with growls. I'd finally stopped asking. I knew my father's parents were from England and came to the States via Canada. They were older when they had him and had no other family that he knew of. Both had died when he was a young man. Dad had settled in California after being discharged from the Army. Mom, on the other hand, had refused to say anything about her people or her origins. It was as if she'd been left behind by aliens — like E.T., but not as wise or as entertaining.

"So you popped Clark out on demand, then hit the trail with cash in your pocket."

"Don't be so crass, Odelia." My mother's eyes sparked with a flash of indignation. "I stayed for a couple of years. I didn't have the best upbringing, and Leland was a kind, decent man, a lot like your father. I thought maybe I could make a home with him, be safe and secure for once, but, quite frankly, I was much younger than Leland and far too restless for life here in the sticks. I left before I did something that might jeopardize him and Clark."

"Does Clark know about his father? About his being gay?"

"Yes, both he and Grady finally figured it out, but I don't think anyone outside the house knew. To everyone else, we appeared to be a normal family." My mother laughed. It came out as a cackle worthy of a Halloween witch. "To the town, I was the prodigal wife who'd finally come to her senses, returning to her loving, long-suffering husband with a bastard child in tow."

"That must have been difficult for you."

"Better than living on the street. And I did have a secure life with Leland, although hardly a conventional marriage. We even became close over the years."

As I readied to approach the next topic, I wrapped my arms around myself, more for protection than for warmth. "I understand you told your sons about me — but you also told them I was dead." I didn't want to ride the slippery slope to whiney bitch, but I couldn't seem to help myself. "How convenient."

"I never told the boys you were dead."

"But you led them down the path to believing it, didn't you?"

She said nothing but at least had the decency to look down.

Putting my hands on the back of a pew, I stared at the large cross hanging behind the altar. After thirty-four years, I finally had the answer to the question that had haunted me. Now I had to ask myself a difficult question: Was it enough? Could I return to California and not look back? I still wasn't sure.

A glance at my watch told me our fifteen minutes were long gone. The orderly would be returning any moment. I turned back to the waiting Grace Littlejohn. "And what about the murder, Mom?"

My mother looked at me, her jaw set, her eyes watery. "You know, you and Clark are a lot alike — single-minded, like a broken record. Not Grady, though; I'm not sure any solid thoughts go through that good-looking head of his."

I kept my broken record of a brain on track. "The murder, Mom."

"Whatever you think of me, Odelia, I'm no murderer."

"I believe you. But I'll bet those six boxes of Thin Mints back in California that you know who did it."

"Nonsense. How could I possibly know that?"

"What were you doing in the corn maze? Weren't you supposed to be running the food booths across the street?"

"I was just trying to help that poor man. See if he was still alive."

"You didn't answer my question, Mom.

Why were you in the corn maze to begin with?"

"Why shouldn't I be there? Lots of folks go through the maze."

"By yourself?"

She kept her weak eyes on me. "You were alone in the thing, weren't you? At least that's what I remember."

She had a point. "Yes, I was alone. I was curious about it and killing time before going back to the food booths to look for you again." I sat down on the pew across from my mother. "But I had a flag. No one remembers signing you into the maze, Mom. If you had a flag, it could have been number one, and that flag was found stuck in a man's chest."

"I had no damn flag."

"Who had number one, Mom?"

"Quit badgering me. I've said all I'm going to on the matter."

When Willie and I met up at the restaurant, I'd told him about the whole ordeal. It only made him more determined to get me on a plane back to California. We both tried calling Greg — me to spring the news that I would be staying longer, and Willie to beg Greg to talk some sense into me. We both got voice mail and left messages.

"You don't have to stay, Odelia." Willie

took a drink of coffee. "They don't need you."

His voice was low and controlled, like the warning growl of a lion before he strikes. I'd never heard this tone from him before, so unlike his usual joking manner. It was the voice of the fugitive that lurked beneath the surface . . . the voice of a man who had fleeced thousands of ordinary people out of their hard-earned nest eggs, seemingly without so much as a twinge of regret.

"No, but my mother does."

"Your brothers are cops. CPAC is on the case. What services could you offer that they could not?"

When I didn't answer, he came in for the kill. "You're not disposable, Odelia. This woman's already cast you aside once like yesterday's news for her beloved sons. Don't let her use you and dump you again."

While intellectually I understood what Willie was saying, in my heart I felt the need to help my mother — even after everything she'd done, and even if she didn't want my help. I was positive she knew who killed McKenna, and I told her so. When I begged her to at least talk to her lawyer about it, she again refused.

"I don't care what they do to me, Odelia," my mother had said. "I told you, I'm not saying anything more."

"But Mom," I'd reasoned, "there's a killer out there still on the loose. They might kill again."

She'd shaken her head in disagreement. "I don't think they will, Odelia."

Willie took both of my hands in his. He was still irritated by my decision, but he'd packed away his anger, trying a different tack to get me on a plane. "It sounds like your mother's protecting someone, little mama. And if that's the case, you're not going to budge her."

"But maybe I could budge Troy. He might have seen something. When I asked my mother about Troy — whether or not she'd seen him prior to the rest of us getting there — that's when she zipped her lip good and tight. I'll bet he saw something important. I was told he's been nervous and had a nightmare last night."

"He's a kid. If he saw a murder in progress, you can bet your booty he's having nightmares."

I pointed an index finger at Willie. "Especially if he saw who did it and knows them."

He nodded in agreement. "He might be frightened of that person finding out he knows something, or even frightened that someone else might find out who that person is. Depends on his relationship with whoever did it."

"Speaking of Troy, did you get a chance to check out his family's produce stand?"

"That I did. I sat on the porch of the Blue Lobster and nursed a beer while I did surveillance."

"Tough work, but I guess someone's gotta do it."

Willie winked at me and took a sip of coffee. "And my hard-core investigation concludes that you are probably right, little mama. They are selling more than corn and tomatoes from that place. The drive-through traffic was far too high for a simple stand of that type. What's more, Cathy had help today."

"Really? Maybe her sister-in-law, Tara Brown?"

He shook his head. "No, a guy. Kind of brawny."

"Probably one of her brothers."

"Definitely one of the farmers. He drove a truck up to the stand and unloaded some things. A boy was with him. Kind of gangly but strong. Fair hair. Early teens, maybe a bit younger. Hard to tell. There was a dog, too. A shepherd."

"The man was probably Clem. He had a German shepherd with him last time I saw him. The boy could have been Troy or maybe a cousin. I don't know much about the whole family situation."

"After he finished unloading his truck, the farmer helped service the drive-up customers. The way he was joking around with some of them, I'd say they were definitely long-time regulars. After helping unload, the kid disappeared into the stand."

I swished the information around in my head to blend it with the other data already stored there. "Drugs, Willie. Something is telling me this is all about drugs."

"Seems like a good possibility."

"But it still doesn't explain what my mother was doing crouched over the body of a drug dealer from Boston if the Browns are the local drug contacts."

The waitress cleared our salad dishes and refreshed our coffee. "Would you folks like anything else tonight? How about some dessert?"

"I'll take some coffee," we heard a voice from behind me say.

Turning, I laid my sorry eyes on Brenda Bixby, the pain-in-the-ass reporter. The last thing I wanted was for her to meet up with Willie. I'd told him about her during dinner and about her promise to dig up whatever she assumed I was hiding. He didn't seem alarmed, just amused.

When the waitress left to get the coffee, Brenda tried to scoot into my side of the booth. I scooted towards the outside, making sure there was no room. "I don't recall inviting you to sit with us."

Brenda ignored me and held out her hand to Willie. "Brenda Bixby, reporter."

Willie took her hand and started moving over to make room for her. "Come on, Odelia," Willie said, a big smile on his face. "We can't have this lovely young lady having her coffee all alone, especially since she's a friend of yours."

"My friends have more manners than Ms. Bixby."

Ignoring my slam, Brenda flashed a toothy smile at Willie and sat in the booth next to him. The waitress brought her a cup of coffee.

"Now, isn't this nice?" Brenda put two packets of artificial sweetener and two creamers into her coffee and stirred while Willie and I looked on — me with a scowl, him with the same delight a kid displays on Christmas morning. I couldn't tell if his foolish grin was the result of Brenda's youth, her looks, or the fact that he might be contemplating some cat-and-mouse fun with her.

"Since there's no wheelchair present," Brenda began, looking at Willie, "is it safe to assume that you're *not* Greg Stevens?" She looked at me and winked. I wanted to club her with my heavy coffee mug.

"Pretty safe," Willie answered. "I'm William Carter, Odelia's cousin. Actually, her husband's cousin."

"So she's traveling with you and left hubby home to fend for himself. How convenient for the two of you."

Willie laughed. "You are a nosy little tart, aren't you? And not very tactful or tasteful, besides quick with assumptions. Mind those traits don't get you into a peck of trouble."

"Tact and taste don't sell stories, Mr. Carter."

"Please, call me Willie."

"Okay, Willie." Brenda batted her eyelashes at him before looking my way.

I wanted to vomit.

"I'm still Mrs. Stevens to you."

"Whatever." Her lips were smiling in my direction, but her eyes were not. They were cold and calculating.

SIXTEEN

"Did you have a nice visit with your mother, Mrs. Stevens?"

Her question didn't surprise me. The only way she would have known I was at this particular restaurant would have been if she'd followed me. Then the thought crossed my mind that if she had followed me from the hospital, why was she showing up now? Why not earlier, while we were eating dinner? Unless she'd had the good grace to at least wait until we'd finished to pounce. I studied Brenda Bixby while she studied me. Nope, I determined, etiquette was definitely not one of her priorities.

"Isn't stalking against the law?" I asked her.

"If you're implying that I've been following you, don't flatter yourself. I do have other leads to pursue. I just merely mentioned to Cathy Morgan when I interviewed her that I needed to find you tonight. She suggested I try here."

Cathy Morgan. Of course — she's the one who'd given me the name of the restaurant.

"You interviewed Cathy Morgan?"

"Right up until her brother ran me off."

I shot a glance at Willie. "Which brother was that? Clem or Buster?"

"It was Clem. I tried to talk to the boy, but Clem made him get in the truck and stay there until I left."

"Can't blame him," said Willie. "He's just looking after his nephew. The kid's been through a lot."

"Well, that's not my problem, is it? I'm just here to get the story."

Willie and I exchanged glances once more. Could this young woman really be this obtuse and insensitive?

She leaned towards me. "But I did learn that Cathy Morgan sure does hate your mother. Any idea why?"

Her look was a lame-ass attempt to intimidate, making me wonder how long she'd been a journalist and if she practiced her look in the mirror. It took all of a split second for me to decide she was a newbie, and yes, she probably did practice her facial expressions alone in her room. I also decided she'd learned most of her techniques

208

from watching TV shows. She struck me as a kitty playing king of the hill in the jungle-cat cage.

"Lots of people don't get along in this world. Or don't you watch the news?" I stared back at her with an expression that let her know I had more than enough gumption to take her on.

"She's convinced the old lady is the killer. What do you think?"

"I told you, Ms. Bixby, I'm not talking to you about anything. And I mean it."

She turned a plastic smile Willie's way. "She always like this?"

He returned the smile. "Sugar, you are way out of your league."

"Speaking of which," I said, holding out my right hand, palm up. "May I see your credentials again?"

Brenda blanched at the question. "Why? I showed them to you yesterday."

"No, you flashed them at me while I was trying to get by you at the police station. Hardly the same thing."

"Mrs. Stevens, are you questioning my journalistic integrity?"

My hand still outstretched, I wiggled my fingers in a *come on, gimme* gesture. "Big time, Ms. Bixby. You see, I have a hunch you're either not a reporter at all, or you've only been one a very short time."

"Better give her what she wants," Willie warned her. "I'd hate to have to send you back to your parents in an envelope."

The girl reporter looked from Willie to me, her face a mix of indignation and fear. Deciding it was better to comply with my request than fight it, she dug around in her handbag and produced the same plastic card she'd shown me yesterday. It definitely claimed she worked for the news station. I turned it over in my hand and studied it, then handed it over to Willie for his inspection.

"This," I said to her, "is simply a magnetized employee card. I have one just like it for my law firm back home. If I'm not mistaken, this will get you into your office building, your parking garage, and probably the elevator after hours. But it definitely is *not* a press card."

She snatched the card from Willie and stuffed it back into her purse. "I'll have you know that I graduated the top of my class in journalism at Boston University."

"And I was at the top of my art history class — which still doesn't make me Picasso."

The mood at the table was awkward. Willie and I sipped our coffee while Brenda took time to mull over her next desperate move.

"I do work at the station." She stuck out her chin. "And one day I'll be a newscaster, you just wait and see. A national anchor, just like Katie Couric. I'm —"

Willie broke in. "But they didn't send you here to cover this story, did they?"

Her lips pursed as she paused to formulate her answer. "No, they didn't. I work on the set. The very bottom rung, a gopher." She turned to Willie, sensing he was the more understanding one of the two of us. At least she was right about that. "You see," she explained, trying to win him to her side, "this could be my big break. Everyone did coverage on the murder, but no one is sensing the story underneath."

"My story?" I suggested.

Brenda looked at me. "Yes. Yours and your mother's. It has a great human interest element: 'Mother and daughter reunited over dead body.' "

Willie laughed. "News at eleven!"

Even as I shot Willie a scolding look, I felt it melt into a slight grin. The whole idea did have one of those "believe it or not" twists to it. I would just prefer that I not be the star.

"Brenda, the truth is I did come to Massachusetts to find my mother. Pure and simple. It's purely a coincidence about the timing. There is no sensational story. I'm sorry."

"But what about your connection to those other murders in California? More unfortunate coincidences?" She rolled her eyes. "Come on, there just aren't that many flukes in the world."

It wasn't the first time she'd hinted that I might have something directly to do with the murder. "You do realize that you're implying, and not for the first time, that *I* had something to do with Frankie McKenna's death?"

"Did you?" She steeled her shoulders and locked onto my eyes, her foolish bravado returning. "Maybe you were involved with those other deaths, too, but no one's caught on to your game yet. Maybe you just seem to be solving them, when really you're just covering your tracks."

At that point, any sliver of sympathy I was starting to have for Brenda Bixby got flushed. In the back of my mind, I heard the sound of water being sucked down a sewer pipe.

"Brenda," Willie interrupted. "Once again, dear, you are letting your assumptions run away with your brain and your mouth. I can assure you that Odelia just has an unfortunate knack for getting her nose caught where it doesn't belong."

She turned her focus to Willie. "Yeah, and what about you? There was no mention in any of the coverage yesterday about you. And my local source said nothing about her traveling with a cousin." As she said the word *cousin,* she made obnoxious quotation marks with her fingers.

I was about to blow my stack, but Willie remained cool and collected, which was annoying in itself.

"Because of Odelia's penchant for finding murders," he explained, "I was sent here by Odelia's husband to keep her out of trouble as much as possible and to give her family support during this difficult time. Being in a wheelchair, it would have been difficult for Greg to tag after her himself. I'm sure you understand. I only arrived last night. Check with the B & B if you don't believe me. Better yet, call Greg Stevens. I'm sure you're resourceful enough to already have his phone number."

"Don't, Willie." I started to scoot out from my side of the booth. "Don't give her any explanation. We don't owe her one, and she doesn't deserve it. She's too stupid with ambition to believe anything not on her own personal agenda."

Willie gave Brenda a thoughtful look. "I fear Odelia may be right. So if you'll just move so I can get out, we'll be on our way."

After a slight hesitation, Brenda Bixby scooted out of the booth so that Willie could exit it. He glanced at our tab, put some bills with it, and handed it off to our waitress, telling her to keep the change. While I waited, my cell phone rang. It was Greg. I flipped open my phone and stepped outside of the restaurant.

Without an invitation, Brenda moseyed up close to me. I turned my back and walked towards the door. She followed. She was a dog on the hunt, and our earlier swat on her snout had done no good to deter her.

"Do you mind?" I snapped at her. "It's my husband."

Willie joined us and took Brenda gently by the elbow. "Let's give them some privacy. Unless you'd rather spend the next ten to fifteen minutes in the trunk of your car?"

"You wouldn't dare." The comment was accompanied with a challenging look and hands on her slim hips.

I stopped talking to Greg for a second. "If he doesn't," I said to Brenda, "I will."

From her look, it seemed she believed it

more coming from me. She dropped her eyes and defiant chin and moved away. I went back to my call.

"Hi, honey. I'm back." I tried to sound cheerful and upbeat. Greg would have received my voice mail saying I was staying a few more days, and I was pretty sure he'd be angry.

"Is Willie with you?"

I motioned to Willie to join me. "Yes, he's right here."

"Then, if you can, put me on speaker." Greg's voice sounded tense.

I ran my eyes up and down Brenda, who stood next to Willie, her ears as big as satellite dishes.

"Hang on, honey. We're in a parking lot. Let us get into the car first." Unlocking my rental car, I slid in and indicated for Willie to do the same. Once the two of us were inside with the windows closed, I hit the speaker feature on the phone.

"Hey, Greg," Willie said in the direction of the phone.

"What in the hell is going on out there?" Greg yelled. "First, I get a call from Odelia saying she's staying. Then a call from you telling me to knock some sense into her."

"I am staying, Greg. Just for a couple more days."

"Did you finally meet your mother?"

"Yes."

"And did you talk to her about why she left you? You know, clear the air?"

"As much as it's going to be cleared."

"Then there's no reason for you not to get your ass on that plane tomorrow."

Willie gave me a told-you-so look.

"My mother needs my help, Greg. It'll only be a few extra days. I promise."

"Does this help involve finding the killer?"

"Not exactly. You see, Mom doesn't want anyone to find the killer."

"But you're going to find the killer anyway, right, *sweetheart?*" Greg's tone was strained and sarcastic, in spite of his attempt to keep it even. "Even though no one wants you to."

"You see what I'm up against here, Greg?" Willie chimed in.

"I'm disappointed in you, Willie. With your resources, I was rather hoping you'd be a bit more creative. Maybe you could drug her. Or perhaps try tying her up and throwing her into the trunk of your car. Have one of your people drive her back to California."

Trunk of a car. With my luck, they'd double me up with Brenda.

"I'm a thief, Greg," Willie said, defending himself. "Assault and kidnapping aren't really within my expertise, though that last idea doesn't sound too bad. Kind of like a cult intervention."

I knocked my knuckles on the dashboard for attention. "Hey, I'm serious, you guys. My mother needs help, whether she wants it or not."

"And I'm serious, too, Odelia. It's one thing when people ask you to help, but this is different." Greg hesitated, then added in a softer tone, "I know this is difficult for you, sweetheart, but helping your mother isn't going to make her love you any more than she's capable. Especially if she doesn't want your help."

Sensing husband-wife talk starting up, Willie exited the car. He went over to his own vehicle and unlocked the door. Blood-hound Brenda sidled up to him.

"I know that, Greg." A lump formed in my throat. "Believe me, I know that." In the warm confinement of the car, I held my husband close, even if only through the medium of a phone.

Quickly, I gave Greg a rundown of what my mother had told me about her life and how she came to have three children from three different fathers. I also told him what little she'd offered up about the murder. I topped everything off with news about the drugs and the pesky Brenda.

"You know, Greg, this isn't just about looking for the real killer. I don't know anything about my mother's life prior to what she's told me about marrying Leland, but I'm guessing it might have been pretty bad or unstable." I adjusted my position. "She's also not well-liked, and most of that is her fault, I'm sure. She doesn't seem to want to make the effort to let people know her in a good way. And maybe there isn't any good, fuzzy part of Grace Littlejohn. I don't know. But I do know that she feels alone in the world. Even with her two sons, it's plain they aren't close emotionally."

"That's not your problem, Odelia. She chose to keep away from you for a reason. And it sounds like she did it to keep you safe from her instability, even if it did start with abandonment. Think about it. Had she not led your brothers to believe you were dead, they might have tried to find you. She felt she'd left you in good, or at least better, hands with Horten."

"She's old, Greg. Old and fearful. If I stay for a few more days, I might be able to bring her some peace, if only for a little while. And maybe she'll talk to me some more about what happened in the corn maze. If I can find out something, maybe it will lead the police to the killer, and Mom won't have to feel so afraid."

"But if the killer is one of your brothers, she may be afraid of the police finding out, as well as afraid of them personally. There are a lot of different reasons to feel fear. And this drug angle brings a whole new level of danger to it. Those guys don't mess around. And if Grady's fiancée is selling drugs, don't you think Grady knows about it? Possibly even Clark? Especially with that situation in Boston years ago."

"That's true, but it's also all the more reason to stay and help my mother. If she's afraid of her own sons, then she definitely needs one of her kids in her corner."

"You have a good heart, Odelia. It's one of the things I love most about you." Greg laughed softly. "Of course, I'd rather that heart of yours not lead you into so much danger. Maybe when you get home, we can find some way to channel that goodness into something less risky, like reading to the elderly."

"So, you're okay with my staying a few more days?"

"No, I'm not, but I understand why you want to."

"Now I just have to tell Steele. I'll call the office first thing Tuesday morning."

"I'll make the call to Mike Steele, sweetheart. I'm not his employee, so he'll be less of an ass with me. I'll call the office on Tuesday when it opens. Leave all that to me."

I started sniffling. "Greg, I love you so much. What would I ever do without you?"

"Without me, you'd still be getting into mischief, just more often and with less backup."

After giving each other vows of love, Greg reported on the photos.

"There might not be anything hidden there. There is one shot, though, probably taken very early, which shows Grace with her hands clutched around the pole shaft. But she might have been trying to pull it out, not push it in. From the way she was kneeling, I don't think she would have had the leverage to effectively do either in that position. I'll send the enlargement to you so you and Willie can check it out on the laptop."

"Okay, we can do that tonight."

"And speaking of Willie, he can't stay by your side forever, especially with that reporter clinging to you like plastic wrap."

"Willie will have to do what he has to do. I understand he might not be able to stay with me and help." I looked out the window.

Willie was helping Brenda into her car. The two of them seemed to be laughing. "As far as the reporter goes, she's a novice — not even a real reporter. I'm sure he'll be able to sidestep her, and she'll find out nothing."

"Problem with people like that, Odelia, is that sometimes they stumble onto the truth through sheer dumb luck. I'd hate to see Willie's safety compromised after everything he's done for us."

"Me, too. Criminal or not, he's a good and loyal friend."

After hanging up from Greg, I watched Brenda flirt with Willie through the window of her car one last time before driving off. I had been afraid that she would dog us all evening, but somehow he'd convinced her to move along, at least for tonight.

Willie had brains and cunning and had managed to thrive for years flying under the radar. But even I knew that beginner's luck was not to be trifled with.

"You and the girl reporter seemed rather chummy." After sending Brenda on her way, Willie had returned to my car. With his hand resting on the edge of the window, he bent down so that his face was closer to mine.

"The minx actually hit on me." He gave me the news flash with a silly grin plastered on his face.

"You're joking!"

"What? You don't think I'm proposition-worthy?"

"Come on, that's not it, and you know it. It's just that you're twice her age. She have a daddy complex?"

Willie laughed. "More like she'll do anything to get the story she's after. She invited herself back to my room for a nightcap."

"You biting?"

He laughed again. "As tempting as it was, I've made other plans. Remember that waitress from the Blue Lobster?"

I thought a minute. "The young one in the hot pants? Or the middle-aged one with the cleavage?"

"The age-appropriate one."

"Uh-huh, that would be Ms. Cleavage. What about her?" I studied him and his silly grin. "Don't tell me you have a date with her tonight?"

Willie chuckled. "When I went back to do my surveillance, she informed me that she bar tends at a local joint at night — someplace called the Kettle. Suggested I stop by if I had the chance." He winked at me.

"What? She saw us together earlier. Didn't it even occur to her that you might be my husband?"

"It did, so she came right out and asked." He flashed me a shit-eating grin.

"Rather cheeky of her, wasn't it?" Before he could answer, I added, "So, you're taking her up on her not-so-subtle invitation?"

"These small-town bars are hotbeds of information, and bartenders generally know everything about everyone. Might be a good place to find out a few things."

"Not to mention you might get lucky."

"One can only hope, little mama."

SEVENTEEN

Before he left me to head for his semi-date at the local bar, I told Willie about the photos Greg was sending. Willie went to his SUV and retrieved his laptop, handing it to me through my open window. "Greg must have noticed something interesting. Let me know what you find out, and I'll give it a look-see in the morning."

I also told Willie about Greg's concern about Brenda.

"Greg's right about the dumb-luck thing." Willie scratched his chin. "No telling what that hungry gal's going to dig up. She's definitely a loose cannon. Smart enough to know something's cooking. Too dense and single-minded to understand the ramifications of her behavior. In the long run, I think it might be smart to keep her close, but not too close."

"You mean help her? I don't think so."

A couple parked their car near us. We

waited until they got out and went into the restaurant. The beep of their car alarm being set gave us the green light to continue.

"Not help her, but don't antagonize her either. She might uncover something very useful to us, you never know. She's sticking her nose into places we might want to go, but no one would ever suspect a reporter of being too nosy. It's their job. Right now, you and I might be the only ones who know she's bogus."

He had a point. Brenda just might stumble onto something, especially with the scattered way she was going about things. She was beginning to remind me of a bulldog with attention deficit disorder.

"Be nice to her, little mama. Just not too nice. That would raise her suspicions. After all, she sees me as the good guy of this team."

"And I'm the bitch."

"The best parts to play are always the villains. Remember that." He leaned through the window and pecked my cheek.

Back at the inn, I slipped into my nightgown and settled at the desk in my room with a cup of tea and the laptop. I was the only one in the entire B & B, and the large and usually homey building had taken on an empty-shell feel.

Greg had sent the promised photos. I opened each one and studied them, not sure what I was looking for. I wished Greg had at least given me a hint, but he probably wanted to see if it was as noticeable to me as it was to him. There were two photos, both looking like the same pose. In each, my mother was kneeling next to the body, in the same position I'd seen her when I first laid eyes on her in the corn maze. I scrutinized the photos, especially her hand position. She had both of her hands clenched around the flagpole, one on top of the other, like she was churning butter.

At first, I thought it looked like she was trying to pull the pole out of McKenna's body, then it struck me that her angle was off. Maybe that's what Greg had noticed. As soon as I was sure, I would call him and discuss it.

Going downstairs, my lone footsteps echoing softly on the polished wood, I located a broom in the kitchen. In an attempt to replicate the scene, I got down on my knees on the tile floor and held the broom in the same angle as the pole in the photo. I tugged up, but my balance was too off to do it properly. Kneeling was not the way to go for pulling a pole out of someone's chest. To do that, it would be best to be stand, get a good grip, and yank straight up. Bracing a foot against the body would even help with leverage. The same was true for stabbing. If my mother was stabbing McKenna, she would not have been able to do it effectively from this angle. That would have required McKenna laying on the ground and my mother standing over him and driving the pole straight downward.

No, whatever Grace Littlejohn was up to, I was pretty sure it wasn't stabbing or pulling. So what in the hell *was* she doing?

Again, I assumed the position on my knees and simulated the grip on the pole. My mother's hand-over-hand grip and the blood smear on the pole suggested she was running her hands up and down the pole, spreading the blood with each movement. All that blood must have been slippery to the touch.

The blood. That was it. I slapped my head as a possibility became clear. By moving her hands up and down the flagpole, my mother could have been smearing the blood. And smearing the blood would probably smudge any fingerprints on the pole. But whose fingerprints? Her own — or someone else's?

My mother had said she wasn't the killer, and I believed her. Still kneeling on the tile, I changed my handling of the broomstick.

Instead of pulling or pushing the pole with my hands, I ran them loosely up and down the shaft. Even with a dry pole, the friction would have distorted any fingerprints already present. With a fluid such as sticky blood, it might have done it faster and more efficiently. My conviction that my mother knew the killer was stronger than ever, and whoever it was, my mother was protecting them by erasing the fingerprints on the murder weapon.

My mind didn't have to go far to settle on the names of people Mom would protect. It had to be either Grady or Clark. I couldn't see any reason for her to protect anyone else. Of course, I didn't know everyone in town and her relationship with each of them, but considering that most of the people Willie spoke to didn't think that highly of my mother's lack of self-control when it came to her temper, I wasn't sure there was anyone else she might shield.

I was still on the floor with the broomstick in my hand when I heard a vehicle pull into the driveway. That was followed by a single door being opened and closed. Soon the back door to the inn opened. I glanced at the clock on the wall. It was only nine thirty. Willie's date must have been a bust.

"Willie," I called. "I'm here in the kitchen.

I think I've found something." I went back to concentrating on my theory about the pole and the cover-up.

"Who's Willie?"

My head snapped up to find Clark Littlejohn at the doorway looking down at me. He was out of uniform, wearing jeans and a loose gray sweatshirt. The sleeves of the sweatshirt were pushed up almost to his elbows. On his feet were athletic shoes. Exhaustion hung heavy on his face like the jowls of a basset hound.

"Clark! What are you doing here?" I got up from the floor, leaning on the broom for assistance.

"What are *you* doing down *there?*"

I brushed off the front of my nightgown and pulled my robe closed, fastening it with the belt. "Exercising. Stretching for my back." The words spilled out with such ease, it surprised even me.

"Uh-huh." I could tell he wasn't buying it. He looked me up and down, his eyes settling on the broom. "Looks like you were trying to figure out something about the murder." His thin lips moved into a smirk. "Solve it yet?"

I kept a firm grip on the broom. If Clark was the murderer and my mother was protecting him, who was going to protect

229

me if he got it in his head I was onto something?

When I didn't answer, he returned to his original question. "Who's Willie?"

"Personally, I'm more interested in why you're here and how you got in."

"Around here, people don't lock their doors."

"I locked that door when I came in tonight, Clark. Mrs. Friar gives all her guests keys and insists it be locked at night."

"I'm the chief of police, Odelia. I know where everyone keeps their spare key." He opened his right hand to show me a key. It looked just like the one I had for the inn.

I held out my hand. "I'll take that key, Clark. And please tell me where it belongs. I'll make sure it gets back there — in the morning."

His mouth twisted in amusement as he handed me the key. "It goes under the cement frog — the one next to the shrub, to the left of the door."

I put the key in my robe pocket. "Were you just going to waltz in here and bang on every room door until you found me? You should have called first. I could have been sleeping. Who knows, I might even have called the cops."

He almost laughed. "You could have been,

but it's unlikely. It's not even ten yet. Besides, I'll bet your internal clock is still on West Coast time, three hours earlier." He was right about that. "And I did call — just about ten minutes ago. I saw the lights on and your car in the driveway, so when you didn't answer, I decided to check on you."

The phone. I must have left it upstairs.

Clark took a step back from the door, rather than towards me. He seemed to be making an effort to put me at ease. "Let's go into the parlor and sit. I have something to discuss with you. Does Mrs. Friar still keep hot coffee around the clock?"

I nodded, unsure what to do. If I showed fear, Clark might jump me, providing he was the murderer and was worried I was getting too close. But on the other hand, I didn't relish sitting down to coffee with a murder suspect, at least not one of my suspects. In the end, I settled on proceeding with caution.

I motioned for him to go down the hall to the living room. "Why don't you take a seat, and I'll bring you your coffee. Black, right?"

With a nod, he took off down the short hallway to the parlor. I poured him a mug of coffee and fixed a fresh cup of herbal tea for myself. When I entered the room and placed them on the coffee table, Clark repeated his first question. "Who's Willie?"

He was seated on the sofa. I took the chair across from him. "He's my husband's cousin." I was telling the lie so often, I was starting to believe it myself. Come November, I would half expect Willie to be sitting at Renee Stevens' Thanksgiving dinner table. "He was in the area on business, so Greg asked him to stop by."

"To keep you company or keep you out of trouble?"

It was my turn to offer a small smile. "A little of both, but tonight he had plans after dinner."

"Should I be worried about you, too?"

The question stumped me, seeing that it could have several meanings. "Worried about me? In what capacity?"

It was a multiple-choice question. Should Clark be worried about me as his half sister, his mother's daughter, a visitor to his town, or as someone who might turn up evidence against him and/or his brother? If prompted, I could also add a box for *all of the above.*

"According to Detective Frye back in California, you have a habit of getting yourself into danger."

"Not by choice, I can assure you."

"Danger is danger, Odelia, no matter what

the intent. I'd hate to see you come to harm, especially since we're just getting to know each other."

I searched his face for any sign of threat or menace but found none, only deepening fatigue.

"Would you excuse me a minute, Clark?" I got up and started out the door. "I should fetch my phone. I'm expecting a call from Greg." He waved me off and stuck his nose into his coffee mug.

Upstairs, I grabbed my phone and checked for recent calls. There was one missed call, and it was from Clark. He'd left a message saying he was in the area and needed to speak to me. If not tonight, then to call him in the morning anytime after seven.

If he was the murderer and was looking to do me in, I doubt he would have left a message that could be traced back to him, letting everyone know we might have hooked up. It gave me some comfort, but still I kept an ear tuned for footsteps on the stairs. Then I called both Willie and Greg and left messages letting them know Clark was with me. If I did get in trouble or worse tonight, I was going to point all fingers in his direction. Before I went downstairs, I shut down the laptop.

When I returned to the living room, Clark

was slouched on the sofa with his head thrown back. He was snoring softly — hardly a sign of the wound-up anxiety you'd expect from a killer. He snapped out of his snooze as soon as he heard me sit down.

"Sorry, Odelia. It's been a bitch of a day." He rubbed a hand over his eyes.

"Actually, two days."

He snorted out a chuckle and straightened himself back into an upright position. He reached for his coffee. "Right, two days. Feels more like a whole damn month."

"How's Mom?"

He took a drink. "That's what I came to talk to you about."

Uh-oh. He must have found out I was at the hospital today. I waited for the interrogation, but none came.

"Mom's home now. They released her a couple of hours ago."

"That's good, isn't it?"

"Yes, seems she's fine, at least physically. She's still singing the same old song. Insists she's not the killer. That she just happened upon the body."

I leaned forward. "Do you believe her?"

"Yes and no. I still don't think she's the killer, but I know better than to believe she was in the maze for a stroll. I think she knows who the killer is. I think CPAC is sure of that, too."

"What are they telling you?"

"Not much. But the big news is they've taken Cathy Morgan in for questioning. She's there right now."

"Cathy?" My voice broadcast my surprise.

Carl nodded. "Seems the vic wasn't Frankie McKenna after all. Fingerprints came back that the stiff was actually Les Morgan, Cathy's ex-husband. They found McKenna's ID on the body. The two looked enough alike, I guess. Seems the real Frankie McKenna has been missing for about a month."

"No one recognized the body as being this Morgan guy?"

"Morgan wasn't from around here. Seldom came with Cathy when she visited her family. In fact, I'm not even sure anyone ever met him except for her family. I met him once, right after they were married. They weren't married more than five or six years to begin with."

"You don't think Cathy killed him, do you? I mean, I don't recall seeing her anywhere near the maze that morning."

"Cathy was at Buster's stand at the time of the murder. Several customers recall her waiting on them. CPAC wants to know why her ex was in town in the first place, though I don't think she even knew he was here."

"Did CPAC tell you this, or did you do some digging on your own?"

"I'm a cop, Odelia. It's what I do. You think I'm going to sit on my hands while the state boys handle everything and feed me scraps?"

Clark was a cop, all right, as well as a former detective. So why was a full-blown drug enterprise going on right under his nose? I looked him over. He wasn't a stupid man. He either had to know about the drugs and ignored it, or he was involved. Just when I was starting to feel comfortable with him again, my danger detectors buzzed. I knew I should tread lightly with the thoughts running around in my mind, but I was eager for some information. I beat down my nosiness in favor of safety. Then I had another thought, one I found truly disturbing.

"Troy," I said, bringing a hand to my mouth in horror. "Troy saw his father's murdered body. Does he know that?"

"We're not sure what he saw. He's with his Uncle Clem and Aunt Tara right now. Grady went with Cathy."

"You left Mom alone? If she knows who the killer is, she might be in danger." *Un-*

less, I thought, *the killer is either you or Grady.*

"I asked Joan Cummings to stay with her a bit. She works with us at the station."

"I remember meeting her. I also heard that it was her son who was supposed to be watching the maze that morning and was found stoned to the gills in a porta-potty. He's the kid you took in."

"You heard that, did you?" Clark went on alert.

"I've been told you can't keep anything secret in this town." I paused. "Guess that's true. It also seems like Joan owes you big time for keeping her boy out of trouble. No wonder she was glad to watch Mom."

"And it's no wonder you keep getting into trouble."

"My mother was found crouched over a dead body." I strained to keep my voice from cracking. "I'm simply asking a few questions here and there."

"Well, stop it!" Clark got up and started pacing. "We have a killer out there, Odelia. A killer that quite possibly is one of the people living in this town. Someone who is here, among us, right now." He ran a hand through his thinning hair. "If flushed out by your questions, he might become even more dangerous."

At this moment, Clark reminded me of Dev. The looks were different but the tune was the same, like fraternal twins separated at birth. Guess it's a cop thing.

"Whoever it is, Clark, I believe Mom not only knows who it is, but is protecting him or her from being discovered. And possibly not out of fear for her own safety but out of some sort of loyalty."

He stopped pacing and turned on me. "Did she tell you that when you sneaked in to visit her today?"

Crap. Caught. "I didn't sneak in. I went right through the front door."

"If that's the case, seems funny no one saw you."

"Then how do you know I was even there?"

"A little bird told me."

For a minute, I wondered if it was the orderly. I was sure Willie had paid him to bring my mother down to the chapel, but maybe he was also spying for Clark. Then I thought of someone else.

"This little bird — was she young and cute with long blond hair, name of Brenda Bixby?" Clark avoided eye contact, so I continued. " 'Cause this same little bird has been dogging me for information about Mom. She has it in her head that there's a hot human interest story unraveling here. She even barged in on me and Willie during dinner tonight and ended the evening by making a very forward proposal to Greg's cousin."

"Wish he'd taken her up on it." Clark gave off a short bark of a laugh. "At least then she wouldn't have been at the hospital tonight when I was leaving with Mom. Hounded us all the way to the car. Thought I was going to have to run her over to get out of the parking lot."

"Yes, I was at the hospital, Clark. Mom and I had a nice talk about a lot of things. But Brenda doesn't know that for sure. She's only guessing."

"Frankly, Odelia, I'm not sure which of you is the more dangerous."

I leaned forward. "Is that why you told Mom I had left already for California, because you think I'm dangerous?"

"You're dangerous because you're going to stir up the killer like a hornet in a nest, just like that damn reporter!" Clark hovered over me, yelling. He noticed what he was doing, backed off, and took a minute to settle down before continuing. "I told Mom what I did to calm her down. She was very nervous about meeting you. I thought if she thought you'd gone home, she'd relax and maybe cooperate with CPAC and her attorney."

"And that's the only reason?"

He plopped down again onto the sofa. "Honestly, no. I thought if you didn't see her, you would go home and not meddle. If you went home, you'd be out of danger. Then, when all this blew over, maybe you could come for a proper visit, or maybe Mom could fly out to California."

Just then we heard a vehicle pull into the driveway. I glanced out the side window and saw Willie's SUV. Soon after, the back door opened.

"We're in here, Willie," I called.

Willie covered the hallway at a fast pace before making an appearance at the doorway to the parlor. I noted that his right hand rested on his waist, just inches from the gun concealed at the small of his back. He looked at Clark, then to me for assurance that all was well. I nodded and introduced the two men.

Willie grinned and extended his right hand towards Clark. "Well, isn't this a cozy family gathering?"

EIGHTEEN

The sight of my chief-of-police half brother shaking hands with Willie almost made my heart stop beating. I hoped that Willie was right, that he and his escapades had fallen off police radar, and that while Clark was busy Googling me, he hadn't come across any mention of my connection with William Proctor, former CEO of Investanet.

"Nice little town you have here, Chief," Willie said, coming to stand by my chair. "I've never been out this way — mostly spent time in Boston and the Cape."

"You staying long?"

"Odelia's supposed to go home tomorrow." Willie made a point of looking at me when he answered Clark. "So I'll probably head out then, too. I have some business in upstate New York."

I cleared my throat. "Clark stopped by to tell me that Mom's out of the hospital. She was released tonight."

"Well, that's great news, isn't it?"

"He also told me that the police are now questioning Cathy Morgan. Seems the dead guy is actually her ex-husband."

"Morgan?" Willie plastered on a thoughtful look that almost even fooled me. "Is that the woman you told me about — the one who runs the vegetable stand?"

"Yes," I confirmed, "that's her. The one with the boy who was in the maze." I didn't know if our little act was convincing, but I appreciated that Willie was a quick study.

"Actually, that's only part of why I dropped by." Clark picked up his mug and took a few quick, small sips of coffee. He seemed to be stalling, unsure of what he had to say next. "Seems Mom has a hankering to see us all together. All three of her kids." He gave me a tight smile.

Clark scooted forward on the sofa. He perched on the edge, leaned his forearms on his thighs, and clasped his hands between his knees. I wasn't sure if he was readying himself or us for his announcement. "Mom would like to know if you're interested in staying a few days longer . . . at our house."

"Your house?" I didn't dare look at Willie, even though I was dying to know if he was just as surprised.

"Yes. We have plenty of room. It's just me

and Mom. Grady lives with Cathy Morgan and her son out near the Brown place."

The invitation took me by surprise. Staying longer was part of my plan. Getting to the bottom of the murder of Frankie McKenna/Les Morgan was part of my plan. Staying with my mother and half brother was not. And I wasn't sure I wanted to. Family or not, they were strangers, and I hadn't decided yet if they were friendly or murderous. And I wasn't just thinking about the body in the corn maze. My mother's home could be toxic on many levels.

Clark continued on his mission. "Mom specifically said she wanted you at the house." He turned to Willie. "We have room for you, too, Will."

Willie had a look of eager attentiveness splashed across his face. I knew that look. It was the look of a boy looking at a new toy — the kind of toy that made messes and involved small explosions.

"That's very kind of you, Clark. Like I said, I have some business in upstate New York, but I can probably stay a day or so longer."

If I hadn't been afraid of Clark catching me, I would have shot Willie a rude facial gesture. What in the hell was he thinking? It was one thing for me to stay with my mother and Clark, but for Willie it could be dangerous. Unless, of course, he was doing it just to be a wise-ass. A nationally known fugitive staying in the home of the chief of police — Willie's personal "screw you" to law enforcement. If Willie came with me, I'd be a nervous wreck, even if he was cool as a cucumber.

"Though," Willie added, "as much as I appreciate your generous offer, Clark, I'd prefer to stay here at the inn. A lot of my business is international, and I'm up all hours on the phone and computer."

"What kind of business are you in, Willie?"

"Venture capital mostly."

Quickly, I added, "I can vouch for his odd hours. Willie's very nocturnal." Inside, I relaxed a bit, at least about Willie being under Clark's roof.

"Great," proclaimed Clark with a faux enthusiasm that was epidemic in the room. "Then it's all settled. You'll both stay a few extra days, and Odelia will come to our home."

I shook my head. "I still don't know, Clark. I'm not sure it's such a great idea for Mom and me to be thrown together like that. It's a whole lot different than a short visit in the hospital."

Although, I reminded myself silently, *it*

might be a great way to get her to talk further about the murder. But on the other hand, I might not be able to come and go as I pleased, which would make talking to witnesses pretty difficult. There was both an upside and a downside to the arrangement, even without Clark and Grady on the suspects short list.

"It will be fine, Odelia, you'll see." I wasn't sure if Clark was trying to convince me or himself. "Mom really wants to spend time with you. And you'll be doing me a big favor."

Both Willie and I looked to the chief for an explanation.

"Considering what's happened, I'm not sure Mom should be left alone too much. I have work to do and so does Grady. You could watch her for us during the day while the two of you catch up."

"Tell you what, Clark," I said, looking directly at him so I wouldn't be tempted to glance Willie's way. "Let me think about it and talk to my husband again. He has his heart set on me coming home tomorrow. But even if I stay a few extra days, I'm not sure I want to be stuck at home babysitting Mom. After all, it's been thirty-four years, and she's not exactly Mother of the Year."

Clark got up to go. "Understood. But

please come by the house tomorrow around one, whether you stay or go." He cast a look at Willie. "Both of you. Mom wants us all together for a Labor Day cookout. Considering the latest turn of events, I doubt it will be very festive. Not even sure if Cathy and Grady will be there. But people have to eat." He turned his haggard face my way. "If you decide to take us up on staying at the house, just bring your things then."

"My plane leaves at four thirty, but let me see what I can do."

"Okay," I said to Willie after Clark had gone on his merry way with my promise to consider postponing my trip home. Of course, I'd already done that, but there was no sense letting him know. "What was that all about?"

"I think your mother wants to spend time with you." He grinned at me. "You must have charmed the support hose off her at the hospital."

"I'm talking about *you*. For a minute, I thought you were going to take Clark up on his offer."

We were in my room. I'd just explained my theory on the smeared blood to him, and he was looking at the enlargements on the laptop.

"I did think about it. Might be interest-ing."

"Are you out of your mind?"

"Don't worry about me, little mama. Last year I dated an assistant DA for two months before she caught on that I wasn't who I said I was." He winked at me while he scrutinized a photo.

"Clark could figure it out, too. And prob-ably in less time."

"What about you? You didn't exactly jump up and start packing your bags."

"And I'm not sure I'm *not* going to, even though I'd already decided to stay a few more days. Until we know what's happen-ing with the Littlejohn brothers, it could be walking into a death trap."

Willie looked up at me, his face screwed in deep thought. "I'm not so sure. Being there might be the safest place for you."

"Huh?"

"If the cops *are* involved, they aren't go-ing to do anything to someone in their own home. If they aren't, it's doubtful whoever did will go there unless they are really cocky. I mean, it is the home of the chief of police."

He went back to looking at the computer. "Problem is, it would be more difficult for me to keep tabs on you when we're not stay-ing in the same place."

"I don't need you to keep tabs on me."

"Uh-huh." Willie didn't take his eyes off the screen. "My guess is, Clark would have liked to see you on that plane tomorrow, but dear old Mom wanted otherwise."

"He knows I saw Mom today, and he wasn't pleased about it. Guess who told him?"

"Better not be that orderly. Otherwise, I'm asking for a refund."

"It was Brenda. She was watching the hospital when Clark left with Mom tonight."

Willie shook his head. "That little girl's everywhere, isn't she? If she doesn't watch out, she's going to annoy someone who's not as nice as we are about it."

Another thought crossed my mind. "Willie, do you ever Google people?"

He laughed. "All the time. I even Google myself on occasion. Everyone does."

"Not *everyone*." I pulled a chair up close to the computer and sat down. "That's how Clark found out about my past activities. If there was any story linking you with me, he might have discovered that, too. If that's the case, it won't take him long to become suspicious."

"I've never seen any connection between the two of us anywhere. Believe me, I've checked that thoroughly."

I thought about Clark's call to Dev. "But if he discovers who you are, he might trace it back to Dev Frye. We can't have that."

"No, we can't. But it won't get traced back to Dev." Willie stopped fiddling with the computer. "Don't worry, little mama. Even if Clark figures out who I am, he'll think either you or Greg contacted me. That's our story, and we're sticking to it. The good detective won't even come up. I promise you."

I hoped Willie was right. Tomorrow was going to be very interesting, that's for sure. The thought of going to that house made me feel like I was going into a lion's cage without a whip or a chair.

"You know," said Willie, back to eyeballing the photos, "I think you and Greg are on to something here. I think the old lady is definitely smearing the prints on the pole. Very clever of her."

I sat down in one of the chairs by the window. I was bone tired but not sleepy.

Willie turned his attention away from the computer. "And I think I'm on to something, too."

"That's right," I said perking up. "How was your date?"

"As fruitful as I expected it to be, but without the happy ending." He laughed. "As

249

soon as I got your message, I made quick apologies and took off, worried I'd find the chief stringing you up by your toes."

"I'm sorry, Willie."

"Not to worry, little mama." He winked at me. "There's always tomorrow night."

"Let's just cut to the fruitful part, shall we?"

"You ever hear anything about your nutty family having money?"

I sat up at attention. "Money? As in serious money?"

"As in kooky, hidden-under-the-mattress-or-buried-in-coffee-cans money."

"What?" I nearly catapulted out of my chair.

"My new lady friend told me that Leland Littlejohn was quite eccentric. Local legend has it that he supposedly invented something and sold the rights to a major company many, many years ago and squirreled his money away somewhere."

In my head, I replayed what my mother had said about Leland. "My mother said Leland Littlejohn was an engineer with a large company. That might fit with the invention theory. He was also a gay man living in secret. Although his sons knew, it sounded like no one else in the community did."

"I think that would have come up in tonight's conversation if the town knew about that. In a town like this, that would be big news — big enough to remember and pass along. Maybe not about a young man today, but fifty years ago, it would not have been accepted."

Willie opened his cell phone and made a call. When the other party answered, he asked them to run a search on Leland Littlejohn and on Les, Lester, or Leslie Morgan. At the last minute, he threw in the name Brenda Bixby.

I played with my hair, pulling an end into my mouth, a bad habit I had as a kid and still did from time to time. "Leland gave my mother money for having Clark, or at least a settlement when she divorced him and went on her way. That couldn't have been cheap, even then. Especially since it also bought her silence about his homosexuality." I brushed my hair out of my mouth. "But what does that have to do with the murder?"

"Not sure, but Sybil — that's the Blue Lobster waitress — told me that Cathy Morgan has been trying to worm her way into the Littlejohn family for quite a while. Sybil suspects it's because of the rumor about money — she said Cathy would latch on to anyone with a healthy bank account. Problem is, she can never get them as far as marriage."

Willie got up from the computer and settled in at the other chair. "Sybil also said a few years ago Cathy had a thing for Clark Littlejohn."

"Clark? But those two can't stand each other. I've seen it with my own eyes." Then I remembered the blush on Cathy's face at the produce stand.

"Maybe not now, but I was told that Clark and Cathy met quite frequently in a corner booth at the bar."

I tried to envision the middle-aged Clark with the red-headed spitfire and couldn't. And it wasn't just the age difference.

"You sure about this?"

"It wasn't just Sybil who told me this. A couple of bar regulars were happy to back it up. Said Clark and Cathy were carrying on at a local motel all the while she was seeing someone else."

"Cathy, a gold digger? Seems a strange place to mine for other people's money, doesn't it? I've seen my mother's house. It's very nice but modest."

"Lots of people in these small towns have money tucked away, little mama. They prefer to live quietly. Many think of extravagance as a sin. I know a multi-millionaire who lives in a two-bedroom bungalow in Colorado and drives a twelve-year-old pickup. Dresses in nothing but jeans and shirts from Walmart." He pointed a finger in my direction. "And remember, Clark had quite a reputation for womanizing when in Boston. He might have a taste for young ladies, especially those throwing themselves at him."

I thought about Brenda Bixby and wondered if she'd thrown herself at the chief yet. "Did the local grapevine say why they broke up?"

"The local grapevine couldn't wait to tell me about it. Seems Cathy broke it off with the guy she was seeing only to be dumped by Clark. No one knows why Clark got cold feet, except to say that they're pretty sure Grace had something to do with it."

"No wonder Cathy hates Clark and my mother."

I got up and fetched the mug I'd left on the desk. The tea was cold but tasted fine. I took a swallow while I processed this new information.

"But, Willie, don't you think it's odd that Cathy is now with Grady? He must have known that Cathy and Clark had something going at one time."

"Maybe he's so in love, he doesn't care."

"Clark said something to me to that effect yesterday at lunch." I shook my head. "Cathy could be with Grady out of revenge against Clark and Grace. And if the money angle is true, she could be trying to get next to the cash if and when my mother dies." I paused to root around in my recent memory. "Just yesterday, Cathy said she was sorry there was no death penalty in the state because she wanted Grace to fry."

"Lovely thought."

"Could my mother have been set up to take the fall for the murder?" I took another drink of tea and paced across the rose-patterned carpet, pushing my tired mind to work harder. "Cathy could be involved with her ex-husband's death and setting up Grace. Killing two birds with one stone, so to speak."

Willie got up and came to me. He took the mug from my hand and placed it back on the desk. "Go to bed, little mama. This isn't going to be solved tonight, and it might never be solved. But we'll try our best to get to the bottom of things tomorrow. And what better place to do that than inside the cuckoo's nest." He started for the door. "As soon as I leave, you lock this door." I had told Willie about the hidden key after Clark left. "I, on the other hand, will be sleeping with my door open, just in case he does come back unannounced."

Willie was just about to step into the hallway when Greg's personal ring chimed on my cell phone. He laughed. "Perfect timing for Greg to tuck you in." He winked and started down the stairs.

Greg was not pleased at all by the change in events from the time he called after dinner until now, just a few hours later. He was angry enough before, but now his frustration had been kicked up several notches, like Thai food going from mild to five-alarm with one jerk of the pepper bottle.

Before we hung up, Greg made one more plea to what sanity I had left, and failed. I had set my course.

NINETEEN

Breakfast was lonely. Willie was a no-show, and I was the only guest. I felt uncomfortable having Mrs. Friar wait on me hand and foot with a gorgeous breakfast when I would have been just as happy with a bowl of cereal and milk. I'd tapped on Willie's door when I came down but received no response. A glance out into the parking lot told me his SUV was missing, too. As soon as I sat down at the dining table, I saw a note leaning against the salt and pepper shakers. It was a small piece of white paper with the inn's logo printed at the top — the same paper I'd found in my desk upstairs. It was folded in half, with my name printed in neat letters across the front.

Just as I picked it up, Mrs. Friar came in with orange juice. "That was on the dining room table when I came in this morning."

Opening the note, I saw that it was from Willie, telling me he had to run an early morning errand but would be back to the inn between eight thirty and nine. He ordered me to go nowhere until he returned.

"No bad news, I hope," said Mrs. Friar, who was hovering in the doorway to the kitchen.

Since the note wasn't sealed, dollars to donuts she'd already read it.

"No, just that Willie had an errand to run this morning."

She poured me some coffee. "Must have been very early. I came in around six, and the note was already there."

As I took a drink of juice, I wondered what in the world Willie would need to do before six in the morning. It was about eight fifteen. Once I'd fallen asleep, I'd slept like a rock.

I was just finishing some spectacular French toast when I heard a vehicle drive up. Looking out the dining room window, I saw that it was Willie. I watched as he got out but was surprised when he didn't head directly for the back door of the inn. Instead, he went around the passenger's side, which was hidden from my view. I went outside to see what he was doing.

Coming around the side of the SUV, I got the shock of my life. With the help of Willie, Greg Stevens — *my* Greg Stevens — was getting settled from the SUV into his wheel-chair.

"Greg!" I screamed in delight. I ran over and threw my arms around my hubby's neck and kissed him soundly.

"Guess you missed me, huh?" He kissed me back hard.

"What in the world are you doing here?" I pointed at Willie, a scowl on my face. "Did he ask you to come?"

"On the contrary, little mama. I tried to talk him out of it."

"I called Willie last night and told him I was catching a redeye to Boston. Told him not to tell you. I was going to take a shuttle here, but he insisted on picking me up."

Willie smiled. "It gave me a chance to fill him in on all the details while on the road."

"Greg, did you make this decision after we talked late last night? I told you I was fine."

Willie fetched Greg's bag from the back of his vehicle. I saw that Greg had also brought his laptop.

Greg took my hand and held it. "I was already on my way to the airport when we last talked. I had made up my mind after I spoke to you earlier, when you told me about the drugs and the reporter. But I have to say, that call about your brother clinched it that I was doing the right thing."

"But you have so much work at home, and there are the animals . . ."

He patted my hand. "It's okay, sweetheart. I can do a lot of work from here. Chris is back from vacation and can handle things at the shop. He even said he'd stay at the house while we were gone." Chris Fowler was Greg's right-hand man at Ocean Breeze Graphics.

"There are quite a few steps in the back," Willie told Greg, "but a ramp in the front. It's the private entrance to the downstairs room I was telling you about."

"Great. Show me the way, cousin."

While the two men went off towards the ramp, I went to the back and replaced the key under the stone frog. Then I went inside and headed for Willie's room. Along the way, I informed Mrs. Friar that my husband had just arrived unexpectedly.

She beamed at me. "Does he like French toast?"

"He adores French toast."

In spite of my worry about things at home, I was excited to see Greg. While I wasn't thrilled that he felt compelled to hop a plane at outrageous last-minute expense, I could feel the excitement of having him with me flush my cheeks with warm and fuzzy joy.

Once Greg was settled, the three of us convened in the dining room, where Mrs. Friar fed Willie and Greg like kings.

"Mrs. Friar," Willie said between bites of cantaloupe, "would you please let me and Odelia exchange rooms? Greg will need the lower room."

"Of course. In fact, Mr. Carter, why don't you take the room right at the top of the stairs. It's already made up. I'll make up the lower room for Mr. and Mrs. Stevens right after breakfast."

It didn't go unnoticed by me that with my husband now present, Mrs. Friar had changed my name to Stevens.

After breakfast, the three of us gathered outside under the trees to talk out of earshot of our host. We compared notes and theories and decided that we were all pretty much on the same page with regard to the blood smears and drugs being run out of the vegetable stand. We all even had the same suspects — Grady and Clark, and now possibly Cathy — although all three of us put Clark at the bottom of the list.

Willie reported that his people found out that Lester Morgan was not a nice guy. No surprise there. He'd been in and out of jail for everything from theft and fraud to assault during the past few years and was currently hooked up with the same drug dealers as McKenna. Where the real Frankie McKenna was, no one knew. Further digging in the drug world had unearthed that Willie's earlier idea that McKenna was probably the contact between Buster's and the drug source proved true.

I scrunched my brows together. "You think Morgan found out and decided to take over the route, seeing it was family?"

Willie hemmed and hawed as he thought about it. "More like Morgan decided to squeeze his family."

Greg wheeled in closer to Willie. "You mean blackmail?"

"It's a distinct possibility." Willie played with a dry golden leaf, stroking its spine and veins as he talked. "From what we can tell, he's only been with this outfit a short time. Say he finds out that one of his new employer's distributors is his former in-laws, including his ex-wife. And that the ex-wife is now playing house with a cop. Seems ripe for blackmail to me."

"But what about the real Frankie McKenna?" I asked.

Willie shrugged, crushed the leaf in his hand, and blew the pieces into the air.

"You mean he's dead?"

"A very good possibility, little mama. He's

261

been missing for a while. He's either dead or decided on a change of scenery. And it might not have been Morgan who did the killing. McKenna could have pissed off the wrong people, got whacked, and Morgan borrowed his identity. They were about the same height, weight, and coloring — even about the same age. But, of course, none of this is solid fact, just a string of possibilities."

"And it still doesn't tell us who the murderer is or why Odelia's mother is protecting them." Greg stroked my arm in a comforting gesture.

"Not really."

"Your people come up with anything on Brenda?" I asked.

"Nope. So far she's exactly what she claims to be — a peon on a TV news show. She's originally from Portland, Maine. Currently lives in Boston with a roommate named Nina Cummings."

"So," Greg said, "where do we go from here?"

"Hold the phone," I said. "I think we've found something." Both men looked at me with expectation while I hooked together a train of information into a viable choo-choo of theory. "Her roommate's last name is Cummings?"

"That's what my guy said. Why?"

"Cummings. Marty Cummings. Does that ring a bell?"

Willie looked at me while he thought about it. I pantomimed someone smoking a joint.

Pointing at me, Willie laughed out loud. "Of course! Marty Cummings, the porta-potty pot head." He quickly brought Greg up to date on Marty's failed gig as the maze lookout.

"Yes," I added when Willie was through. "And his mother is Joan Cummings, who works at the local police department. Cummings might be a somewhat common name, but it could also be how Brenda is getting some of her inside information. After all, Brenda knew I was Clark's half sister and was staying at this particular B & B. She knew exactly how long it had been since I'd last seen my mother. She even knew when Clark was going to pick up Mom from the hospital. Joan could have known all that from her close proximity to both the police and Clark and passed it on." I looked at Willie. "Can your people find out if Joan Cummings has any other children besides Marty? Or where Nina Cummings is from?"

"We can sure try, little mama." He yanked

out his cell phone and hit a speed-dial number.

I slapped my knee and kissed my husband. "I'll bet Nina is Joan Cummings' daughter. And I'll bet she and Brenda have been friends a long time."

Greg looked at Willie in awe. "Where in the hell do you get this information? You secretly CIA or FBI?"

Willie shrugged as if he'd just been asked a question as mundane as his birthdate. "Simple, really: hackers. Highly skilled and well-paid hackers."

Although not a breakthrough on the murder, discovering Brenda's possible secret data bank buoyed my spirits. I looked at my watch. "We're expected at my mother's at one. It's almost ten now. Maybe while we're there, the three of us can each target someone to chat up. Never know who might slip and say something."

Greg yawned. "Unless you two have some unauthorized sleuthing to do right now, I'd really like to grab a short nap before we go. I didn't sleep well on the plane."

"And I'd like to get in a walk before I shower for the day. What about you, Willie? Any more dates with the gossip girl?"

"Later tonight." Willie got up and stretched. "You know, with Greg here now, they won't be pressuring you to stay with them."

"You're right. That's a bonus I hadn't thought of." I turned to Greg with a smile. "Thanks, honey."

"Hey, I'm here to help." Greg studied me. "Are you sure you should go walking by yourself?"

"Don't worry," I assured him. "It's safe. And Willie's been asking most of the questions, so I haven't had the opportunity to really get under anyone's skin."

"Yet." The word came out simultaneously from both men.

While Greg rested and Willie caught up on some work in his new room, I changed and took off down the road with my iPod. It wasn't as humid as it had been when I'd arrived just a few days before. The daytime temperature had dropped today, and there seemed to be more red and gold leaves than green ones just since yesterday. Fall had come to stay.

I had been walking at a good clip for about three songs when I heard a car come up behind me. I was walking on the left-hand side, facing oncoming traffic. The car approached from behind and slowed down. As soon as I glanced over my shoulder, I felt a growl form in my gut. It was Brenda

Bixby, reporter wannabe. I turned back around and kept walking. As before, she slowed her car to keep pace with me.

"Come on, Odelia, talk to me."

I ignored her.

"But maybe, considering the circumstances," she persisted, "I should talk and *you* should listen."

At her baiting words, I felt the rhythm of my gait break but kept walking. Willie had said I should be nicer to her. Keep her close. What's that old saying: *Keep your friends close, and your enemies closer?* I wasn't so sure about that. Brenda wasn't exactly an enemy, more of a major pain in my big butt. In my book, that didn't qualify her for close treatment as a friend or an enemy. I kept walking. She didn't give up.

"Tell me, Odelia. Are you involved in your family's drug business? Or are you here to cash in on the rumored hidden treasure? That alone should be motive enough for an abandoned daughter to suddenly show up."

I stopped. So did her car. Spinning around, I snapped, "Do you have some sort of light on your dashboard that goes on when I take a walk? Or do you lie in wait for me to leave the inn?"

From the look on her face, she knew she'd hit a nerve and was inwardly celebrating. "I was on my way to see you when I spotted you walking down the road. Certainly makes it easier without your curious guard-dog cousin around."

"Then you'll be thrilled to know that I now have *two* guard dogs. My husband arrived this morning."

"He in on it, too?"

"No one is in on anything." I barked at her so hard, my back teeth knocked against each other. *Calm down,* I told myself. *Anger will make you slip, and you're not ready to show your cards just yet.* "You're fishing, Brenda, and you know it. You want a story so bad, you're willing to make up crap as you go, just to get people to react to you."

"Oh, really? So I guess I'm making up the fact that it was Cathy Morgan's ex-husband who was killed and not Frankie McKenna. And I guess I'm making it up that there is a booming drug business going on at Buster's."

Now I was sure Brenda Bixby had an inside track with the local PD. She might have found out about the drug dealings on her own, but not about Les Morgan. That had only happened yesterday afternoon, and it had not been in the papers this morning.

Standing on the side of the road, I pulled out my iPod earbuds and challenged

Brenda. "You seem to know everything. Have you figured out who the murderer is yet?"

The young woman jutted her sharp chin out the car window. "No, but I will. And that's why I wanted to talk to you. You help me and I'll help you, and together we can get to the bottom of this."

I laughed in spite of my resolve to remain aloof and bitchy. "I have all the help I need, Brenda."

"A guy in a wheelchair and that oily cousin? Come on, Odelia. We women can do stuff like this faster and better."

Oily cousin? Little did she know just how slippery Willie could be. And that in him, not me, she had a career-making story.

"Chasing murderers is dangerous business, Brenda. Trust me. I have the bullet wound, broken bones, and emotional trauma to prove it." When she didn't respond, I put my earphones back in place. "As entertaining as this is, I have places to go, people to see, and calories to burn. So go find some other sandbox to pee in."

Brenda flipped me a rude hand gesture and gunned her engine, sending her car speeding down the road.

Well, I *tried* to be nice. At least nice

enough not to return the gesture, no matter how tempting.

TWENTY

A few minutes after one o'clock, we pulled up in front of my mother's in a two-vehicle caravan. Willie decided to take his own vehicle so if things got too close cop-wise, he could take off, explaining that he had other plans. Before we left the inn, we asked Mrs. Friar if we could extend our stay. She was delighted, since she had no other guests besides us until Friday.

Clark was in the garage when we pulled up in front of the house. He waved and walked out to greet us carrying long-handled barbecue utensils.

Clark watched with interest as Greg deftly swung out of the passenger seat of my rental car into his wheelchair. At home, the wheelchair is stashed behind the driver's seat of his specially equipped van, and he can complete the act without any assistance. Because of the rental, I had to pull the chair out of the back-seat area and position it for him. It was a lightweight wheelchair, sleek and compact; one made to handle Greg's active lifestyle.

"I have a big surprise," I told Clark with a smile. "This is Greg Stevens, my husband. He flew in this morning."

Clark stuck the cooking tools under his left arm and held out his right hand. "Nice to meet you, Greg."

"Nice to meet you, too."

"Come around back," Clark directed us. "It will be easier for Greg to get into the house that way."

My mother's house was deceiving. From the outside it looked like a simple two-story bungalow, but inside, it was spacious, extending back into the lot on which it sat. Downstairs there was a large living room, kitchen, and dining room. Just off the kitchen was a den.

The back yard was a nice size, with half of it taken up by a very large redwood deck. Half of the deck was screened in and contained wicker furniture with plump cushions. On the unscreened portion was a gas grill the size of a Smart Car and two patio tables with chairs. A large sliding door separated the two. The steps up to the deck were low and wide. Greg handled them easily with some help from Willie.

"I rebuilt the steps a few years back," Clark explained. "Originally there were just a couple of very steep ones. They were getting difficult for Mom to manage as she got older, so I tore them off and made new ones. These extend out further but aren't as steep."

"Did you build the deck yourself?" Greg asked.

"Sure did." Clark beamed with pride. "First it was just an average deck, then I doubled it in size. Next I screened in half. We get nasty mosquitoes out here. We had a large yard that we never used, but we used the porch all the time except in winter. Better use of space, I think."

Greg nodded in agreement. "Very nice job, Clark."

"Thanks. I love working with my hands. It's a nice break from the stress of the job."

Clark seemed more relaxed today than I'd ever seen him. Perhaps it was because he was at home and in a social situation, or maybe he'd gotten a good night's sleep now that our mother was back home. Whatever it was, his welcome and chat seemed unforced and genuine.

Inside, my mother was bustling around the kitchen. The place was filled with the odor of fresh-baked pie. Strewn across the kitchen counters were plates of raw vegetables, bowls of chips, and two pies cooling on racks. My mother glanced up at me. I handed her the bouquet of flowers we'd picked up on the way over. She took them without a word.

"Hope your cousin likes pie. I made apple and rhubarb. Clark loves rhubarb; Grady, apple." She got down a vase, added water, and put the flowers in it. "There's a lemon meringue in the refrigerator. That still your favorite?" With her head down, she set the flowers on the kitchen table.

"Yes, it is. Nice of you to remember, Mom." We stood near, but not too near, each other in the big country kitchen. "Though you didn't need to go to so much trouble."

"Nonsense. Some things a mother doesn't forget."

"Like favorite pies and cookies?"

Mom moved to a counter and started fussing with raw veggies arranged on a platter. "It's always the little things you remember. Ever notice that?"

I nodded. "Like Dad always adding a spoonful of sugar to his coffee, followed by just a smidgen more. Never a whole second spoon, or even a half." I held up my left hand and pinched the thumb and index finger together. "Just a smidgen."

My mother gave me a weak smile. "That used to drive me crazy. That second bit was hardly enough to worry over. I used to tell him, Horten, why don't you just add more to your first spoonful. He used to do that with other things, too. Like jam. He'd slather jam on his toast an inch thick, then before he'd take his first bite, add just a wee bit more for good measure."

"He did that right up until he died."

My mother stopped what she was doing and looked at me, her face pinched in concern. "How did he go, Odelia?"

"Heart attack at home. Doctor said it was very quick."

"Good. That's the way I want to go — quick. No fussing. No hospitals. No infernal tubes for days and weeks on end."

A thick fog of awkwardness fell between us. I could tell my mother was feeling self-conscious. She went back to rearranging the perfectly aligned carrots and celery. I half expected them to stand up and march off the plate in protest.

"By the way, Mom," I said, breaking the discomfort. "I brought an extra guest. I hope you don't mind."

"Your husband's cousin. Clark told me."

"Yes, I brought Willie, but I also brought

my husband. Greg surprised me by taking a redeye flight to Boston last night. Both of them are out on the deck with Clark."

She peeked out the kitchen window at the three men gathered around the grill, no doubt swapping stories about gas grilling versus charcoal briquettes.

"Clark told me he thought your husband was in a wheelchair." She continued to stare out the window. "Do you love him, Odelia?"

"Very much, Mom. He's my life."

"I married two very nice men, both for the wrong reasons. They deserved better than they got."

I walked over to her and put a hand on her shoulder. "Don't beat yourself up, Mom. It's not worth it. Let's put the past in the past, where it belongs."

She turned to look me in the eye. Her eyes were dry; mine were wet. "Can you do that, Odelia? I'm old and set in my ways. If you're looking for a tearful apology, I thought I made it clear at the hospital that you're not going to get one."

If this were the movie of the week on the Lifetime channel, we'd be dissolving into each other's arms, surrounded by a puddle of our joint tears. But this wasn't a made-for-TV movie. This was my life. Correction: our lives. And it was obvious my mother was staying in character to the end. I might have gotten more emotion from a turnip.

"That's okay, Mom." And it was. "I heard what I came to hear yesterday."

Our emotional headlock was broken when Cathy, Grady, and Troy came through the front door. Grady was carrying two big bags; Cathy, one. My mother seemed relieved to see them.

"Thought you'd never get here with the corn." Fussing like an old hen, she barked orders. "Cathy, Odelia, start shucking those ears. We have to get them on the grill pronto."

"I ain't your kitchen help," Cathy snapped. "You wanted us here, we're here." She pushed past us and went straight out to the deck with her bag. Without saying anything to anyone, she opened it and brought out a six-pack of beer. She took a bottle and twisted the cap off with one angry move, as if wringing the neck of a chicken. Plopping down into one of the patio chairs, she tipped it back until I thought she was going to swallow the bottle with the brew. Grady dumped the corn on the table and joined her, but not before gracing me with a lip-raised look of disgust.

"We're dry in this house," my mother explained. "Cathy thinks it tortures me and

Clark when she brings booze. Only one she's hurting is herself."

I was hoping to get a little one-on-one time with Cathy. But while she was somewhat friendly at Buster's, today she was vile and spitting nails. Guess a night of police questioning could do that to a person, not to mention breaking it to your son that his father is dead. It was anyone's guess how she was feeling about her ex-husband being gone for good. I decided to cut her some slack, and not just out of sympathy but out of self-preservation. If Cathy Morgan ever got it in her head to launch that beer bottle at someone, I did not want to be within firing distance. It made me want to gather up Greg and Willie like chicks and scoot them to safety.

Instead of following his mother out on the deck, Troy stayed behind in the kitchen. He inspected me with sullen, distant eyes. "You're the lady from the corn maze, aren't you."

"That's right, Troy. I'm also Grady and Clark's half sister, Odelia. I'm visiting from California."

Mumbling to herself, my mother started yanking ears of corn out of the bags. The bags were generic plastic shopping bags, not the handled bags I'd seen for special customers.

"Here, Mom, let me clean the corn." I turned to the boy. "Troy, want to help?"

He shrugged. "Sure."

If Troy hadn't been a kid, I might have cut to the chase and asked him about his father and what he saw in the corn maze that day. But even I knew that children had to be handled with care. Troy had just lost a parent. Although it sounded like he hadn't seen him in a while, Les Morgan was still his father, and his death and the boy's memory of him had to be respected. I was dying to know if the boy knew it was his father that morning in the maze or if he had found out along with everyone else yesterday. I also wanted to see if I could jar loose any information about who or what he saw that day. But for now, I would have to be content peeling husks from corn and letting Troy get used to me.

After pushing aside the vase of flowers, we both took seats and began shucking the corn. Troy was an expert at it and finished twice as many ears as I did in the same amount of time. He worked in silence, focusing on the physical task as if it were surgery. He seemed withdrawn and troubled, in a silent battle with internal demons. Little wonder, with what he'd been through recently. It made me consider what his family was doing, if anything, to help him through this ordeal. Or was he simply collateral damage?

"I'm glad you came today, Troy."

He glanced up at me, then refocused on the ear of corn in his hand. "Uncle Clem wanted me to stay with them today." The words were presented in a mumble.

I looked around. My mother had left the room and gone upstairs. "Why?" I asked the boy.

He shrugged and kept shucking. "They don't like it when I come here."

"Your Uncle Clem and Aunt Tara?"

"All of them. Even Uncle Buster."

"But one day your mother is going to marry Grady, and then the Littlejohns will be your family, too." I finished the ear I was working on and grabbed another. "And so will I."

At this last comment, Troy looked up and studied me, his face painted with a frown. "You really live in California?"

"Yep. Right near the beach."

"Could I come visit?"

"Anytime you'd like, if your mom lets you."

With that information tucked inside his head, he went back to work.

When we were done, Troy, Mom, and I joined the others on the deck. Cathy and Grady drank beer, the rest of us lemonade and iced tea, while Clark cooked chicken and hotdogs on the grill, along with roasting corn and other vegetables. Grady and Cathy remained aloof and silent. Troy bonded with Greg, and the two of them were shooting a basketball at a hoop hung from the front of the garage. Willie made small talk with Clark, discussing the rise in white-collar crime. Talk about cheeky.

When Grady joined Clark at the grill, I moved over next to Cathy and tried some small talk. "It's nice that you didn't have to work today. Who's minding the stand? I'm sure Labor Day is pretty busy."

Cathy took a pull from her beer. "Tara and Clem are running it."

"Oh, I didn't realize your sister-in-law was involved. I guess you all take turns."

"Usually it's just me and Clem. Tara does the books." She glanced at me and rolled her eyes. "About the only thing she does do right."

"Buster's not involved?"

"He spends most of his time managing the farm. His daughter used to work at the stand until she married a guy from New York with a big uppity job."

"I haven't met Buster yet."

"He's on vacation right now. He and his wife went to London for their twenty-fifth anniversary."

Cathy wasn't exactly friendly, but she didn't seem to mind my company. I'm sure if it had been Clark or Mom who'd sat down next to her, it would have been a different story.

"I was very sorry to hear about your ex-husband, Cathy."

She didn't look at me but squinted like she was setting her sights on a bug in the distance. "Why? He was a rotten bastard."

"Still, he was your husband at one time and the father of your son."

She snorted. "Some father. Left us flat, then years later turns up here dead." She finally turned to look at me. "Damn police questioned me for hours last night. Troy again, too. Strange thing is, Les hated those mazes. He was a bit claustrophobic. I don't understand why he was in there in the first place or who could have talked him into going in."

I cautioned myself to tread lightly with my next question. "Did Troy know that it was his father that morning in the maze?"

"No." The word came out quick and sharp like a switchblade, making me doubt the truth of it.

Shortly before we sat down to eat, Cynthia Rielley wandered into the back yard. Today she was dressed in navy blue pants with an elastic waist and a floral-print shirt that she wore tucked into the pants. A blue cardigan sweater was draped across her shoulders and on her feet were white sneakers. She looked tidy and crisp and very alert. In one of her hands was a potted purple hydrangea. In her other arm was Coco. He growled at the gathering in general.

"Oh, dear," Mrs. Rielley said when she saw everyone. "I didn't realize you had a houseful of company. I just wanted to drop these off for Grace and see Cathy for a moment."

"Not at all, Mrs. Rielley," said Clark. "Why don't you join us?"

"Thank you, Clark, but Mr. Rielley and I are heading to our niece's for the day. She's having a cookout for the family, too, and asked me to bring a bunch of Cathy's corn to her. She loves the corn from the Brown farm."

Cynthia Rielley spied me and did a double take, as if she remembered seeing me but took a moment to place exactly where. She took a step closer to confirm what her eyes were telling her head. Her lined face broke into a smile as soon as she remembered. Coco remembered, too, and increased his growl.

"I see you finally caught up with Grace, Mrs. Stevens. How unfortunate it had to be this weekend, with everything that's happened."

"Yes, Mrs. Rielley, I finally found her."

Everyone looked at me with surprise except Clark, Willie, and Greg, who already knew that Mrs. Rielley and I had met the morning of the murder.

"I came to the house Saturday morning," I quickly explained. "When I found no one at home, Mrs. Rielley directed me to the fair."

Mrs. Rielley held the flowers out to my mother. "These are for you, Grace. Something to cheer you up after that horrible experience."

Mom took the flowers from Mrs. Rielley. "Thank you, Cynthia. Seems to be my day for flowers."

Mrs. Rielley looked from me to Grace several times. "I just can't get over how much you and your niece look alike."

I glanced at my mother, wondering if she would let Cynthia Rielley assume what she assumed or correct the error. I wasn't going to, feeling it was my mother's secret to keep or not.

After clearing her throat, my mother said, "Odelia isn't my niece, Cynthia, she's my daughter."

"Your daughter?"

"Yes, I was married to her father while I was in California, before I came back to Leland." My mother said the words firmly, without hesitation or emotion, simply clarifying a misconception.

"My goodness," was all Mrs. Rielley could say as she looked at the two of us.

Cathy got up from the patio chair she'd been glued to since she'd arrived. "I have your order in my trunk, Mrs. Rielley. Troy can help us."

"Nonsense," piped up Willie. "Let the boy enjoy himself. I'll help you ladies."

Mrs. Rielley smiled at Willie. "You must be Mr. Stevens, Odelia's husband."

"Actually, he's my husband's cousin, Mrs. Rielley," I explained. "My husband is the one playing basketball with Troy."

Mrs. Rielley looked at our complicated family, her face that of a befuddled puppy. "All very confusing, isn't it?"

With a chuckle, Willie escorted Mrs. Rielley and Coco off the deck. "But then, aren't all families?"

Mrs. Rielley smiled at him. "I suppose

you're right, Mr. . . . uh, I didn't catch your name."

"Willie, ma'am. Just call me Willie. Everyone does."

Twenty-One

Cathy returned a few minutes later, but Willie wasn't with her.

"He said to start without him," she explained in a deadpan voice. "Mrs. Rielley mentioned something about a drippy faucet, and he offered to look at it for her." She grabbed a fresh beer before sitting.

"Quite a handy guy, isn't he?" noted Clark as he pulled chicken parts from the grill. "Where's his family?"

"He's a widower, no children." I tried to sound casual. "He sort of looks out for me and Greg, kind of like a guardian angel."

Later, after we ate, I had a chance to talk to Willie alone.

"I talked to Mrs. Friar about using the washer and dryer at the inn. If we're staying, I'll need to wash the few things I brought. If you have anything you want washed, just leave them by our room door tonight. I'll do them in the morning."

"You don't need to be doing my laundry, little mama."

"I know I don't, but I'm making the offer. Didn't look like you brought much with you yourself."

Willie fixed me with a warm smile. "I miss that, you know."

"Laundry service?"

He laughed. "I hire people to do those kinds of things for me." He sighed softly. "No, what I miss is someone doing them because they want to, not because they're paid to do it."

Willie looked out from the deck over the back yard. Bordering the Littlejohn property in the back was a stand of birch trees. In the silence, loneliness wafted from Willie like the gentle breeze that moved the slender white branches of the trees.

I cleared my throat. "That was a very nice thing you did for Mrs. Rielley. I had no idea you were that handy around the house."

"What can I say, I'm a jack of all trades."

"Right, and I'm the Queen of England." I leaned in close. "My guess is you checked out the bags of corn Cathy brought for the Rielleys."

Still looking out at the trees, Willie smiled. "I did fix her faucet, little mama."

"And?"

He turned in my direction. "And it seems our observations hit a bull's-eye. Cathy is definitely packaging up drugs with the produce — both pot and coke. While Mr. Rielley hunted up some tools for me, I put the bags into the trunk of their car and took a peek. There were about three to four dozen ears of corn, and I doubt the packets hidden in each bundle were oregano. A few smaller bags held squash and coke."

"That sweet little old lady is a drug user?"

"Please, Odelia, all old people are drug users, just that most use prescription drugs. More likely, Mrs. Rielley is a mule."

"She might not even know about the drugs, Willie. Didn't she say her niece ordered the corn?"

"Could be she doesn't. Then again, old people are having a tough time making ends meet, just like everyone else. A little under-the-table money can help a lot."

"For someone who stole millions from retirement funds, that comment seems very out of place."

Willie turned his head so that he was directly facing the trees in the distance, showing me only a profile. "Don't you mean disingenuous?"

"Just making an observation, Willie."

"Stop trying to give me a conscience, little

mama. It's too late for that."

He sounded like my mother.

Cathy, Grady, and Troy took off almost as soon as their plates were clean and their bellies full. A bit later, Willie left, with the excuse he was meeting a friend for drinks. Greg and I knew he was off to do some more digging for information. We decided to hang around and help with the clean-up. Greg was in the kitchen helping Mom, saying it would be a good time for him to get to know her. He also thought she might relax around him, seeing that he wasn't a kid she'd left behind. He had a point and a special way with people. I was counting on his natural charm to garner some results.

"That's a good man you have there, Odelia." Clark was cleaning the grill.

"Yes, he is. The best."

"Wheelchair or not, I'd hate to go up against him on the court."

I beamed with pride. "He's the star of his wheelchair basketball team."

"I'd like to see one of those games." He glanced my way. "Maybe one day Mom and I can come out for a visit."

"Anytime, Clark. We have room for both of you, as long as you don't mind two annoying cats and one overeager dog."

"I love both." He continued cleaning. It

seemed it was taking him a long time, making me think he was using it to occupy his hands while we talked. "That cousin of his is an interesting fellow."

I held my breath.

"He's only been here two days and already he has drinking buddies."

"He and one of the waitresses at the Blue Lobster hit it off. He said she works at a bar at night."

"Ah, that must be Sybil Johnson. She works nights at the Kettle over in Derek's Grove. She's been married three times. One kid, a son. He lives in Alaska." Looking down at the grill, Clark smiled to himself. "That woman sure likes to party."

"Did you ever party with her?"

Clark's private smile turned into a short laugh that dissolved into a self-conscious cough. He turned to me. "Don't worry about Willie, Odelia. Sybil's a very nice person. She just doesn't take men too seriously. Kind of a wild, independent spirit. Always has been."

"Sounds like his type of woman."

Inside my head, I had a laundry list of things I wanted to talk to Clark about but wasn't sure where to start. There was the drug issue. The money issue. And the probable leak in his department issue. *Eeny.*

290

"I need to talk to you, Clark. About several things."

"From the change in your tone, it sounds serious."

"It is."

Clark finished the grill and turned to study me. Then he looked into the kitchen where Greg and Mom were chatting away while they worked. "Would you like to take a walk?"

"Sure."

Clark went inside and washed his hands. He told Greg and Mom that we were going for a short walk together.

"You two are going to talk about me, aren't you?" My mother's words, full of vinegar, drifted out to me through the open window.

"Absolutely, Mom. It's what keeps Odelia and me alive."

As soon as we cleared the driveway, I opened the conversation. "I think you have a leak in your police department, Clark."

He stopped, looked at me in confusion, then fell in step again with me. "That certainly wasn't what I expected you to say."

"It's just the lead topic. A little something to warm you up."

"I see." We took a couple of steps in

291

silence. "So what makes you think there's a leak at the PD?"

I gave him a brief rundown of my speculation on the connection between Brenda Bixby and Joan Cummings, and how much of the information Brenda was spouting could only have come from a police insider.

"Nina Cummings is Joan's daughter." Clark shook his head. "Joan, Joan, Joan," he mumbled to himself. He looked my way. "How did you know that, about Nina and Brenda?"

"You think you're the only one who knows their way around a computer?"

"Fair enough." He blew out a short gust of air. "I can't understand why Joan would do something like that, even for a close friend of her daughter's. It's not like her at all. Especially after everything the department's done for her."

"You mean like not charging her son with possession when he was found all doped up the day of the killing?"

"Yes, that and all the other times we've turned a blind eye to Marty's indiscretions on Joan's promise that he'd change his ways. Marty was a good kid, but after his father left them a few years back, the boy turned to drugs. Dropped out of high school. Stuff like that. No one could reach him." He sighed. "I'll look into the leak issue."

"Now the next topic — money. Did your father hide a large sum of money?" When Clark didn't answer, I added, "Because I don't like being accused of being here for the family fortune — especially that of a family that isn't really mine."

"Brenda give you that scoop, too?"

"It's one of the things she told me."

"That's the story, Odelia. Supposedly, he did hide a bundle. I've never seen it. Have no idea where it might be if he did."

Now it was my turn to stop and stare. A car drove by. Clark gave a friendly wave to the people in it.

"I swear to you, Odelia. I only know as much as anyone else, and it's all based on rumor. I've even asked Mom about it over the years, and she just laughs it off. My father was a loving but odd man. Probably came from not being able to be himself. He was a homosexual. Did Mom tell you that?"

I nodded.

"Except for us, he kept to himself. He had a good job. Traveled a lot on business. Might even have had an out-of-town lover, for all I know. We wanted for nothing but never had any showy extravagances. When the time came, there was money enough to send both of us to college. That money came from college funds he set up for us boys, but how he funded them, I have no idea. I always thought he was simply a good investor and saver."

As he talked, a thought occurred to me. "Grady hasn't been very friendly to me the few times I've seen him. Does he think I'm here for money?"

Clark looked at the ground and hemmed and hawed like an old woman deciding between oatmeal or bran flakes. His hesitation gave me my answer.

"Well, tell him I'm not. If there is any money buried anywhere, I just heard about it." I wasn't sure if I should add anything about Cathy hooking up with the Littlejohns for the money. In the end, I decided, in for a penny, in for a pound.

"Does Grady know that you and Cathy were once an item?"

Clark stared at me, open mouthed. "Guess I shouldn't be surprised that you know that. You seem to have plugged into the local gossip stream." He moved his head to look down the road, then started walking again. "To answer your question, yes, he does."

"Cathy thinks there's a lot of money in the family, doesn't she? Is that why you broke up with her, because you thought she was trying to get her hands on it?"

"One of the reasons." He looked up at the sky and laughed. It wasn't a joyous laugh but one coated with regret. "One day I took Troy out for a movie. He was only about seven at the time. Anyway, Troy ate too much candy and didn't feel well, so I brought him home early. He fell asleep on the way home. Rather than wake the boy, I carried him into their house. The door was open — Cathy hardly ever locked it. I came in quietly so I wouldn't disturb Troy and overheard Cathy talking on the phone in her bedroom. I don't know who she was talking to, but she was saying stuff like as soon as she got her hands on the money, she was leaving Holmsbury. It was clear in the conversation that she was talking about the money she assumed our family had hidden."

"Did you ask her about it?"

"Of course. She wouldn't tell me who she was talking to, just tried to lie and talk her way out of it. I left and never saw her again. I tried to warn Grady as soon as he hooked up with her, but he believed — still believes — that I made it up to keep them apart."

"Isn't it uncomfortable for you to have Cathy and Troy around like they were to-day?"

Clark shrugged. "At first it was. But she's Grady's girlfriend, so I put up with it. I miss Troy. He's a good kid."

"You hardly spoke to him today," I pointed out.

"It's easier for everyone if I keep my distance."

We walked along in silence for several yards. The area where my mother lived was more built up than where the inn was located. The street was busier, with houses neatly arranged on both sides. While still not on top of each other, as in California, they were spaced closer together than on the road I'd walked just a few hours earlier. We passed a middle school with a spacious athletic field. A few steps more, we came across a small post office. That's when I let loose with my largest bomb of information.

"Clark, I know that Cathy Morgan and her family sell drugs out of their vegetable stand." There, it was out.

Clark stopped in his tracks, cemented to the ground like a statue. I stopped, too. We stood like that, frozen, our faces locked on to each other. It seemed like an hour, but in reality it was only about a minute. During that time, Clark's face ran the gamut from anger to disbelief to resignation.

I broke the silence with another question.

I was getting deeper with every comment but couldn't help myself. The local drug business was a delicate egg. Now that I'd cracked it open, the only question was how to cook it — soft-boiled or scrambled. Might as well go for broke and scramble the thing. "You knew about that, didn't you? Are you involved?"

Clark looked around, then headed back towards the field, gesturing for me to follow him. I wasn't sure I should. Ninety percent of me trusted him, but it was that pesky ten percent I was worried about. Quickly, I did some calculations. Greg was back at the house. If Clark showed up without me, he'd have some big-time explaining to do. I took off after him, quickening my steps to catch up.

Clark stopped when he reached a baseball diamond a short ways from the street. He climbed a few steps of the bleachers and entered a row, sitting down about midway. I did the same. Clark gazed out over the playing field before turning to me.

"Odelia, you're messing with things that could get you hurt and cause a lot of trouble for a lot of people."

"So you know about the drugs?"

"I know about them." He turned his face back out towards the field. "I can't tell you the number of games I played here as a kid."

"So, are you involved with the drugs, or are you simply looking the other way, like you did with Marty?"

He looked back at me, his face set like stone, his eyes dark pools. "Neither. I'm trying to shut it down, but there are complications — one of them being Mom found with a dead drug dealer."

"Are you talking about Frankie McKenna or Les Morgan?"

"Both, but the body being Cathy's ex kicked up the investigation."

"How about Grady living with Cathy?"

Clark rubbed his face with both of his hands. "Another major fly in the ointment."

After a minute of weighing his thoughts, he turned and pulled a leg over the bench so that he was straddling it, facing me directly.

"Odelia, between you and me, I'm working with the state on this drug thing. Have been for a while. Just me, off the record. None of the other officers are involved and certainly not Grady. But we're not after the Browns, we're after their suppliers — the guys Frankie McKenna worked for. Or maybe he still does, who knows? He's disappeared. It's our guess Les Morgan worked for them, too. If they fall, the Browns will too. We want the head of the snake first."

"And what about Grady and Cathy?"

"If Grady's involved, he'll go down with them. There's a slim chance he might not know."

"Are you kidding me? One afternoon of watching the comings and goings in that stand alerted me. Willie, too."

"Grady may have gotten the looks in the family, but we got the brains. Until I got him into the police department here, he couldn't hold a decent job."

"So you gave him a badge and a gun?" An image of Barney Fife, bumbling deputy on the old *Andy Griffith Show,* came to mind.

"He's actually a pretty good cop, at least when it comes to traffic and minor scuffles. He handles himself well enough, and people like him. But as far as the drugs go, neither CPAC or I are clear on what he knows. And if we alert him, he'll alert Cathy and her brothers." Clark ran a hand through his hair. "Believe me, Odelia, it wasn't easy going to the state boys with my brother possibly involved. And with my past relationship with Cathy, it looks like revenge. But I had to do my job, and bringing CPAC in made it easier for me to operate under the radar."

"Brenda Bixby also knew about the drugs.

I'm not sure if she figured it out on her own, like we did, or if Joan Cummings alerted her."

"I never told Joan about it. All my calls to and from CPAC went through my cell, not through the main desk. Doesn't mean she didn't figure it out, like I'm sure some other folks in town have. But those would mostly be the ones buying the drugs, like Marty."

"And Mrs. Rielley."

"Mrs. *Rielley?*" Clark looked at me like I'd lost my mind.

"Those bags of corn and squash Cathy brought for her contained drugs. Willie checked them out when he unloaded them from her car."

"Jesus." There was more rubbing of his face with his hands, like he was sanding it down smooth. "We were actually making a lot of progress until this murder. I can't help but think the drugs and Morgan's death are related, but I need to know why Mom was in the corn maze that day and what she knows about the killer." He gave me a look of expectation. "Is there any chance you could worm that out of her?"

"I tried, didn't work. I'm hoping my husband can charm it out of her over dishes — or at least put her at ease enough for her to drop some unintentional hints."

After a short silence, Clark swung his leg back over the bench and stood up. He stretched, twisting his torso first one way, then the other. He did the same with his neck. His body gave off a short series of cracks and pops. Finished, he stepped down and offered me his hand in assistance. I took it and started down the bleachers to the ground. Once there, Clark didn't let go of my hand. He held it firmly, bordering on tight.

"Except for trying to get Mom to talk, I want you and your posse to stay out of this investigation, Odelia. And I mean it. You already know too much."

I started to ease my hand away, but he tightened his grip.

"And I need you to keep quiet about what I told you tonight. The drug investigation has intensified with the murder. If we close in on anyone, I can't have you and Greg in the way. Willie either. The three of you need to sit back and enjoy your visit or get your asses on a plane back to California. Understand?"

"You're hurting my hand."

"Tell me you understand."

I said I did, noting to myself that understanding wasn't the same as agreeing to stay out of it.

TWENTY-TWO

After we left my mother's, I drove Greg to the Tyler farm and showed him the layout of the maze. Along the way, I told him about my conversation with Clark but left out the part where Clark held my hand in a vise until I said I understood that I was to keep my nose out of the murder investigation. Considering it was a promise extracted under duress, I didn't plan on taking it seriously, but I was worried Greg might. One way or another, I was going to find out who and why my mother was protecting someone at a great cost to herself. It had occurred to me that Mom knew about the drugs and was protecting Grady. Whether he knew about it or not, I doubted he had much of a future with the police after this came to light.

Once at the Tyler farm, I pulled into the makeshift parking lot and down the short dirt road so Greg could see how it was set up from outside. We couldn't get up close to the maze because barricades and police tape were still in place. A freshly painted sign announced that the corn maze would be back open for business the following weekend.

"What's on the far side of the field?" asked Greg. "It looks like a river."

"It is. Not a wide one, but wide enough that you'd need a boat to cross it. See, there are boats on it now."

Greg craned his neck out the window. "Follow this road as far as you can."

While Greg kept watch, I continued down the narrow dirt road, driving slowly over the uneven terrain in the rental car. No one seemed to notice or care. The fair across the street was in the midst of being broken down. People were busy packing trucks and vans with everything from tables and chairs to products that didn't sell.

The road took a sharp turn to the right, then turned left at the border of the maze. It was a service road, dividing the maze from the unplanted field next to it. Down this far, there was no yellow tape warning people to keep out. I took the left and followed the road until I reached the end of this side of the maze. The road ended just short of the river, giving us the choice of turning left and following it behind the maze, or turning right alongside the empty field. We turned left.

"It looks like it circles the maze, doesn't it, Greg?"

"Yes, and I noticed a couple of small openings cut into the maze on these sides. Probably additional exits."

The wall of cornstalks to my left stood straight and tall like soldiers in close rank, while the smell of corn and earth, mixed with the loamy scent of the river, drifted through my open window.

"You know, Greg, it would have been easy for someone, anyone, to have slipped in here Saturday morning unnoticed." Not paying attention to my driving, the car hit a pothole. Both of us bumped up and down inside as we went through it. "In fact, this is a perfect place for a murder."

"Or a secret rendezvous," Greg added. "People could have easily slipped in and out of there before the thing opened."

"Then why the pole in the first place? If someone slipped in from one of the back exits, why would they need a flagpole?"

"Does seemed kind of silly. Those are used to help people find their way out, aren't they?"

"Yes, the flags help the maze people keep

304

track of how many people are in the maze and are devices for people in the maze to call for help. Although," I began, taking my eyes off the bumpy road just long enough to glance at Greg, "Cathy told me tonight that Les hated corn mazes and suffered from claustrophobia. Maybe he's the one who had the first flag."

We continued along the road, turning left at the end of the back of the maze.

"You thinking he took it when no one was looking?"

"Could be he grabbed it as a safety net so that after his meeting he had a way to get out, just in case he couldn't find one of the exits on his own. Willie was told that poles sometimes get misplaced, so maybe no one cared when flag number one wasn't there when they opened."

Greg craned his head to get a good look at the barrier of corn outside my window. "If what Cathy told you is true, Les Morgan had to have had a pretty compelling reason to throw his fears to the wind and enter this thing."

When we reached the end of the far side of the maze, the road went past the area where the concessions and picnic tables stood, then forked again. To the right, the road led to farm buildings. To the left, it headed back towards the entrance and parking lot. We turned left again and completed our circle.

I pointed out the car window at the lookout tower. "That's where Marty, Joan Cummings' son, was supposed to be that morning."

"That's the kid who was found stoned, right?"

"Yes."

"Wonder where he got the pot?"

I cocked an eyebrow at my husband. "What?"

"The pot. Was Marty a customer of the Browns, or did he have another source?"

"You think there might be drug turf issue in this small town."

"Could be, but I'm thinking more along the lines of who actually gave it to him. Was it something he already had or was he recently given it? You know, sweetheart, someone might have slipped him some fresh weed to get him out of the way that morning — after all, everyone knew he did drugs, right?"

"I hadn't thought of that." I leaned over and gave Greg a quick kiss. "You're getting good at this."

"I had to be a quick study to keep up with you."

"Willie tried to talk to Marty, but he wasn't here yesterday. Maybe one of us should try to locate the kid, preferably without his mother around."

Greg rubbed his beard. "Troy told me he starts back at school tomorrow. Marty probably does, too. He in high school or college?"

"Clark said he dropped out. We might have to track him down at his mother's while she's at work, or find out where Marty works, providing he has a job."

"Too bad you can't ask that reporter. I'll bet she'll know, but it would tip her off."

"Yeah, the less she's involved, the better."

I turned the car back up the dirt drive towards the street. A small group of older teens was coming into the parking lot from the fair area. Greg asked me to stop.

"Hey, man," he called out the window to two boys walking together. They were joking around and laughing. "Hey," Greg called again, "I was wondering if you could help me."

One of the boys broke away and came up to our car. "If I can." He was tall and thick, with meaty arms poking out from his tee shirt.

"I'm looking for a kid named Marty Cummings. Know where he is?"

"He's not here, mister. Old Man Tyler fired him yesterday."

"Know where I can hook up with him?"

The kid thought about it a minute, then turned to his companion, who I recognized as the pimply faced boy who'd directed me in the parking lot on my first visit to the farm.

"Hey, J.P.," he called to his friend. "You know where that loser Cummings is?"

J.P. came up to the car and scratched his head in thought. "Hard to say, but he might be at work. He's been working nights at that new home improvement store over on Bank Street."

"Got the name of the place?" Greg asked.

"It's one of the big chains, not sure which one," J.P. told him. "Only one like it in the area. It's on the corner of River Street and Bank in Thomasville, just off the main highway. Can't miss it."

"Thanks, guys."

The boys walked away to join their friends at a small cluster of vehicles still left in the parking lot.

Greg grinned at me. "Who says men don't ask for help."

"Shall we head for Thomasville?"

Greg answered by punching the intersection and city into the GPS. After a short search, it came up with directions.

The store was still open, but the parking lot was nearly empty. Greg and I entered the huge building stacked with everything from toilets to drill bits, plants to paint, and looked at each other for the next step.

"Might be difficult to find him." Greg rolled into the main aisle and glanced up and down it.

"I sort of remember what he looks like. A tall, skinny kid, straight brown hair on the long side. About eighteen to twenty years old."

"Should we have him paged?"

"Might scare him off. I also don't want to bring any more attention to him than necessary."

"Good thinking."

Greg came up with a plan to divide and conquer the space of the warehouse-sized store. I went to the large horizontal middle aisle and started at one end. He stayed in the front horizontal aisle and started at the other end. From opposite directions, we walked down our respective aisles towards the center with our cell phones connected to each other. It was clear that the place was operating with a lean sales staff. Along the way, I saw someone helping a customer with paint chips, and a husband and wife deciding on kitchen cabinets, but no Marty Cummings and no alert from Greg.

I was starting to think Marty wasn't scheduled to work when I heard Greg say through the phone, "Hey, man, can you help me with something?" I trotted past a couple more aisles and finally spotted them both, Greg and Marty, halfway down the aisle containing electrical fixtures.

As I approached, Greg introduced me. "This is my wife. She has some questions."

One look at Marty, and I knew he was stoned. Maybe not fully baked, but I was pretty sure he wouldn't be able to pass a urine test. He shifted from foot to foot in a blatant display of lack of attentiveness and over-relaxation, waiting for me to ask him something about home improvement, which I doubted he knew much about.

I didn't mince words. "Who gave you the drugs Saturday morning, Marty?"

His mouth fell open enough for me to catch sight of fillings. "What?"

"Saturday morning at the corn maze. Did you have those drugs on you when you went to work, or did someone give them to you?"

"Who the hell are you?" The question was laced with wonder, not anger.

"Friends, Marty," Greg added. "We just need to know who hooked you up with the pot. We heard from J.P. it was great stuff."

At the sound of a familiar name, Marty gave us a lazy smile. "The best. Better than the shit I usually smoke. Can't afford the good stuff, you know."

"Where'd you get it?" Greg pressed. "We were told you were the man to help us out." Greg was doing such a fine job of communicating with the druggie, I was impressed and worried at the same time.

"The old lady gave it to me."

Old lady? Did he mean Mrs. Rielley? From the way Greg looked at me, I knew his brain had made the same leap.

"What old lady, Marty?" Greg asked.

"You know, my old lady."

"Your girlfriend?"

"Nah, dude, my mother."

I held up a hand, index finger pointed at him. "You're telling us that your mother, Joan Cummings, gave you the pot on Saturday?"

He gave us a sloppy nod. "Yeah, ain't that the shit? She bitches at me all the time. Yakkity, yakkity." He made talking movements with one hand. "Always on my back about not doing drugs, then shows up with a bag of primo weed and tells me to knock myself out. Says it's a special day."

Greg moved closer to him. "The stuff

you're on tonight — get that from your old lady, too?"

"Same stuff. Cops confiscated my stash, but I didn't take it all with me Saturday." He gave us a slow half-wink. "I ain't stupid, you know."

We thanked him and started to leave when an idea hit me. I went back to the kid. "Marty, do you know Brenda Bixby?"

"Bren, sure. She's smokin'."

"I heard she was in town. Is she staying with you and your mother?"

He shook his head. "No, says I'm a creepy perv." He snorted. "Just because last time I sneaked a peek at her in the shower. I'm a guy, for crissakes."

"Okay, thanks again." I started to walk away.

"Try the North Woods Motel over on Spencer Street in Derek's Grove."

"Excuse me?" I turned around.

He shrugged. "Bren came to the house to see Ma. Could've sworn she said something about the North Woods. It's over by the Kettle."

TWENTY-THREE

"The Kettle is where Willie went tonight," I told Greg. "That's where Sybil works. If he wasn't on a date, I'd call him and have him check out the North Woods Motel."

Greg was fussing with the GPS. "Guess we'll have to do that ourselves." He tossed me a grin.

"You are starting to enjoy this stuff way too much." As he chuckled, I started the car.

Derek's Grove was a tiny town located two towns north from Thomasville and one town east of Saxton. If you blinked, you'd miss it. Following the GPS, we maneuvered through a web of country roads that turned into streets through small-town business districts, then dissolved again into sparsely populated roads until the next small town presented itself. None of the roads we traveled were straight but meandered, curving around bends, up rises and down hills, until we saw a small sign announcing Derek's Grove, founded in 1790, population 862. We arrived just as the sun went down.

We had keyed the GPS for the North Woods Motel. Once in Derek's Grove, the device took us through the middle of the town's small city center with its picturesque town hall and few businesses. We followed the directions around a small rotary that spit us out on the other side, onto Spencer Street. Shortly after that, the GPS mechanical voice alerted us that our destination was a mile on the left. About a hundred yards before the North Woods, we spied the large lit sign for the Kettle on the right. The bar was larger than I expected, and the parking lot held a good number of cars. As we drove by, Greg pointed out Willie's SUV.

The North Woods Motel wasn't really a motel at all but a cluster of tiny cabins scattered throughout a wooded grove with a narrow drive going through it. The cabins and their surroundings were a bit on the shabby side, but not horribly so; "rustic" might be the better word. I counted ten cabins. About half appeared occupied, with lights on and cars parked in front. The office was located in a large cabin nearest the road. It was well lit, and a neon sign announced vacancies, but I couldn't see anyone through the window. The manager or owner could have been in the back watching TV. With today being the last day of the long weekend, I doubted that the North Woods expected any new guests tonight, and it wasn't like it was located on a busy highway.

Just past the motel, I pulled the car into the driveway of a closed auto repair shop. "What do you think?" I asked Greg.

"Did you notice Brenda's car anywhere?"

"No, but she drives a dark blue Honda. Might be tough to see in the dark, especially with all those trees." I unbuckled my seat belt.

"Where are you going?"

"I'm going to check out the cabins, see if I spot her car."

"Don't, Odelia. We can just drive slowly through the road that goes through the property."

"She knows my car, Greg." I started to get out. "I'll only be a minute. She's probably at dinner anyway."

"And if you find her, what then? You going to question her?"

I thought a moment. I really didn't want to leave Greg alone in the car. "Maybe I should drive to the Kettle and park there; that way, you can wait for me with Willie."

Greg looked skeptical. "Honey, you can't come with me, and I need to find out if that's where she's staying. I can come back tomorrow and talk to her."

Greg reached out to grab my arm, but before he could I was out of my seat.

"Ten minutes, Odelia. If you're not back in ten minutes, I'm calling Willie."

"Make it fifteen."

"Fifteen, but take your cell. Put it on vibrate."

I switched my phone to vibrate and stuck it into the pocket of my jeans. I heard Greg swear as I quietly shut the door.

It took me just a couple of seconds to cover the few yards from the car to the motel grounds. It was much darker in the bosom of the property, which was sprinkled with low-level security lights that did little except mark the progression of the private drive. Counting on this darkness for cover, I tiptoed my way to the first cabin with a car. Not Brenda's. Then to the next. Again, not hers. I made my way deeper into the property. The next two cabins both had two cars parked next to them. As I started for the closest of the two, something small scurried past me in the dead leaves at my feet. I nearly died of fright, but at least I didn't shriek like a schoolgirl.

316

Making my way as quietly as I could over the crunchy autumn fallout, I finally reached the first cabin with two cars — a silver mini-van and a black truck. Neither vehicle was familiar to me. Just as I started for the next cabin, the door to this one opened. I ducked behind a couple of large trees and waited, knowing that my precious time was ticking away.

A man came out first. He looked up and down the road before the next person followed him out. It was a woman of average build, with shoulder-length hair. She looked vaguely familiar, but I couldn't be sure. They walked to the driver's side of the mini-van and kissed long and hard before opening the door. As the woman got into the van, the light inside illuminated her face. I wasn't positive about her identification, especially since she wasn't screaming hysterically at the moment, but I could have sworn it was Tara Brown. Interesting.

As soon as the minivan left and the guy went back into the cabin, I made for the next cabin with two vehicles. It appeared to be the last one on the property. One of the cars was a dark-colored Honda that I recognized as Brenda Bixby's.

All the cabins had a shallow porch in front with two plastic chairs and a nice-size window. The shades to the front window of the cabin with the Honda were closed, as were the shades to the cabin next to it. Slinking around the side of the cabin, I made my way to the back. There was a small, high window in the back wall, and it was open. Through it, I could hear water running, a shower, and two voices — a man's and a woman's. The woman's voice morphed into giggles. It was Brenda, and she was obviously with a close friend. I pressed myself against the wall to the cabin and strained to listen.

"We're almost there, baby," the man said. The voice sounded familiar, but it was difficult to tell over the sound of water. I dug into my brain to see if the other car I'd seen out front, a late-model SUV, was one I'd seen before, but came up empty. A few seconds later, the shower stopped. "Soon we'll be long gone from this dump."

"You're sure about the money?" I heard Brenda ask.

"Yep, the old lady led me right to it when she took out that fifty grand for Morgan. Never saw me, but I saw everything. Looks like a whole lot more is there. Just have to wait until the time is right."

"Goody for us." Brenda's words were followed by noisy moaning and kissing.

I was hoping to hear more when a car pulled into the drive and stopped in front of the cabin. Using the sound of the car's engine to hide my footsteps, I slid alongside the cabin walls to the front. A few feet away was a large, thick stand of evergreen shrubs. I darted behind it to get a better view of the new arrival and the porch.

The car that had just pulled up was a beat-up subcompact with a magnetized sign on the door announcing Rinaldi's Pizza. A kid got out of the car and retrieved a large pizza hot sack from the back seat and a six-pack of soda. He looked from one cabin to the other, unsure of which was his destination. He was about to head for the other cabin when the door to Brenda's opened and a dim yellow porch light was switched on.

"Over here," someone from Brenda's cabin called to the kid.

A man dressed only in a towel greeted the delivery guy and took the pizza and sodas, then he called back into the cabin. "Brenda, you got a couple singles? He doesn't have enough change."

The man went back into the cabin and returned a second later to pay for the pizza. I peeked around the shrub as far as I dared to get a better look. When the man in the towel turned to go back inside, the weak glow from the porch light caught his face. It was Grady Littlejohn.

The North Woods must be the local No-Tell Motel.

While I waited out the departure of the delivery car with nervous energy, I turned and scanned the area, looking for a quicker escape route than the road. It was then a slight movement at the other cabin, the one Tara had left, caught my eye. The blinds were parted and a man was looking out, the dim light in the cabin behind him creating a silhouette. He was watching Grady, same as I was. As Grady closed the door to his cabin, the man caught sight of me. I ducked back farther behind the shrubs. When I poked my nose out again, he was still there — still staring in my direction and making no attempt to hide from me. I just about peed in my pants.

Afraid that the man in the other cabin was going to call someone and report a peeper, as soon as the pizza wagon left, I started slinking my way from tree to tree in the direction of the exit. The phone in my pants vibrated, but I didn't dare take the time or make the noise necessary to answer it. As soon as I felt it safe, I made for the road and Greg, hurrying before he called out the militia.

"Grady?" Greg shook his head. He had repeated the name in surprise several times since I'd returned to the car and sped out of the parking lot as if we were being chased by a T-rex. I'd filled Greg in while I drove, my mouth moving as fast as the car.

"Seems little brother isn't as dumb as people are making him out to be."

"So the legend about Leland Littlejohn's money is true."

"Seems possible. And from what I over-heard, Mom was digging out fifty thousand dollars for Morgan. I'm assuming he meant Les Morgan, not Cathy."

"Sounds like Cathy's about to be dumped by a second Littlejohn."

"Sure looks that way."

We were back at the inn after picking up a pizza and sodas of our own for dinner. Greg had also wanted an order of fried zucchini sticks, but I insisted on a salad.

"Hold off on the fried food," I told him. "Before we go home, I'm taking you to the Blue Lobster."

"What's the Blue Lobster?"

"Trust me, you'll love it."

We were eating in the kitchen at a small wooden table. I didn't think Mrs. Friar would mind. It was less stuffy than the formal dining room. I'd pulled dishes and utensils from the cupboard. We were about to start eating when a car pulled into the driveway. I peeked out the window.

"It's Clark," I announced to Greg. I went to the back door and let him in. He didn't seem happy as he followed me to the kitchen.

"Want some pizza and salad?" I asked.

He shook his head. "I'll take a soda though."

I handed him a can and a napkin. He popped the top and took a long drink.

"We're surprised to see you tonight, Clark," said Greg as he dished up salad.

"Can't get enough of us?" I joked.

"This isn't a social call." Clark was using the same tone he had used at the field. "I thought I told you to keep your nose out of things."

"What are you talking about?"

"Are you telling me you did not go for a joyride around Tyler's farm tonight?"

"Are you having us watched?" I stared at my half brother with indignation.

"No, I'm not. Though it might not be a bad idea. But that farm and field are being watched. A car with your plates was seen driving around the maze earlier tonight.

When I received the call, I about blew my stack."

"Calm down, Clark," I told him. "I was just showing Greg the layout, that's all."

"Well, cut it out. Don't go near that farm ever again. Got me?"

I agreed, then turned to Greg. "Doesn't he remind you of Dev Frye, honey?"

"Yes, kind of. Just not as big."

Clark eyed the pizza. "That from Rinaldi's? I grew up on that stuff."

I got up and retrieved another place setting from the cupboard. I slipped a slice of pizza onto the plate and held it out to Greg to add salad.

"No salad for me," said Clark. "Should have tried the fried zucchini instead. Best anywhere."

Greg cocked an eye my way.

"You'll take salad and eat it," I ordered. "Both of you."

While we ate, I glanced off and on at Greg, using eye movement and facial gestures to ask if we should tell Clark what we found out. He was doing the same back at me.

Clark stopped eating and wiped his mouth with a paper napkin. "Okay, you two. What's up?"

"What do you mean?" I asked, reaching

323

for another piece of pizza.

"You two either have contagious facial tics or you're sitting on information. Out with it."

I looked at Greg just as he stuffed his mouth with pizza and made gestures that he couldn't talk with his mouth full. Yeah, right. I turned to Clark.

"You're right, Clark, we did find out a few things tonight."

"I thought you promised me to keep out of it."

"I made that promise under coercion and police brutality."

"What?" Greg asked, suddenly finding his voice.

Clark rolled his eyes. "Police brutality, my ass." He put down his pizza and crossed his arms across his chest. "What in the hell am I supposed to do with you? Lock you up like that cop in California suggested?"

Greg took a drink of his soda. "Just go with it, Clark. It's what I do. Life's a lot easier that way."

Clark glared at Greg. "And how are you any better? You're riding right along with her on this. Hell, I'm surprised Willie isn't here, adding to the problem." He paused. "Or is he off doing his own investigation?"

I straightened in my chair. "He's on a

date, Clark. Just like I told you."

"Clark," Greg began, "it's true, Odelia can't seem to stay clear of murder and mayhem. I came here to keep her safe. That's why Willie's here, too. I've learned it's more productive that way. If I tied her up and locked her in a room, I'd probably go to jail, and she'd divorce me. I don't want the former and couldn't live with the latter. Understand?"

Clark got up and went to the kitchen sink. With both hands on the edge of the sink and his back to us, he huffed and puffed his way through his thoughts. Greg gave me a raised eyebrow. I shrugged. Who knew what Clark was thinking, but I was now very sure we needed to tell him what we knew.

A minute or two later, he returned to the table and sat down. "Okay, shoot. What have you got? Although something tells me I'm not going to like it."

He devoured three slices of pizza and two helpings of salad while I talked.

TWENTY-FOUR

Greg was in bed reading. I was at the desk doodling names, listing possible motives, and drawing connection lines from one individual to another. It was beginning to look like a spider's web. As soon as the clothes in the dryer were done, I was calling it a night.

Willie had come back to the inn to change before his date. When we got home, I had found a small stack of dirty laundry neatly piled by our door with *THANKS!* written across a piece of paper on top. He had called a few minutes ago to say he wouldn't be back tonight and not to worry. He said he was doing some important undercover work, then he laughed. I asked him to check with Sybil about any gossip regarding Grady Littlejohn, Brenda Bixby, and Tara Brown.

We'd told Clark everything we'd found out — about Joan giving her son drugs the morning of the murder in the maze, and about Brenda and Grady's relationship and what was said about the hidden money.

"Okay," Clark said, trying to wrap his head around all the information. "Assuming Mom does know where that money is, why would she be giving fifty thousand dollars to Les Morgan?" Before we could say anything, he added, "The only reason to pay that kind of money to creeps like him is for blackmail."

"If Les was working for the same outfit as McKenna," I said, "then he knew about the Browns' drug business. Those are his former in-laws. He might even have a grudge against them. And Grady, a cop, was going to marry his ex-wife."

Greg added his thoughts. "Seems like a lot of people knew about that hidden money, or at least the rumor about it. Cathy could have told Les while they were married, and he remembered. She seems fixed on it."

Clark shook his head slowly. "How ironic. Cathy's been after the Littlejohn hidden treasure for years. Now Grady's planning on stealing it and leaving her flat."

He got up and paced the kitchen floor, running his hands through his hair. "Grady and I have never been close. Probably the age difference, but maybe not. He's agreeable enough, just never seemed very motivated. Never finished college. Couldn't keep a job. Always looking for the easy way out. Used his looks as far as he could. As much as I try to pass it off as him being kind of dull, he's not. He's just lazy. I've always covered for him, for Mom's sake."

"So you really do think he knows about the drug business?"

"Yeah. He'd have to be deaf, dumb, and blind not to, living with Cathy as he is." He shook his head. "I'm almost tempted to give him cash so he and his secret honey can leave town and start fresh. Maybe it's what he needs." Clark said it more to himself than to us.

"You know, Clark," I began, not relishing bringing up my current thought, "it could be Brenda's informant at the station isn't Joan, but Grady."

Clark looked at me, his eyes dull and lifeless. "Or both. Some chief I am, huh?"

After an awkward silence, I got up and moved the dishes to the sink for washing. "Okay, let's say Les Morgan contacts Mom and tells her unless she pays up, he's going to finger her fair-haired son for drugs. It would not only ruin his career as a cop, it could also endanger yours." I ran some hot water into the sink and added dish soap that

I had found under the counter. "If she had the money, she'd pay up, wouldn't she?"

"Yes, especially after what happened with me in Boston." Clark sat down heavily in his chair. "During a drug bust that went wrong, I shot and killed one of my informants. People said it was to cover up the fact that I was on the take from drug dealers. I wasn't. The investigation cleared me, but that was a tough time for Mom. I'm sure if Les told Mom that Grady was involved in drugs, she'd do most anything to make sure it didn't come to light."

Clark looked at me with a sad grin. "As ornery as she is, Mom does love us all in her own way, including you."

I swallowed hard and turned back to the dishes.

Greg rolled over to the sink, grabbed a dish towel, and started drying the dishes as I washed them. "That could explain why Grace was in the maze," he said. "She was paying off Les Morgan."

I stopped washing and turned to Clark. "But there was no money found in the maze that day, was there?"

"Not that I know of."

"And that still doesn't explain why Mom was erasing the prints on the pole or who killed Les Morgan." I went back to washing, talking over my shoulder. "All we may know now is why Mom was there in the first place."

"What about Marty and his mother?" The question came from Greg. "How do they fit into this?"

"Yes," I said, "we seem to have forgotten about them. Why would Joan give dope to her space-cadet son on that particular morning, especially considering how hard she was trying to keep him clean?"

"Puzzles the hell out of me," said Clark. "She had to have known he'd smoke out right away and be useless."

Greg and I had finished the dishes, and I was wrapping up the leftover pizza and salad. "Unless," I said, "she wanted to make sure he was useless that particular morning."

"What do you mean, sweetheart?"

"Maybe Joan knew something was going to go down in the maze that morning. She might have thought that if her son was stoned, he wouldn't go to work, keeping him out of harm's way. He seems the type to just blow off a job, especially one like working the maze. But instead, he went to work and got stoned there."

"That line of thought, if true, would mean Joan might be involved with the killing."

Clark said the words slowly, like each one was horrible and nasty to his taste. "Or knew it was going to happen."

"If she was feeding Brenda Bixby information, why couldn't someone have fed Joan information, maybe in an effort to keep her son out of the way?" I leaned against the kitchen counter. "I wish Mom would talk. I still think she knows a lot about all this."

I looked around the kitchen, making sure it was as spotless as when we'd found it. "Either way," I continued, "Marty saw nothing." I paused. "Unlike Troy, who apparently is having nightmares. Makes you wonder what he saw, doesn't it?"

Clark answered. "We're not sure he saw anything except a dead body and our mother bent over it."

"Clark," Greg began, his face squeezed in concern, "do you think when Troy saw the body, he knew it was his father?"

"Cathy claims Troy hasn't seen his father in several years. With the shock of seeing a body, especially one impaled like that, he might not have noticed the face." Clark played with the salt and pepper shakers on the table. "We've asked him, but he says he didn't know. But my gut tells me he's lying, at least about something."

Soon after, Clark said goodnight, but not

before admonishing us to keep out of it. We'd helped enough and he thanked us for it, but he'd take it from here. It was police business, not ours.

Humph. Clark was forgetting something. This wasn't just police business, it was family business. Therefore, it was my business.

Tapping my pen against one of the names on my list, I mulled over a thought. "Greg, Willie said that Frankie McKenna was a liaison between the drug supplier and the drug dealer. Would you assume that meant he picked up the cash from their retail outlets?"

"Retail outlets?" Greg gave me a strange look over the top of his book. "Jesus, Odelia, you're making it sound like a Gap franchise."

"You know what I mean. If the Browns are selling the drugs for a supplier, how would they exchange the money for more drugs?"

"I guess they would either go to the supplier or the supplier would send one of his people here." He thought a minute. "So McKenna could have been the go-between. He could have delivered more product and picked up money. Sure."

"Cathy said that Tara keeps the books for the farm and the stand. I wonder if she also keeps them for the drug money. I don't recall seeing Cathy put that money in the same till, but Tara could still keep the books on it."

"Sweetheart, I doubt the books on the drugs would be kept in the same ledger as the farm's accounting."

"Silly, I know that. And they wouldn't be that extensive — just an accounting of outgo versus income and the divvying up of the profits. They would run all expenses through the farm for tax purposes. Anything from the drugs would be unreportable. But I'll still bet that somewhere there is a journal of some kind tracking it. Just wondering if Tara kept that as well, or if someone else did."

"If drugs are a family business, like the farm, she might keep the figures on both."

"So the question is, what was she *really* doing in the maze? Was she simply taking her nephew through it early in the day before the crowds, or was she making an exchange of money for product?" I got up and sat on the edge of Greg's bed. "Doesn't it seem odd that the bookkeeper of the Brown family enterprise was one of the people who found the body?"

"You think she was there to make an exchange? Odd place, don't you think? That maze doesn't run all year. Much easier to do it someplace more convenient, like at the stand itself."

"I agree, the maze is an odd choice, but I doubt the Browns would meet with the supplier at their place of business. Too risky for exposure. I'll bet the exchanges usually took place somewhere inconspicuous, like a mall parking lot or something like that. And don't you think the Browns would use someone who could go virtually unnoticed for the exchange — someone like Tara, who, again, is their money person?"

Through our open room door, I heard the dryer stop. "Be right back."

"Before you go, can you grab me my laptop?" Greg put down his book as I handed him the compact computer.

A minute later, I came back with the clean, dry clothes in my arms. After kicking our door shut with a foot, I tossed them on my bed and started folding and hanging. Greg had booted up the laptop and was maneuvering it, looking for something.

"Think about it," I said as I folded one of Willie's tee shirts. "The people here are nosy by nature. They know everyone and almost everything about each other. The farmers might be noticed and are busy with the farm. Cathy is busy with the stand. And people might take note of two cars meeting on a country road. But a housewife in the parking lot of a grocery store or mall, or someplace like that, would go virtually unnoticed. She'd be the perfect one to be the liaison on the Brown side."

I put Willie's clothing in a pile on top of the dresser and put ours in the drawers and closet. "If that's the case, I wonder if Tara knew that it was Les Morgan and not Frankie McKenna she was meeting in the maze."

"*If* she was meeting him in the maze. We don't know that for sure. Maybe she was meeting her lover." Greg continued to tap away at his keyboard.

"With Troy in tow, unlikely. And why would she have Troy tag along on a drug deal unless it was to provide cover?" I paused. "Seems like none of the Browns are concerned about Troy being exposed to all this."

I'd told Clark that I thought I saw Tara Brown leaving a rendezvous at the North Woods. He didn't seem surprised.

"I'm almost glad," he'd said. "Clem's been slapping her around for years. Although if he found out, he'd probably kill both of them. Did you recognize the guy?"

I shook my head. "He drove a black pickup truck, not old, not new."

Clark had laughed. "Well, that narrows it down to half the guys in the county."

While I finished getting ready for bed, I continued presenting my case to Greg. "For the sake of argument, say it was a meeting. She takes Troy as cover and goes into the maze like any auntie showing her nephew a fun time, when in reality she is making a drug exchange."

"Look at this, sweetheart."

I sat on the edge of his bed as he turned the computer screen towards me. On it was one of the photos Ollie had taken. It was an enlargement of a couple of people gathered in the maze by the murder scene. Greg pointed at a woman.

"Isn't this Tara Brown?"

"Yes, it is."

"Look at her closely, particularly her bag."

I squinted. Tara was carrying a large, ugly messenger bag. It was hanging across her body bandolier-style.

"You know, Odelia, I think you may be right. I'm no fashion expert, but wouldn't that be the perfect bag for transporting drugs and money?"

"It sure would. I mean, it doesn't prove anything, but most women wouldn't carry a bag like that. Generally, men carry messenger bags. Women would be most likely to carry a shoulder bag, tote bag, or maybe even a cute backpack." I paused to think it through. "Or no bag. When I went into the maze, I left my purse in my car and only carried water. My phone and some money was tucked into a pocket."

Greg brought up another couple of photos with people. In another of Tara and Troy, Tara appeared to be clutching the bag close to her body. He pointed at the photo. "But even with this, why the maze? Seems like too much trouble to me."

My tired, middle-aged brain tried to sort out the facts into complete thoughts and sentences. It was difficult. "Les was already meeting Mom in the maze, so why not kill two birds with one stone? He may have told Tara to meet him there, too." Another thought, an offshoot of the other, presented itself. "And maybe Les asked Tara to bring Troy so he could see his son."

"So you think Tara killed Les?"

"In front of her nephew? Again, unlikely." My shoulders sagged with exhaustion. "Like with Mom, it's only a theory on why she was there."

I went back to the desk and started drawing on a clean sheet of paper. In the middle, I put a square and put Les Morgan's name in the center. I wrote down Tara's name to the side and drew a line from it to the center of the square and wrote "exchange" across the line. Next, I wrote my mother's name on the other side with a line to the square and labeled that "blackmail."

"Had Les made it out of the maze," I began, concentrating on the new drawing, "he would have had a lot of cash on him. Cash from the blackmail and cash from the drugs. But Clark said no cash was found on him or anywhere. I'm guessing the drug exchange didn't happen before Les was killed, but there were no drugs found either."

"Unless there were drugs found, and Clark didn't tell us."

I grabbed my cell phone.

"What are you doing?"

"Calling Clark."

"Odelia, it's late. Ask him tomorrow."

I looked at the clock. It was nearly eleven, and Clark did look like he was about to drop when he was here. Reluctantly, I put down the phone. Instead, I drew a big question mark above the square on the paper and drew a line from it to the square. On the line, I wrote "took cash and drugs" with another question mark. As a last flourish, I added another question mark several inches above Tara's name with a line to her that was marked "lover."

"Whoever killed Les probably knew about the drug and cash exchange and about the blackmail money Mom was going to pay him. Les could have been killed for both."

Greg raised an eyebrow. "By Joan Cummings maybe? After all, she got her son out of the way."

"Joan was working that morning at the police station." I rubbed my tired eyes. "And Les was killed before he met Tara, so the killer didn't get that money. Or did he?"

I circled the question mark indicating Tara's on-the-side affair. "I wonder if Tara's lover had anything to do with the murder?"

Greg closed his laptop and put it on the floor next to the bed. "Come to bed, Odelia. You're going to blow a fuse in that busy head of yours. We can go over it all tomorrow. Willie might have a fresh perspective."

He was right. My head did feel like a balloon with too much helium. I eyed the twin beds with disfavor. Greg noticed and laughed.

"Come here, sweetheart." He patted the narrow space beside him. "There's plenty of room for both of us."

"I seriously doubt that."

"Then at least climb into my bed for a snuggle." He extended an arm to make a nook for me. I got into his bed and nestled against him. He kissed my forehead and held me close.

"Tomorrow, I think we should hunt down Tara Brown, don't you?"

Greg gave me a squeeze. "Uh-huh. Sounds good."

"And visit Mom. Maybe I can try water boarding to make her talk."

"Whatever you say."

Greg's mouth traveled down from my forehead to my cheek to my mouth. He kissed me firmly while his hand found and fondled one of my breasts. It was a familiar signal of an amorous advance. But as much as I wanted to dive right into his sexual invitation, I held back. Sensing my hesitation, he leaned his head back so he could look at my face.

"What's the matter, sweetheart? We're all alone in the place." He chuckled. "Why should Willie have all the fun?"

"It's not that, honey. It's the bed. With my size and your limited movement, it's kind of small for this, don't you think?"

"No different than the back seat of a car."

"Um, hate to tell you this, but I've never, um, had sex in the back seat of a car. The front seat either."

"You haven't?" He seemed genuinely surprised.

"Nope. I'm a back-seat virgin."

Greg pushed my nightgown down off my shoulder and kissed my neck. As his kisses moved south, he mumbled, "We'll have to remedy that when we get home."

TWENTY-FIVE

Greg and I had just sat down to breakfast when Willie came sauntering in from outside. I was drinking my juice. Greg had his nose stuck in the morning paper.

"Why, Mr. Carter," we heard Mrs. Friar say with cheer as he came down the hallway and entered the dining room. "You're up and out early this morning."

"That's me. Got that early bird and worm thing going on."

I pressed my lips together to keep from laughing. Greg snickered from behind his newspaper.

"I am making mushroom omelets for Mr. and Mrs. Stevens this morning. Would you like one? I also have fresh blueberry muffins. My grandkids picked the blueberries just yesterday."

"Sounds divine, Mrs. Friar. Thank you."

Willie sat down. I picked up the coffee carafe and poured him a cup. He looked like he could use it. Chipper or not, he looked a bit ragged around the edges.

"Rough night?" I asked when Mrs. Friar went back into the kitchen.

"Nah, Sybil's not into the rough stuff."

Greg snickered again. No matter what their age, when it comes to sex, men are adolescents.

I lowered my voice. "Before or after your nocturnal shenanigans, did you learn anything new?"

"About Sybil, plenty." He hoisted his cup into the air. "I may have found a kindred spirit in that woman."

"You mean, she's on the run?"

Willie laughed so hard he sloshed his coffee. "Not sure about that yet." He grabbed a napkin and wiped the dribble from the side of his cup. "Let's just say Sybil shares my rather loosey-goosey moral fiber."

"That's okay, cousin," Greg said, folding and putting aside the paper. "Odelia and I were pretty loosey-goosey ourselves last night." He winked at me.

"I thought I noticed a fresh glow about her." Willie smirked into his coffee cup.

I was about to deliver a suitable retort when Mrs. Friar waltzed through the swinging door with our breakfasts. "Yours is coming up in a jiffy, Mr. Carter."

After Mrs. Friar served Willie, she brought in a basket of a dozen freshly baked blueberry muffins. "I have to scoot on over to my house for a moment. My husband just called and said he needed help with something. Just help yourself if there's anything you need."

Willie grabbed a hot muffin, dancing it from hand to hand until finally dropping it on his plate. "Last night I got to sample some of the pot being sold from Buster's stand. I must say, it was primo stuff."

Willie sliced open the muffin. Steam rose from its fluffy insides as he slathered it with butter. His cholesterol was really taking a beating this trip.

"Some of the best I've ever had." Willie looked from me to Greg with a big grin. "I had to try it, you know, in the spirit of my investigation."

Greg picked up his own muffin. "Did you bring us any?"

After slapping Greg's arm, I said, "We talked to Marty Cummings last night. He was waxing poetic over it, too. I thought it was just the ramblings of a stoner."

Willie waved a table knife in my direction. "Never underestimate a pothead's sense of quality, little mama. At least not when it comes to cannabis." He took a bite of muffin. "Anyway, the high quality gave me an idea. I asked Sybil if she'd ever heard of the Browns doing any growing of their own." Willie talked with his mouth full. He swallowed. "Damn, I don't know when I've tasted better muffins. I could eat the whole batch."

"Over my dead body," Greg said, his own mouth stuffed with blueberries and dough.

Not to be left out, I buttered up one of my own and took a bite. It was heavenly. Let's see, a dozen muffins and three of us; that seemed about right.

Breaking the spell of the magical muffins, I got the discussion back on track. "You think the Browns are growers?"

"When you think about it, it makes sense. They're farmers. It's what they do. Seems a natural step for them. But, alas — Sybil said there's been no rumor to that effect. Doesn't mean it's not happening, but she was pretty sure that isn't the case. So I had my people check, and they also came up with nothing on it."

"Clark didn't say anything about growing, just selling."

Willie stopped stuffing his face and stared at me. "So the chief *does* know about the drug biz?"

While Willie moved on to his second muffin, I gave him the condensed version of our latest discussions with Clark, then gave more thought to the idea of the Browns growing. "It would be pretty risky and stupid for them to grow their own weed. They'd not only be naturals at it, they would be natural *suspects*."

"Good point." Greg started on his second muffin.

"In fact," I continued, "legally, it could jeopardize their whole family enterprise, couldn't it? I mean, if they're growing and get caught, they could lose their entire farm, and everyone connected with the farm could be charged." I made sure the guys were following me, in spite of their blueberry muffin haze. "But if they're only selling product out of the stand, they could pass it off as something only Cathy and a few others knew about and possibly save the farm and the family business. Selling the product of others might minimize the farm's exposure, don't you think?"

"Quite possible, little mama." After buttering a third muffin, Willie started on his eggs. "By the way, I like your ideas about the blackmail and Joan Cummings' involvement. Nice work. I think it's becoming clear that Les Morgan could have been there on several missions. His bosses could have sent him to do McKenna's old job with the Browns, and he thought why not shake down the old lady at the same time. It's not like anything would get back to his big bosses through her. He'd do his job and make some quick cash for himself on the side, not to mention stick it to the Little-john family over Cathy."

He plowed through half of his omelet before speaking again. "I also asked Sybil about the Cummings kid. She said he's the local dropout poster child. That his mother's tried almost everything to straighten him out. Frankly, I'm surprised he has a job."

"Don't you think it's odd that his own mother gave him drugs?" Holding myself back at only one muffin, I started on the cantaloupe on my plate.

"Not if you consider your theory about her wanting to keep her kid out of the way. Question is, who gave her a heads-up about something going down in the corn maze that morning? Was it Brenda? And if so, how did she know — unless *she* was involved? And if she's involved, is Grady? Maybe the two of them are into more than just fleecing Grace out of that money."

With Greg's mouth full of muffin, I kept the conversation going. "Did you ask Sybil about Grady and Brenda?"

"Yes. She knows Grady and says he hasn't been in the Kettle for quite a while. Brenda, on the other hand, she wasn't so sure about. Could be those two are keeping their relationship way under the radar."

"Seems strange, doesn't it, that she came on to you when she had a thing going on with Grady?"

Willie shook his head in amusement. "If she wanted information bad enough, a girl like that wouldn't think twice about bed hopping to get it." He took a bite of muffin. "Could be the thing with Grady is fairly new. She could be working him."

"I hadn't thought of that. Maybe to get her hands on the Littlejohn money. Or maybe a twofer, the money *and* information."

Willie continued. "Nothing either on Tara Brown stepping out, but Sybil did say she wouldn't be surprised. Said that Clem Brown is a real bastard to his wife."

"Clark told us that last night, too," Greg added.

I took one last bite, my brain moving in sync with my mouth. "After seeing Grady and Brenda so cozy last night, I wonder if they're the ones behind all this. Maybe little miss I-wanna-be-a-reporter didn't come down to cover the story as much as to *cre-*

ate the story."

I pushed my plate away and pulled my coffee close. "I think it's time I have that heart-to-heart talk Brenda's been asking for. I also still think we should talk to Tara Brown." I gave Willie an update on my theory about Tara possibly being the money link and go-between.

Willie listened closely while he finished his breakfast. "Sounds feasible, especially since she was in the maze near the time of the murder."

Greg leaned back and patted his full stomach. "After looking at the maze last night, it's pretty clear that almost anyone could have slipped into it from one of the other openings and slipped out again virtually unnoticed. They could have even approached it from the river."

"I definitely want to talk to my mother again. Old lady or not, I want to push her about the blackmail theory and the fingerprints."

Willie grinned. "There's that take-no-prisoners spirit I love."

Greg placed a hand on my arm. We looked at each other before Greg turned to Willie, seated across the table. "Willie, Odelia and I were talking. We think you should leave."

Willie, his nose deep into his coffee cup,

looked up at us. "What? You don't love me anymore?"

I leaned forward. "Willie, it's *because* we love you that we want you to leave."

"From what Clark told Odelia last night, CPAC is all over this case, and not just because of the murder. They're investigating the drugs, too. They've been working with Clark on it for quite some time." He paused. "We don't want anything to happen to you."

Willie leaned back in his chair, his eyes hooded in thought. "Leaving is definitely something to consider, under the circumstances."

"And," I added, "you've already told Clark you have business in New York, so it wouldn't look suspicious for you to up and go."

After breakfast, Willie excused himself. "I'm going to grab a quick shower and think about the leaving issue." He grabbed another muffin and wrapped it in a paper napkin. "For the possible road," he explained.

"I have your clean clothes," I told him as I got up. "Follow me, and I'll get them for you."

Greg clapped Willie on his arm as he passed by. "I can't tell you how much we appreciate what you've done for us, Willie — now and in the past. Know that you're always welcome in our home." The two men shook hands. "And while you're upstairs, don't forget to rumple your bed. Wouldn't want Mrs. Friar to wonder where you spent the night."

"You're right about that. Although in this town, I'm sure many people already know."

After giving Willie his clothes, I cleared off the table and took our breakfast dishes into the kitchen for Mrs. Friar. Greg brought his laptop to the dining room table to work where there was more room. Since Greg was with me, I had to do my own calling to the firm. I left our office manager, Tina Swanson, a voice mail message that I needed to take a few more days off, but that I'd be available via my BlackBerry. I left a similar message for Steele.

While Greg worked, I went to the kitchen and rummaged around for a phone book. Finding one, I took it back to the dining table. It wasn't very large and covered many of the small towns and villages in the area. I opened it to the listings for *Brown.* There were quite a few.

I was running an index finger down the page looking for Clement or Clem when my BlackBerry went off. It was Mike Steele.

I didn't answer it. A few minutes later, my cell phone rang. It was him. I didn't answer it. Greg's cell phone rang. Before I could warn him, he answered it.

"Hey, Mike," my husband said. "Yes, I know she's staying a few extra days. I'm with her. Yes, I am. I flew in Sunday night on a red-eye. No, she's okay. It's just complicated."

I couldn't help but laugh.

Greg finished his call. "Mike's not happy, but he'll live."

"Humph, too bad."

I went back to the phone book. "I know that Tara is married to Clem Brown, but his real name is Clement."

"You're kidding me."

"Here it is: Clement Brown. Looks like it's on the same road as the Blue Lobster."

Digging a pen and scrap of paper out of my purse, I wrote down the address and phone number for Clem Brown. At least with a name like Clement, there shouldn't be an issue of contacting the wrong person.

We were about to leave when my cell phone rang. It was Dev. "Should I answer it?" I asked Greg.

"Don't be silly, of course you should. He's our friend."

Friend, yes, but at times like these he was

usually an angry friend.

When I hesitated, Greg said, "I'll get it, if you'd prefer."

"No, I'll do it. He's calling me, and I need to face the music." I flipped open my phone just before it went to voice mail and said hello.

"It's Tuesday," Dev said without preamble. "You'd better be back in Cali."

I squared my shoulders before responding. "Well, I'm not. In fact, Greg's here with me now."

"Greg flew out there?"

"Yes, he's here right now. I'll put you on speaker." I pressed the speaker feature and held the phone out between us.

"Hi, Dev," Greg said. "Not to worry, I'm here with Odelia and keeping an eye on her."

"And who's keeping an eye on *you*?"

"Very funny. But we're fine. We had a barbecue with Odelia's family yesterday."

"What about the murder and her mother?"

"Murder is unsolved, but the police don't seem to think Grace did it." Since Greg was doing such a nice job side-stepping the situation, I didn't interrupt.

"Well, that's a start."

"How's your case going? Double homicide, right?"

"Easy one. Family member cracked as soon as we brought him in. All locked up except the paperwork. Had a minute and thought I'd check on Odelia." There was a pause. "You two sure you're okay?"

"We're fine, Dev," I said. "We should be home in a day or two."

"Good. When you get back, dinner's on me. I want to hear all about your trip. Is Greg's *cousin* still with you?"

Greg looked at me and smiled. "I think he's addicted to the blueberry muffins here. Might never get him to leave."

"He's even found a lady friend," I added.

Dev chuckled. "Well, if he has time for blueberry muffins and romance, and you're going to family barbecues, I guess there's no need to worry."

Twenty-Six

The home of Clem and Tara Brown was not only near the Brown farm, it was on the Brown farm. The house was located on a private road called Farm House Road that connected with the main road just about a mile from the intersection that held Busters, the Blue Lobster, and the ice cream stand.

"There's the Blue Lobster, and over here is the vegetable stand," I said to Greg as we passed by. Of the three, only the vegetable stand appeared to be open.

Farm House Road was really a long driveway that ended at the top of a small hill with a cluster of farm buildings, including a large old farm house and farm buildings. About halfway up on the right side, a shorter drive branched off and led to a single-level, ranch-style house painted blue. Closer to the main road, on the left-hand side, was another driveway that led to

355

another single-story ranch home in white. Both homes were landscaped with nice yards and trees. Acres and acres of farmland surrounded the residences. I spotted a silver minivan parked in front of the garage belonging to the white house.

"That looks like the van I saw last night at the North Woods." I pulled the car over to the side of the main road and studied the layout. "But I hadn't planned for all this togetherness."

Greg agreed. "It could make it difficult to see her without anyone noticing."

"Buster and his wife are gone. Clem could be out in the fields, but I'm sure they have other farm workers besides just them. It's too big of a place not to have hired help. I'm also not sure if Clem and Tara have kids."

"Most kids will be in school today."

"That's true, but they could have older children who are home or in the business with them, or little ones, which means someone will have to be home to care for them. Also, there's Mrs. Brown, their mother. I got the impression she's a widow, but who knows where she is."

At that moment, I wished we'd assigned this task to Willie and that Greg and I had taken on the task of watching my mother.

As soon as he'd finished dressing, Willie had come downstairs with his laptop and his duffel bag and announced that he had a plan.

He dropped his bundles by the door and handed me an envelope of cash. "I've already paid Mrs. Friar for Saturday and Sunday nights," he explained. "This is for last night and tonight."

"So you've decided to go?" Greg asked.

"Sort of. My bags are packed, and I'll keep them with me in case I need to vamoose. If so, you can give Mrs. Friar my apologies for giving her no notice and this money. If not, I'll stay one more night and leave like a normal guest tomorrow morning after breakfast."

Greg nodded. "Sounds like a good plan. We'll tell people you got called to New York a bit early."

"Okay," I said, happy with the solution. "That's settled. We're on our way to track down Tara Brown. What's on your agenda for today?"

"I have a bit of personal business to do." Willie gave us sly look. "Then I want to drop by Mrs. Rielley's."

That piqued my curiosity. "You going to drill her about the drugs?"

"Yes and no. You see, when I was fixing

her faucet, she mentioned a few other things that needed repairing around the house. Seems Mr. Rielley doesn't see that well anymore, and money is tight, so little fix-it things have gone to pot — so to speak." He chuckled at his own joke. "I thought I'd go by and surprise her, providing she's home."

I gave him a sly wink. "And while you're there, you can have a cup of tea and a nice chat. Right?"

"Brilliant," Greg announced.

Willie held up an index finger. "Ah, but wait, there's more." He paused for dramatic effect. "At the same time, I can keep an eye on Grace's house in case that skunk Grady drops by to try and cash in."

"Thank you, Willie." I sighed with relief. "That's something I'm worried about. It sounded like whatever plan he and Brenda had, it's happening in the next day or so."

"I might even drop by and see if little mama senior needs a handyman, although with Clark around, I doubt it."

As my eyes surveyed Farm House Road for signs of life, I tried to figure out our next move. "I wonder where Cathy lives? Clark said she and Grady had a place near the farm. One of these could be theirs."

"Sweetheart, this isn't near the farm, it's *on* the farm."

"Hmm. Maybe we should visit the vegetable stand and have another little chat with Cathy."

"Not a bad idea, but what's your reason for stopping by when you just saw her yesterday?"

I dug around in my brain for an excuse to stop at Buster's. When I grinned at Greg, he knew I had one.

There were only two vehicles in the parking lot when we pulled into Buster's. One was the old truck with the Brown Bros. logo and the other was a late-model silver sedan. As Greg and I were getting him situated in his wheelchair, a gray-haired woman in a denim skirt and green tee shirt sprinkled with daisies came out of the stand with two big bundles and climbed into the sedan. That left just the truck.

"At least she won't be busy," I whispered to Greg as we entered the building.

Looking around, I didn't see Cathy, or anyone for that matter. Greg and I poked around the few aisles. From behind the counter came the German shepherd I'd seen before. He walked up to Greg, who cooed at the animal and cautiously held out a hand for the dog to sniff. When its tail started to wag, Greg scratched it behind its ears.

"Good boy," he told the animal.

"That's Clem's dog," I told Greg in a whisper.

"You folks need help?"

It was Clem. He came through the back lugging a crate of fresh green beans. When he saw me, he stopped and glared. "What do you want?"

"I just stopped by to see Cathy a minute."

Clem Brown's eyes trailed from me to where Greg was patting the happy dog. "Digger, here." The animal immediately left Greg and went to his master.

"This is my husband, Greg Stevens."

Greg gave him a nod. Without a word, Clem returned his eyes to drilling through my head.

"What do you want to see Cathy for?" He carried the green beans to one of the displays and dumped them out on top of others already in place. "Thought you folks all got together yesterday." He mixed the new beans into the others with his hand.

"We did." I took a few steps closer. "But I forgot to give her my contact information. We're going home soon, and I wanted to stay in touch with her." I gave the surly farmer a big smile. "After all, she's going to be my sister-in-law soon."

Clem scoffed. "Don't bet on it."

"What do you mean?" Greg moved towards us.

"What I mean is that I doubt Grady and Cathy are ever going to get married." He walked over to the register and started fiddling through some receipts.

I followed. "Has something happened?"

Clem slapped the receipts down on the counter. "Do you see Cathy here?"

"No, I don't."

"That's because she's home worried sick, leaving me to do this instead of my own work. Seems Grady left shortly after they got back from the Littlejohns' last night and never came back."

I glanced over at Greg. The two of us went wide-eyed at each other, knowing what we knew.

Turning back to Clem, I said, "Did she try the station or his mother's?"

"Don't you think she's smart enough to do that early on?" His lined face twisted like an annoyed pretzel.

"Yes, of course. I'm sorry." I took a deep breath before I hit him with another question. "Did they have a fight?"

"According to her, they didn't." He started for the front of the stand. The dog followed. We followed behind the dog. "Who knows why he took off. Even the chief doesn't

361

know where he is."

"Where does Cathy live, Clem? I'd like to drop by and see if there's anything I can do."

Clem turned on me with vicious speed. "There's nothing you can do, Miss Nosy." When I looked surprised, he continued. "Yeah, I know you've been buddying up to Cathy and Troy. Asking them questions about that murder and about us." He moved closer. "Better be careful, or you could get hurt."

With astounding speed, Greg got between us, pushing me several steps back while he faced a red-faced Clem Brown. "That's my wife, Mr. Brown. So just back the hell up!"

Clem looked down at Greg in angry surprise, his fists clenched. The dog went on alert, a low growl emitting from its gut. I noticed Greg's back stiffen and his hands go tight. If Clem Brown threw a punch at Greg, wheelchair or no wheelchair, dog or no dog, Greg would respond in a like manner. I'd once seen Greg get so angry he threw an able-bodied man into a wall. The man had been J.J., my ass of a stepbrother.

It was Clem who backed down first. "Get the hell out of here, both of you." As we retreated, he called after us. "And tell the whole Littlejohn family to stay away from us."

"I think you should forget about Tara Brown, Odelia."

It was the first words either of us said after leaving the vegetable stand two miles back in the dust. I pulled off the road into the empty parking lot of a small church and let the engine idle.

"Greg, I'm worried that Grady and Brenda have already put their plan into play. If so, Mom might be in danger." I looked at the clock on the dash. "I doubt Willie is at the Rielleys' yet. Let's give Clark a call."

Clark still didn't know where Grady was. In addition to not coming home last night, he hadn't reported for work this morning. Unofficially, Clark had people on the lookout for both him and Brenda, including cops from other districts.

"He's a grown man," Clark told us via the speaker on Greg's cell phone. "If he decided to run off with that chippie, not much we can do about it. But I'm pretty angry about him not showing up for work today. My ass is on the line enough over him, and we're swamped. And Mom's worried as hell."

"Do you think he'll stop by Mom's? She might be in danger if he comes by to get the money."

"I really don't think he'd hurt her, Odelia. Take the money, yes, but Grady's never been the violent type. By the way, I asked Mom about the money, told her what you overheard. She told me it was all nonsense. Said she's never had fifty thousand dollars in her life."

"You believe her?"

"Not sure. I don't know who or what to believe anymore." We heard him say something to someone in the background. "Sorry, I'm being called into a meeting. Don't worry about Mom. I'll send someone over to look after her."

"Joan Cummings?"

"Not until I know what she's hiding. Besides, she's on vacation today. There's a woman I hire once in a while to take Mom shopping or stay with her when I go out of town. I'll call Mrs. Spaulding and ask her to stop by the house for a few hours."

"We could go over," Greg offered.

"I'd rather you two stay out of it and keep low. You've already kicked up the Browns, and, believe me, you don't want to do that."

We called Willie and gave him an update. He said he still planned on swinging by to see Mrs. Rielley and would meet us at the inn later.

Greg closed his phone. "Guess we should head back to the inn and wait."

I stared out the window of the car while I mulled over what we knew and what we didn't know. I felt like there was still something missing, like I'd baked a cake but forgotten an important ingredient. My hands clutched the steering wheel — one hand in concentration, the other in frustration. Waiting wasn't my strong suit.

"Oh, no," Greg said with a shake of his head. "I know that look. We're not going back to the inn, are we?"

I looked over at my husband and gave him a coy smile, or as coy a smile as it was in my power to muster. "Honey, would you mind terribly if we made one teeny-weeny little stop?"

"Who are we going after?"

Without a word, I put the car in gear and turned out of the parking lot, heading back in the direction we'd just come.

"Back to the vegetable stand?"

"Nope. I have questions for Tara Brown, and I'm going to ask them."

TWENTY-SEVEN

With my foot heavy on the pedal, I covered the two miles back to Buster's, but instead of stopping, I continued on to Farm House Road. Once again, I pulled over to the side and looked up the drive. The silver minivan was still parked in front of the white house.

Greg craned his head this way and that. "Doesn't seem to be much activity from any of the other houses."

I pointed to the group of farm structures at the end of the drive. "I just spotted someone going in and out of those buildings, but they're probably busy with their usual chores. Not even sure if it was a man or a woman. Most of the workers could be in other fields."

I nosed the car up the drive and turned towards the white house. "Not exactly any place to park and sneak up, is there?"

Parking behind the minivan, I got out and helped Greg. We approached the house like

366

we were simply making a social call. After ringing the bell twice, Tara Brown opened the door. She was dressed in jeans and a baggy shirt that looked like it might belong to her husband. Her blond hair was pulled back, and she looked tired. One arm was clutched around a loaded laundry basket, which she balanced on a slim hip.

"Hi," I said in a pleasant, perky voice, like I was delivering a Welcome Wagon basket. "Do you remember me? I was in the corn maze with you on Saturday."

She looked at me, then poked her head a bit out the door to look up and down the road. I wasn't sure if she was worried someone might spot us or if she was afraid I'd brought reinforcements.

"I remember you." Unlike the other Brown family members, her voice was quiet and timid. "You're related to the Littlejohns, right?"

"Yes, that's correct. And this is my husband, Greg Stevens." On cue, Greg gave her one of his award-winning smiles. "Can we come in, Tara? We're going home soon, and I'd really like to clear up some things before we do."

I'd added the part about going home because I thought it might encourage her to talk. After all, what harm could I do if I was back in California?

"I don't know. Now's not a good time."

"It won't take long." I indicated the laundry. "You can throw that load of clothes in and visit with us while it's washing."

I could tell she wanted us to disappear, but she didn't have the gumption to say so. Questioning her might be easier than I had thought, or at least easier than I had hoped it would be. I didn't want our rental car sitting outside her house any longer than was necessary.

I made a slow move towards the door. Looking past her, I saw that the house looked tidy and that there were no toys strewn about. Nor did I hear the sounds of any young rugrats. "You have children?"

"No." She dipped her head slightly and knitted her brows in thought. When she raised her head, I could see in her eyes she'd made a decision. "Why don't you come in — but just for a minute."

She backed away from the door, and I helped Greg guide his chair over the small lip of the entry. Once inside, Tara guided us through to the back, where there was a large family room that opened into a big modern kitchen on one side and a deck on the other. The deck was small compared to Clark's, but the yard was large and sloped. The view from the deck was of farmland. In the far distance, I could see a tractor pulling something behind it. The house was homey, with large, open rooms. Photos were scattered about in frames on various surfaces. One large photo showed a young Tara and Clem on their wedding day.

Tara put the laundry basket down on a nearby table. "Is this about Grady's disappearance? If so, I don't know anything about it."

"You talk to Cathy today?"

She shook her head. "My husband told me this morning before he left for work."

"You haven't called your sister-in-law to see how she's doing?"

Tara shrugged and picked at a sock on top of the laundry pile. "We're not close."

"She live nearby?"

"The house across the street."

"The blue one, right?"

Tara nodded. There hadn't been any signs of life at the blue house when we drove up.

"It didn't look like anyone was home when we drove up. You have any idea where she might be?"

Tara continued looking down at the laundry. "Troy's probably in school. Cathy might be up at the big house with her mother. Or out looking for Grady."

Greg looked up at me, clearly wondering what I was going to say next. I wasn't sure myself. I'd tuned my ears for sounds of someone else in the house but heard nothing, just the low murmur of a small TV perched on the kitchen counter facing the family room. The volume was turned down. Onscreen was a popular women's talk show. I decided to get right to the meat of the matter.

"Who's the guy you met last night at the North Woods Motel?"

Tara's eyes shot up from the laundry to meet my own. Her simple, open face, with its perky nose and large blue eyes, fell like rocks off a dump truck. Her bottom lip quivered, then stilled. To her credit, she didn't try to deny it. "How could you possibly know that?"

"I saw you. I was there —" I hesitated. "Um, visiting a friend."

"It was no one."

"Didn't look like 'no one' to me."

"Stay out of this, please." She dropped her eyes. Unlike the harsh warnings of Clem, her request for us to butt out was delivered in a low, shaky voice.

"Grady was at the North Woods last night, too."

Tara's eyes latched on to mine again. "He

370

was? Did he tell you he saw me?"

"No, I saw him just as I saw you. He was in the last cabin — probably why you didn't see his vehicle. Who knows if he saw your minivan."

I had hoped that by now Tara would have crumbled into a puddle of tears and confessed to everything. It would have been too easy, but there's always hope.

"Who's the guy, Tara? He a local? One of your husband's cronies not above doing his pal's wife on the side?"

"No!" For the first time her voice had some meat to it. "It's not like that. He's not like that." Her words drifted back into their previous soft tone.

I waited, giving her time to offer up more, like professing her love for the guy. And, who knows, maybe she *was* in love.

"Please don't tell anyone. Forget you saw me there." Tara's eyes went wide with fear. "My husband would kill us both if he knew."

"Then it seems rather risky, doesn't it?"

She looked around her own house as if she expected spies to be lurking in the corners. "I'm leaving soon. So please, just mind your own business and don't say anything."

"You're leaving with him? The guy from the motel?"

She said nothing.

I hated to hit her when she was down, but I knew now would be the best time to throw out my next probe. Taking a deep breath, I blurted out, "I know about the drug business at Buster's stand, Tara."

She went pale.

"And I know that you're the one who exchanges the money for the drugs with your dealer."

She sat down heavily in a nearby wooden chair. After a moment of silent reflection, she looked up at me, then over at Greg. "What do you want? Is this blackmail? If so, you'll have to deal with my husband and his family. And they're not easy to deal with, believe me."

Greg spoke up, his voice soothing. "No blackmail, Tara. We're just trying to get to the bottom of the murder in the corn maze. What do you know about it?"

"Nothing, I swear. I was just there with Troy."

I played my bad-cop part. "I don't buy that, Tara. I think you were there to make a drug exchange with Les Morgan. You knew it was Les in the maze that morning, didn't you?"

She remained tongue-tied.

"We know Les worked for a drug dealer

372

in Boston. The police know it, too. How long do you think it'll be before they make the tie-in to you? We did."

She started sobbing and covered her face with her hands. "I never wanted to do this. I knew one day it would catch up to us."

Greg moved closer. "Did Cathy know that her ex-husband was involved with your supplier? Did she know he was here in town that day?"

With her hands still over her face, Tara shook her head. "No," she squeaked out from behind her hands before bringing them down.

I grabbed a nearby dishtowel and handed it to her. She wiped her splotchy face. "Cathy didn't know. When Les started working for the people who sold us the drugs, I was his only contact. He kept asking to see Troy."

"You brought Troy to the maze to see his dad?"

"Yes. Les said it was a perfect place to meet and both do business and let him see Troy."

Looking at Greg, I gave him a smile with my eyes.

"Did you see Les alive in the maze, or was he already dead?" The question came from Greg.

Tara thought a moment, her eyes darting back and forth. "He was alive the first time I saw him."

I looked at her. "The first time?"

"When we made the exchange. I gave him money. He gave me the drugs."

"You exchanged messenger bags, correct?" asked Greg.

"How do you know that?"

"You had a messenger bag in the maze, Tara," I explained. "Not a typical bag for a woman to carry. But it's also a bag no one would think twice about a man carrying."

"Yes, we had identical bags and exchanged them."

"And you'd already made the exchange that morning?"

"Yes. Les had flag number one. That was the plan. He raised it so I could see it and find him once I was inside. I had flag two. We were the first ones in the maze that morning."

"So Troy knew that was his father?"

"I don't think so. Les looked different, and it had been years since Troy had seen him. And Les didn't say anything about it. Just looked the boy over while he and I talked."

"So you let Troy see you exchange the bags?" asked Greg.

"No, after a minute, I told him to find the next puzzle. He ran off, and Les and I did business. After, Troy and I circled through the maze, playing the puzzle game. When we came across Les again, he was dead. I thought he'd already left."

My mind was in overdrive. "I was told that Troy was running through the maze on his own and found Les."

"Yes, he got quite wound up and was ahead of me. When I caught up to him, he had already found Les." She started to cry again. "It was only about fifteen to twenty minutes after we'd done the exchange."

"And you didn't hear a struggle or shouts or anything like that?"

She shook her head. "By then, other people were in the maze."

"What about my mother?"

"That's all I know, really." Tara stood up. "Now if you'll excuse me, I have to go. I have a lot to do."

I was not about to be dismissed that easily. "My mother, Tara. What about my mother?"

"She was found with the body." She looked away.

"Yes, but I don't think she killed Les Morgan, do you?"

She looked away. "That's all I know. Now

please go."

As we drove down Farm House Road, Greg looked back at the white house. "She's going to run."

"That's what I'm thinking. Sounds like she was planning to bolt anyway, but I'll bet now she's gone by sundown." I felt bad that our pushing might cause Tara to hit the road prematurely. But if we knew about her affair, it was only a matter of time before someone else found out and told her husband. Leaving was probably the safest avenue for her right now.

"There's still something fishy about her story, don't you think, honey?" I looked over at Greg.

"Absolutely. She never came right out and said she saw Grace herself."

"Exactly."

"And I think she may know who the killer is."

By the time we returned to the B & B, Mrs. Friar had already tidied up our rooms and the kitchen. She was busy dusting the parlor when we came in.

"There you are," she said when she saw us emerge from our room. We'd come up the ramp and entered the inn via our private entrance. "Has Mr. Carter left? I saw that his things were gone when I made up his room."

I dug into my bag and produced the envelope of money and handed it to her. "He's not quite gone, Mrs. Friar. He's packed and ready, though. He's waiting on a call from his office. If it comes in, he must leave immediately. If not, he'll be here through tomorrow morning. He's sorry he can't be more specific. Either way, here is your money for last night and tonight. He wanted to make sure you got it."

Bonnie Friar checked the money in the envelope. From the way her eyes widened, Willie must have given her a bonus. She tucked it into her apron pocket. "Such an odd and interesting man, isn't he?"

Greg headed for the dining room to work. "Never a dull moment, that's for sure."

Sitting around and waiting for a call from Clark was driving me nuts. Greg busied himself with his work. I tried to read but couldn't concentrate. Bits and pieces of information, along with faces and names, clustered inside my head like debris caught in a storm drain. I would have scrubbed the inn from top to bottom to alleviate my stress, but it was already spotless. I finally decided to go for a walk.

TWENTY-EIGHT

I was going to miss these morning walks in the country. At home, I walked along the beach with Wainwright tugging me along on his leash. Not too shabby by anyone's calculation, but it was nice to have this change of scenery. After making a U-turn, I took a big slug from the water bottle in my hand and headed back, feeling pretty good and perky. About halfway back to the inn, I heard a vehicle approach from behind, then slow to a stop. I didn't turn around.

Damn. As much as I wanted to talk to Brenda Bixby, especially after last night, I didn't want to do it while walking along a back road listening to my favorite music and feeling good about life in general. No, I wanted to have it out with her on *my* terms, when I was geared up to take her on and get to the bottom of things. I put one foot in front of the other, moving my legs faster, with determination. From the sound, the vehicle was still stopped.

This is stupid, I told myself. I *had* to talk to Brenda, especially now, with Grady missing. They were probably together, and maybe both of them were in the car stopped behind me. Suddenly, now seemed as good a time as any.

Just as I spun around to head towards the car, I heard an engine being gunned. It wasn't Brenda and Grady, or even a solo Brenda. It was a rusty old truck, and it was coming straight at me. I did a swan dive into the bushes next to the road and tumbled over them. Dazed, I lay on the ground and got my bearings. My face and extremities stung from sharp scratches.

The truck turned around and came back for a do-over. Behind me a few feet was a broken-down rock wall hardly two feet high in some places. I barely had time to scramble over it and take refuge behind a tree before the truck crashed into the bushes and stopped right over where I'd been a minute before. The driver, who was wearing a ski mask, put the vehicle in reverse and backed it out to the road. I didn't wait around to see if he would make it over the wall. Screaming, I ran along the fence towards the inn, keeping the jagged-toothed stone barrier between me and my assailant for as long as I could. The vehicle tried ramming me again, but again the old truck couldn't penetrate the brush and broken wall. The sound of metal meeting stone vibrated my spine like a tuning fork. I had already passed the closest residence to the B & B when the truck made its first bid to land me as a hood ornament, so my best course of action was to continue to the inn while threading through the sparse woods.

When the wall ended, the beat-up truck made another run at me and missed. I started running, going deeper into the woods, using the trees for cover. This time the truck didn't back up. Fear covered me like a gummy film when I glanced over my shoulder and saw the driver get out and start after me on foot. There was no way I was in shape to outrun anyone, except maybe another fifty-year-old with a penchant for cookies.

I was too tired and frightened to scream anymore. Bobbing and weaving through the trees, I hoped I was still heading towards the inn and safety. As I ran, branches snagged my clothes and skin, holding me back like accomplices to the crime. My ears caught the sound of my tracker closing in on me fast.

As they lost their juice, my legs slowed

from a slow run to a raggedy jog to just a bit faster than a walk. My heart was pumping like a steam engine, my breath labored. I had pushed my body to its limit, demanding that it increase its speed. It had responded, but not enough. Just as the inn came into view in the distance, he took me down like a wounded wildebeest.

I hit the ground hard, face first, with him on top of me. Pain rocketed through my body. Turning me over, he straddled me. I thrashed beneath him until he backhanded me hard across my already tender face. My teeth rattled in their sockets. He struck me again, sending my face in the opposite direction. Then he hit me the other way. My head and neck felt like one of those red balls on the end of a rubber band, his hand the paddle. Blood gushed from my nose.

When the slaps stopped, he held my arms above my head and leaned in close. My hands dug into the dirt and debris, scooping it up, looking for something, anything to use as a weapon.

"I'll teach you to keep your fucking nose out of everyone's business, you pathetic fat bitch." His breath was heavy with the smell of coffee and bacon mixed with wet wool.

I whimpered in response.

He let loose one of my arms to hit me

again. Shattered light, like bits of broken glass, entered my vision with the blow. I shook my head to clear it. Before he could hit me again, I threw the dirt in my freed fist straight into the eye holes of the mask. Yowling, he dug at his eyes with both of his hands. Still pinned under him, I grabbed for anything I could get my hands on — dirt, twigs, pebbles, leaves — and threw it at him. When he lowered one hand from his eyes, I let loose with one more handful. Bull's-eye.

"Bitch! I'm gonna kill you!" His eyes closed, his hands searched for my throat.

Beneath him, my exhausted legs bucked while my hands continued to claw the ground. One hand finally connected with a rock the size of a softball and clutched it. As his hands found my neck and started to squeeze, he leaned forward. When he was within range, I slammed the rock against the side of his head as hard as I could with my last bit of strength.

The blow stunned him. He rolled off me. He was on his knees, shaking his head and still trying to clear his vision, when I struggled to my feet. Using both hands, I brought the rock down hard but was off balance. It glanced off the side of his head but still did the job. He flattened to the ground.

I started for the inn, dragging myself the rest of the way, stumbling over the ground as I fought to remain upright. I just wanted to get back to Greg.

As I staggered from the woods into the parking lot of the inn, Willie's SUV drove up. He hopped out and ran to me as he yelled for Greg. I collapsed into his arms. Willie half-carried, half-dragged me into the inn and deposited me on the sofa in the parlor.

"Sweetheart!" Greg was next to me immediately.

"Knocked him out." I choked the words out through bloody lips. "Back there."

Willie pulled his gun out and took off out the door at a dead run.

"What happened, Odelia?" Greg held my hand and wiped my hair out of the way.

Mrs. Friar hovered above us, her face the color and texture of school paste. "Did Mr. Carter have a gun?"

Greg turned to her. "Can you get me a wet cloth, Mrs. Friar?"

She looked down at my battered face. "Oh my, yes, of course."

"What happened, Odelia?" Greg repeated.

"Someone." I gulped some air and tried again. "Someone tried to run me down. Not far from here. Then he chased me. Beat me.

Told me to mind my own business."

"Didn't you have your phone with you?"

"Yes." I patted the side pocket of my capris. "Didn't have time. Just ran."

"Did you get a look at him?"

I shook my head. "He had a ski mask."

Mrs. Friar returned with a pan of warm water, soap, a facecloth, and a towel. She placed them on the coffee table. "Maybe I should call an ambulance."

"No," I told her. "It's just scratches and bruises. Not as bad as it looks."

Greg soaped up the cloth and patted it against my bloody, bruised face. It stung like hell. "I'm afraid you might have a black eye, sweetheart. But I don't think your nose is broken."

He dabbed the soap and water on my legs and arms. More stinging, like I'd fallen on a colony of fire ants.

Willie returned. "Whoever it was is gone. No truck anywhere along the road." He looked me up and down, taking in my torn clothes and bruised face. "Did you see who tried to kill you?" Willie's voice was as pointed as a sharpened stake.

I shook my head. "Like I told Greg, he wore a ski mask."

"Could you identify the vehicle?"

"I think so." I took several deep breaths

and put a hand over my heart. The beat was returning to normal. "It was an old truck and rusty or rust in color, hard to say."

Greg opened his cell phone and made a call. He asked for Chief Littlejohn. When told the chief wasn't available, he asked the clerk to get a message to Clark as soon as possible. "Tell him someone tried to kill his sister."

"Oh, my." Mrs. Friar wobbled. Willie gently helped her to a chair. "These things have never happened around here before. First the murder. Now this." Confused, she looked at Willie. "Did I see you with a gun, Mr. Carter?"

"Certainly not, Mrs. Friar. I'm a business-man."

Through all this, Greg remained silent. He fussed with the facecloth, continuing to pat down and clean my various injuries. I stopped him.

"It's okay, honey, I'll just take a hot shower and survey the damage."

He looked me in the eye. "No, Odelia, it's not okay."

I ran my hands through my hair. A few leaves and twigs fell out. "I'm fine, Greg. Just cuts and stuff. Mostly, it just scared me."

He tossed the facecloth in my lap and

rolled away. "And damn well it should!"

"It's not like I went looking for this, Greg. I was just out getting some exercise." I could tell by his face that he wasn't placated. In my usual bullheaded way, I pushed. "Whatever happened to *just go with it — life's easier that way?* Isn't that your new motto?"

Mrs. Friar started to her feet. Willie helped her. "Perhaps Mrs. Stevens would like some tea. If you'll excuse me, I'll make her a pot."

When she was gone, Greg answered me. "Bravado over pizza is one thing. It's quite another to see the woman you love nearly become roadkill."

I looked to Willie for support, but he had turned away. "And what do you say, Willie?"

He glanced back around. "Sorry, I never get involved in domestic squabbles." To make his point, he started for the stairs. "Just let me know who gets custody of me in the event of divorce."

Greg and I remained silent, not looking at each other. I patted a few of the deep scratches on my arms with the cloth and wondered what to say without my usual foot-in-mouth disease.

"Greg," I started, "I'm sorry. I know this is difficult for you, but I honestly don't know how not to get involved. Especially when it's someone close to me."

He took several deep breaths, his solid chest rising with each. Then he squared his strong shoulders and turned back around, wheeling up to the sofa next to me again.

"I know you don't." He took my hand. "I'm actually angry at myself." He swallowed hard. "You see, sweetheart, I'm a fraud. The truth is, I rather enjoy bumming around with you on these adventures."

I started to speak. He gently placed a fingertip against my swollen lips, stopping me.

"It's true. It's like playing some fantasy sleuth game. Digging around for clues, interviewing people, and uncovering bad guys. It's fun. Until something like this happens, and it always does." He squeezed my hand. "I came here for two reasons, Odelia. One, to take care of you, first and foremost. And second, because I didn't want to be left out of the game." He looked down. "How selfish of me."

I pulled my hand away from his and stroked his face, running my fingers from his soft hair down across his cheek and through his beard until they rested on his chin. I lifted his face up and gazed into his lovely blue eyes.

"You're not being selfish, honey. And I'm

so happy you did fly out."

"But it's no game, Odelia. I'd forgotten that until I saw you stagger in here all tore up. It wasn't a game in El Segundo, and it's definitely not a game now." He clutched my hands and brought them to his mouth for a kiss. "I couldn't bear to lose you, Odelia." His voice cracked.

"Danger or not, Greg," I told him in a soft voice, "I have to finish this."

"Then we'll finish it together."

We both leaned forward, our mouths meeting for a few quick kisses, followed by one long, deep one. Kissing was painful, but I didn't care.

TWENTY-NINE

After two cups of soothing tea, I hauled my sorry ass into the shower. Then I pulled on the only dress I'd brought with me. With my black eye starting to blossom, my fat lip, and numerous scratches, scrapes, and bruises covering me from head to toe, I thought the dress might at least help me to feel a little pretty, but it didn't; instead, I felt grotesque. I changed into khakis and a shirt.

I was drying my hair when Greg stuck his head in to say that Clark was in the parlor. Clark would want to know every detail, and I was trying hard to remember them all. After popping some ibuprofen and taking one last glance in the mirror, I made my entrance.

Willie and Greg were waiting for me, but instead of Clark, a young uniformed police-woman I'd never seen before was with them. Greg and Willie were nursing beers from a six-pack Willie had picked up on his way back to the inn earlier. He'd stopped by the Rielleys' but no one had been home, so he'd come back to the inn. I was glad he had. I sat in a chair near Greg. He took my hand. Except for the beers, the two of them looked like they were at a wake. The young officer sat stiff and official.

"We made you a fresh pot of tea," Willie said. "Unless you'd like something stronger."

"Tea's fine." I looked at them each in turn. "And I'm fine, guys, really. Where's Clark?"

Greg nodded in the direction of the young officer. "Clark got called away, sweetheart. He'll be back later. This is Officer Marlaine Burbank. She's going to be taking your official statement." Officer Burbank stood up and came to me, offering her hand. She was in her thirties, trim and tall, with medium brown hair pulled back at the nape of her neck. After greeting me, she sat back down on the sofa and pulled some papers from a folder.

"Anything new about Grady?" I asked the cop.

"We'd like to get your statement out of the way, Mrs. Stevens, if you don't mind. I believe the chief will fill you in on the rest."

For the next hour, I retold the events of the attack to Officer Burbank, trying to remember and relate every detail of the truck and my attacker as clearly as possible, including the earlier threat made by Clem Brown.

"Who knew that you took these daily walks, Mrs. Stevens?"

"My husband and Mr. Carter, of course. And Mrs. Friar." I paused, then added. "And Brenda Bixby. She has stopped me during my last two walks. I thought it was her again this time."

I seriously doubted that Greg, Willie, or Mrs. Friar had anything to do with my attack, but Brenda was another story. Was my attacker Grady? My own brother? I didn't think they saw me lurking around the motel last night. Then I remembered the man watching me from his cabin window — the man who'd been with Tara Brown. I wasn't proud of the fact that I was skulking around a sleazy motel in the dark and almost didn't say anything, but I knew Clark would want me to be honest with the officer and in my report. When Greg squeezed my hand, I knew he was thinking the same thing. With her head down in concentration, Officer Burbank scribbled detailed notes while I talked.

Afterwards, she, Willie, and I trekked out to the road so I could show them where the truck had slammed into the bushes. I spotted the water bottle I'd dropped during my leap to safety and picked it up. We followed the path of the truck's several attempts to hit me. Officer Burbank marked each spot for further investigation. Then we walked through the woods, trying to follow the path I'd taken during my flight. Along the way, I spotted something on the ground that didn't fit in with the usual forest debris. It was my iPod. Like the water bottle, I'd forgotten all about it.

Before I showered, Greg had taken photos of my battered face and body with a digital camera borrowed from Mrs. Friar. While we walked through the woods, he was going to upload those to his laptop and sent them to the e-mail address the officer had given him.

When we returned to the inn, Officer Burbank gave me her card and told me to call if I had anything to add. With a final reassuring smile, she left.

I looked at Greg. "No word from Clark while we were outside?"

"Just a quick call to see how it was going with the report. Clark said there's been no sign of Grady or Brenda. They've even gone to the North Woods Motel. Brenda's stuff is still in the cabin, but there's no sign of her or her car. Manager said he doesn't recall her being with a man — Grady or otherwise."

I let out an unladylike snort. "Places like the North Woods would lose their customer base if they paid attention to things like that."

My stomach growled like a mean dog guarding a junkyard. It was mid-afternoon, and breakfast was almost ancient history. "I'm starved. How about you guys?"

"Want me to go get some take-out?" Willie offered.

"Sounds good to me," chimed in Greg.

I thought about it. "Why don't we go to the Blue Lobster?"

"No way." Greg moved in close and fixed me with a determined eye. "I know that look, and it's a lot more than hunger. You want to spy on that vegetable stand. Haven't you had enough for today? Or are you looking to get the other eye blackened?"

"I told you I'd take you to the Blue Lobster, didn't I?"

"No. If the Browns see you there, who knows what they will do next time."

"You're assuming it was one of them who attacked me, Greg. It could have been that guy at the motel, or even Grady."

"Maybe so, but the Browns are at the top of my suspects list." He looked from me to Willie. "And don't tell me they aren't at the top of yours."

Willie got up and stretched. "I was actually thinking of going to the Blue Lobster later today myself."

Greg narrowed his eyes at him. "I thought you didn't get involved in domestic squabbles."

"Not when it doesn't suit me." He laughed. "Today is Sybil's last day at the place. It would be kind of nice to go see her and mark the occasion. She's been there ten years."

"Wow," I said. "That's a long time. She have a new job, or is she just going to work at the Kettle?"

Willie gave us a sly smile. "Neither. She's coming with me."

"What?" I looked to Greg, but he was silent, his mouth hanging open like he'd been scared to death.

"That's where I went this morning after breakfast, to talk to her."

Greg shook his head in disbelief. "You just asked her to drop her life and follow you? Does she know anything about you?"

"I told her everything. And, yes, she's closing up her house, leaving her two dead-end jobs, and coming with me. For how long, who knows, but she was ready for an adventure."

I smiled to myself, remembering when Willie had invited me to do the same. Then a worry scuttled my happiness.

"Willie, can you trust this woman? You haven't known her very long. What if she turns you in for some reward?"

"That's the chance I'll have to take, little mama. So far, the cops have only shown up here looking for you." He winked at me. "That's a good early sign, at least for me."

Greg wheeled over to Willie and put a hand on his shoulder. "Are you sure?"

"This is only the second time I've asked a woman to come with me." He looked my way before continuing. "It's not something I do lightly. I'm pretty sure Sybil is just as trustworthy as the first one who turned me down."

Willie left for the Blue Lobster. I told him we'd meet him there after I plastered some makeup over my still-swelling face. I finally gave up before the layers of foundation turned me into the bride of Chucky. On the way in the car, Greg extracted the promise from me that I would leave the vegetable stand and the Browns alone. He had no worries there, but I did wonder if Clem was sporting a concussion this afternoon.

"Were you the other woman Willie asked to go with him?" From the way Greg had switched his eyes back and forth between Willie and me back at the inn, I knew it wouldn't be long before that question popped out.

"Yes, Greg. I was the one he was referring to. The first one."

"He knew about me when he asked, didn't he?"

"Yes, but it was after the shooting incident, when you and I were sort of on the outs. More me than you."

We rode a mile or two in silence before he asked the next expected question. "Why didn't you go with him?"

"Couple of reasons." I glanced over at my husband. "But don't think it wasn't tempting." My eyes went back to the road. "Willie didn't love me; he was lonely. And I was in love with someone else." Greg reached over and gently squeezed my thigh. "And, while my moral standards might be a bit on the goosey side, they weren't loosey-goosey enough for that lifestyle."

We were almost to the Blue Lobster when my cell phone rang. Greg dug it out of my bag and answered. It was a woman asking for me. Greg put it on speaker.

"This is Odelia," I said, aiming my voice at the phone while I drove.

"This is Stacia Spaulding." The woman snapped off her name like she was breaking a stick. "Chief Littlejohn hired me to watch Grace today."

I yanked the car over to the side of the road and parked. "Is Mom okay?" I took the phone from Greg.

"I tried calling the chief, but they said he was on some police emergency. He had given me your number as backup."

"My mother, is she okay?" My voice was shrill. Greg leaned in to hear better.

"That old woman needs to be put away, if you want my advice. She's been throwing tantrums ever since I got here."

"About what?"

"I've had enough, I tell you. She threw a book, and it hit me in the back of my head. About knocked me out."

"I'm sorry, Mrs. Spaulding."

"Sorry isn't enough. You tell Chief Little-john that he's not to call me anymore. I never want to see the old witch again."

"We'll be right there to relieve you."

"You're crazier than she is if you think I'm sticking around. I'm already on my way home."

I gave the phone to Greg. While he called

Willie to say we'd be late, I turned the car around and headed for my mother's house.

On the way, we hatched a plan. Greg would stay in the car while I went inside and nicely invited Mom to lunch — emphasis on *nicely*. In reality, we were getting her out of the way in case Grady did come for the money. Once she was with us, we'd call Clark and let him know where she was. Problem was, I didn't expect my mother to come willingly, but I was prepared to do my best to woo her into it. I promised Greg that clubbing her would be my last resort.

I went to the back door and knocked. No answer. I knocked again; still no response. I tried the door and found it unlocked. Opening it, I called to my mother. There was no answer. I could hear the TV blaring in the living room. I dashed inside, expecting to see her sprawled facedown on the floor. Instead, I found her in her rocking chair watching TV, as composed as a pastor's wife sitting in church.

"You didn't hear me calling to you?" I asked in a raised, vexed voice.

Her face remained turned towards the TV. Her hands were in her lap, clutched around the TV remote. "Didn't want to miss my program."

When the show went to a commercial, my

mother's eyes remained glued to the TV.

"Mom, Greg's outside in the car. We want you to go to lunch with us."

"Why?"

"Why not? You're my mother, and I don't know when I'll see you again after I return home." I moved into her line of vision. "Come on, it will be nice. We were going to meet Willie at the Blue Lobster."

No response.

I glanced at the TV. "Could you turn that down while we talk?"

When she made no move to do so, I pushed on, determined to remain calm and nice. *Nice, Odelia,* I reminded myself. *The operative word here is nice.*

"Or we could go someplace else. Anywhere you'd like."

"Haven't been to the Blue Lobster in years." Her voice held no emotion. "Doctor won't let me have fried food." She turned to me with a scowl. "I'll bet Clark took you there, didn't he? He's not supposed to go neither, but I know he sneaks off every chance he gets."

"They have other food besides fried stuff. Come on, it will be fun."

She turned back to the TV. The commercial was over, but a different program had come on. "No. You only want to grill me about the maze. That's all anyone wants me for these days, to question me about things that are none of their business."

I scrunched down to get eye-to-eye with her. "No, Mom. We'll just have a nice lunch. I'll button my lip about the murder. I promise."

I was selling my soul making that promise. There was so much I wanted to question her about. But, then again, the promise was for during lunch. I didn't make any such promise about questioning her after we ate.

She turned off the TV and started to rise. "Well, all right, but no questions. I like to eat in peace. And I'll want a lobster roll and fried scallops both, doctors be damned. Won't be around much longer. Might as well go out with a happy belly."

After fussing with her hair and locating her purse, Mom was ready. We shuffled out the back door, across the deck, and down the wide, easy steps. When we came around the side of the house, I felt like I'd dropped into the *Twilight Zone.*

Greg and the car were gone.

THIRTY

"Maybe Greg took the car for gas."

I spun around from the empty driveway to face my elderly mother. "In case you hadn't noticed, Mom, Greg's in a freaking wheelchair!"

Seems nice had flown the coop, along with my husband.

"There's no need to yell at me, Odelia."

I spun back around to where I'd left the rental car and studied the empty space, half expecting to see it there. That maybe I'd had a moment of insanity or early senility. It was there, after all. Had to be. How could I miss seeing something that weighs two thousand pounds?

But it wasn't there.

Walking over to where I'd last seen the car and Greg, I spied something on the ground. It was a cell phone. No, correction: *two* cell phones, mine and Greg's, side by side. They were acting as paperweights, holding down a piece of paper. I stared at the paper like it was a bomb before finally bending down and picking it up. On it was just a single telephone number, no message or instructions.

Standing in the middle of my mother's driveway, I studied the number. It wasn't familiar, and it wasn't the local area code. I wasn't sure what to do. Do I call the number? Do I call Willie? Clark? I started to cry, my salty tears burning the scratches on my face. I reached for a tissue, then realized my tissues were in my bag — in the car.

"What?" I screamed down the road in front of my mother's house. "You couldn't leave my damn bag?"

"Odelia," I heard my mother say from behind me. "Quiet! Someone will hear you."

I turned on her. "I hope everyone hears me!" I shook a finger at her. "A lot of this is your fault, you selfish old woman. If you'd just told the police what you know, this would be behind us, and Greg and I would be home now, not mixed up in this living hell."

"No one asked you to get involved."

That stopped me cold. "No, no one did, but you're my mother, for gawd's sake. How could I *not* get involved? Tell me that. You think everyone has a heart of stone and no sense of responsibility like you?"

"That's unfair, Odelia."

"Is it?" I pointed at my battered, swollen face. "You haven't asked yet what happened to my face. Don't you even care why I look like something that ran full frontal into a bus?"

"None of my business."

I walked up to her and got almost nose to nose. "This is *all* your business. Running away doesn't change that. I'm still your daughter. I'm still your business, just as you are mine."

I was about to say more, much more, but decided it wasn't worth it. Looking down at the number on the scrap of paper, I punched the numbers into my cell phone. It was picked up on the second ring by a voice I didn't recognize.

"About time you called. Was beginning to think you didn't want your husband back."

"Is he okay?"

"He's fine. Got a little rough with us, but it wasn't anything some rope and a few punches couldn't cure. Bit of a tough guy, isn't he?"

"Please." I started to cry and stopped to get a grip on myself. "Please don't hurt him. What do you want?"

While I was talking, the cell phone beeped

that another call was coming in. The display said it was Willie. I ignored it.

"The old woman with you?"

I looked over at my mother. She stood near the house, clutching her handbag, looking as shrunken as the day I saw her in the hospital.

"Yes."

"Get her to tell you where the money is. When you deliver the money, we'll deliver your husband."

"Grady? Is this you?"

The person on the other end laughed. "Sorry to disappoint you, but this is not Littlejohn. And don't even think about getting the chief involved. No police. Just you and the money. You have twelve hours. We'll call you in an hour or so to see how you're doing."

I panicked. Who knew how much money Leland had hidden? After paying off Les Morgan, maybe there was only a few thousand left. "But what if there is no money? Or not enough?"

"Then let's keep it simple." He laughed. "Make it two hundred thousand dollars. Anything left, you can consider it a tip." He laughed again, then was gone.

When the cell phone in my hand rang, I jumped. It was Willie, trying me again.

"What's going on, little mama?"

I started sobbing.

"Slow down and tell me. I heard you were assaulting your mother in the front yard."

"Huh?" Sniff. "How?"

"Mrs. Rielley. I left my number on a note, letting her know I could come by later when she got home. She called me when she saw you and your mother having a ruckus. Said her dog was going crazy."

I looked across the street and saw the Q-tip coiffure of Mrs. Rielley poking out from behind her curtains.

"She also said you struck Grace. I hit the road immediately."

"I did not hit my mother." I snuffled. "At least not yet."

I told Willie about Greg and the car and the phone number.

"Hang tight, I'm almost there. Don't do anything."

While I waited, my mother went into the house, saying she was calling Clark and Grady. I wanted to tell her not to bother calling Grady but didn't. I didn't care who in the hell she called.

Less than two minutes after he called, Willie pulled up in front of the house. I ran to him and told him everything that had happened.

"Is your mother inside?"

"Yes. And I'm about to go inside and beat the location of that money out of her."

"Not sure I blame you, little mama. But let's try a less brutal approach first."

Before I went inside, I held up the phones. "I understand why they left my phone, but why Greg's?"

The left corner of Willie's mouth turned upward. "So you couldn't track him. These phones can be tracked in emergencies."

I stared at him. I'd heard that before and seen it done on TV shows but always took a lot of that with a grain of salt. Until now. "Is it accurate?"

"To within a certain distance, say a hundred meters or so. It's used by emergency personnel like 911 operators and the police."

"Can you do it?"

"It's highly illegal, little mama, except in emergencies, by authorized personnel."

I raised an eyebrow at him. "Can you do it?"

"Without a phone to track, no." Willie pointed at the phones in my hand.

"What about the number they gave me?"

"We can try, but I'm guessing that number and phone are disposables and were tossed shortly after you called them. You watch.

When they call you back, it will be on a different line or from a pay phone." He took the paper from me.

"Oh, Willie, what can we do?"

I took a few paces up and down the drive. Willie got on his phone.

"You calling your people?"

"No, I'm calling Mrs. Rielley." He turned and waved at the Rielley house. The figure behind the curtains waved back. "Hi, Mrs. Rielley. Just calling to let you know everything is okay over here. Grace and Odelia got into a little mother-daughter tussle, is all."

He talked a bit more to Mrs. Rielley, then made another call, turning away from me as he talked to someone in Spanish. Finally, he turned his attention back to me.

"Mrs. Rielley didn't see anything regarding the car. Said she was in the back and only looked out her front window when Coco started going crazy."

"You asked her if she saw the kidnapping?"

"No, I didn't. Just asked if she noticed any cars coming and going in the driveway here in the last hour or so. The other call was to my office, to see about rounding up the cash, just in case the old lady doesn't have it."

I started crying. "Thank you, Willie. Greg and I will repay you once we get back home."

He put his arms around me and held me tight. "It's going to be okay, little mama. We're going to get him back, one way or the other."

"It's the other I'm worried about."

When we ended our comforting embrace, I looked at the phone in my hand, willing it to ring. The sight of it gave me another idea.

"Willie, if I gave you my BlackBerry number, could you trace that?"

He nodded.

"My BlackBerry was in my purse, and they took the purse with the car. I keep the phone in a side pocket, not in the same place as I keep my personal phone, so they might not have spotted it."

"Was it turned on? It has to be turned on to work."

I thought about the last time I had used the BlackBerry, then remembered it ringing that morning when Steele had called and I had ignored it. "Yes, I think so."

While Willie called the magical fairies he kept on retainer and gave them my Black-Berry number and the number on the paper, Clark drove up to the house. Willie walked towards the back of the house to keep his conversation out of earshot of Clark.

"Is Mom inside?"

"I supposed she called you," I said as soon as he climbed out of his car. "Did she tell you that Greg's missing?"

"Greg?"

Clark looked even more haggard than he had the day before. When he saw my beat-up face, he froze in his tracks. "Yes, just minutes ago."

I brought him up to speed. I wasn't going to, considering what the guy had told me on the phone, but I knew my mother would say something.

"Jesus," Clark said. "Could this day get any worse?"

"They said not to get you involved, so don't. Just get Mom to get the money, and Willie and I will make the exchange."

"It might not be that simple, Odelia. These guys mean business."

"If we don't give them two hundred thousand dollars, Greg is toast. You want *that* on your conscience?"

Clark rubbed a rough hand over his tired face. "Odelia, Brenda Bixby's dead. We found her stuffed in the trunk of her car."

The news caused me to stagger. Clark steadied me. "Considering your assault, you're lucky to be alive."

I looked at my half brother, heavy tears running down my face. "I'm sorry about Brenda, but maybe 'these guys' include our brother. Has that crossed your mind?"

Clark blew out air of frustration and looked around for a hole to drop into. As much as I hated being in my shoes with a missing husband, I really didn't envy him either.

I poked Clark hard in the chest several times while I spoke my next words. "Trust me, Clark, I'm going to do whatever I have to do to make sure Greg doesn't join Brenda in the hereafter. And if that means bringing down baby brother, or even you, tough noogies."

THIRTY-ONE

I stomped up the back steps and into the house. My mother was nowhere to be seen. I headed upstairs, where there were three bedrooms. I glanced in the first one. A police uniform in a dry cleaners bag hung from the closet door. Must be Clark's room. A small, unused bedroom was next to it, separated by a large bathroom. At the front of the house was the master bedroom. It was large and sunny and held twin beds with cannonball posts. Each bed had a navy blue bedskirt with matching quilts in rust, dark green, and blue. On one of the beds sat my mother, staring down at her hands as they rested in her lap.

"It's time, Mom," I said, trying to keep my voice even and devoid of the anger and fear eating my gut. "Time for you to come clean about a lot of things — about the money, Les Morgan, everything."

She didn't respond. If not for the occasional blink of an eye, I would have thought she'd expired and forgot to fall over. I fought the urge to grab her and shake her until her dentures were dust.

"Clark's here. He just told me that Brenda Bixby, that reporter, was found dead. She'd been murdered, Mom. And my husband . . ." I had to pause to choke back nervous bile. "Greg might end up the same way."

"How much did they ask for, Odelia? Those people holding my son-in-law — how much?"

"Two hundred thousand. Willie's raising it for us. I'm sure you don't have that kind of money."

"No, I'll cover it. There's enough. That money has been a problem for a long time." She looked at me. "I always knew Leland had money hidden somewhere. He was afraid I'd take it and run off again. Later, he was afraid Grady would take it and leave, or that I'd give it to Grady. Grady was never happy here. Leland didn't tell me where he'd put it until right before he died. I should have taken it to the bank then instead of letting those fool rumors run wild."

I sat on the other bed opposite her. "I overheard Grady talking about it last night with Brenda, Mom. He said he saw you get fifty thousand out for Les Morgan. He knows where it is and is planning on stealing it."

"Grady knows no such thing. I'm not blind. I saw him watching me, so I moved it."

"Was Les Morgan blackmailing you about the Brown drug business?"

"Yes." She moved her head up and down slowly. "He said he'd ruin Clark and Grady if I didn't pay him. I met him in the maze before it opened and handed it over." She paused to catch her breath.

I looked in the mirror of the dresser and saw Clark's reflection. He was standing in the doorway, listening.

"I couldn't find my way out of the maze," Grace continued, rubbing her hands together. Her voice fluctuated, rising and lowering every few words, like she couldn't quite get the volume right. "Kept going around in circles until I thought I'd go crazy. Then I saw him — Les — flat on his back with that spear thing through him."

She looked up and saw Clark. "They're not connected, you know, the money and the murder. Whoever is after Leland's money didn't kill Les Morgan."

"You saw the killer, didn't you, Mom?" I asked.

Her nod was barely visible, but it was a nod just the same.

"And you tried to cover the prints on the pole."

"Yes."

Clark came into the room. "It's okay, Mom. The lab was able to identify some of the prints. We took Troy Morgan into custody a couple of hours ago." He looked at me. "I came by the house to take Mom in for more questioning."

"Troy?" I looked at Clark in disbelief, then back at Mom. "It was *Troy* you were protecting?"

My mother started weeping. "He's just a boy, and a good boy. Closest I'll ever come to having a grandson. If Troy killed his daddy, he must have had a good reason."

I leaned forward and took my mother's hands. She didn't resist. "You saw Troy Morgan kill his father?"

"When I circled back, Troy was standing over Les with his hands on the pole." Her voice cracked. "Then he ran off."

"So you were trying to help Les?"

"I could see he was dead, so I tried to help the boy the best I knew how. I scooped up some blood and smeared it on the pole. I thought it might get rid of Troy's prints."

"Did Troy take the money you gave Les?"

"I . . . I don't know."

I patted my mother's hands. "I'm going to get a call in about an hour about where to drop the money. Can you have it by then?"

She nodded. This time it was a definite, strong nod.

"I'll help you, Odelia," Clark said, moving deeper into the room.

I got up and faced him. "I told you, no police. Willie and I will handle it." When he started to protest, I held up a hand. "No, and that's final. Besides, you have enough on your plate. Why don't you help Mom find the money before you take her to the station?"

Again, Clark started to protest, this time with more muscle. "Odelia, no. This is police work. It's too dangerous for you and Willie."

I grabbed my brother by the front of his shirt and yanked him to me, my face turned upward towards his. "Trust me, Clark, you do not want to screw with me right now. We're going after Greg, and that's final. You do your job. I'll do mine." Renee Stevens wasn't the only one who could wield a machete when the need arose.

We heard footsteps coming up the stairs. I

released Clark from my clutches. It was Willie. He nodded to me. I didn't know if that meant he had the money or Greg's location — maybe both.

"Clark is taking Mom to the station," I told him. "We'll wait for the call and follow the directions to get Greg back."

"Sounds good to me."

Clark stared at the two of us. I could tell he wanted to be the heavy but in the end decided against it. He left the room.

Mom had gone to the window. With her hands on the sill, she looked out, her back with its sagging shoulders turned to us. Clark returned, holding something wrapped in cloth.

"You know how to handle a gun?" he asked Willie.

"I've been to a shooting range a few times. Not a bad shot, if I say so myself."

"Take this. Just in case." Clark opened the wrapping to display a polished handgun half the size of the one Willie usually carried. "It's already loaded."

Willie solemnly nodded in understanding and took the gun from Clark carefully, like it was a newborn babe. "Just in case," he repeated.

"Okay, Mom," Clark said to Grace. "Let's round up that money so these folks can get

Greg back."

Willie and I went back downstairs to wait. I filled him in on the Troy situation.

"Do you buy that the boy broke the shaft of the flagpole and stuck his father with it?" he asked me.

"Not really. Although kids have been known to murder."

I got up from the sofa and paced. The waiting was killing me in a slow, torturous death. I wanted to be on the road, tracking down the scum who had Greg, but I couldn't go anywhere until I had the money and knew where to go. I worked on the murder puzzle to keep my mind occupied.

"And even though Troy was running ahead of Tara," I told Willie, "it wouldn't have given him time to think about it, let alone go back and do the deed."

"That's what I'm thinking."

"My guess," I told Willie, "is that Troy ran back, saw his father on the ground, and tried to help him. My mother, already confused, mistakenly thought Troy had just stabbed Les."

I noticed that Willie was crossing and uncrossing his legs every few minutes with nervous energy.

"You know, Willie, I'm convinced someone knew about the drugs and the blackmail and was laying in wait for Les to cash in."

"A quick kill, so to speak, on many levels."

"So to speak." I stopped pacing and fiddled with some knickknacks on the mantle. "Grady could have known about both. And he might have told Cathy, but she was at the vegetable stand when the murder happened. Tara's mystery man might have known about the exchange, but how or why would he know about the blackmail money?"

"What about Joan Cummings? Any idea yet how she ties into all this?"

"Not a clue. She was at the station that morning, so she couldn't have committed the murder. But someone tipped her off about something so she could get Marty out of the way."

"Grady could have told Brenda, and Brenda told Joan."

"Whoever the killer is, they'd have to have a tie somehow to Joan, either directly or indirectly."

"Hate to say this, little mama, but all roads seem to circle back to Grady."

"Yes, I know." I turned, one hand on the mantle, and looked at Willie. We could hear footsteps crisscrossing the floor overhead. "Maybe the blackmail and drug money wasn't enough for him, and he decided to go after the rest of Leland's stash before hitting the road."

"But how would he know about the black-mail payoff in the first place — unless he and Les Morgan were connected some-how?"

"Grady could have set up the blackmail plan with Morgan to find out where Mom kept the cash, then double-crossed Les at the payoff location, killing him and taking all the money." I held out an index finger, moving it like a baton, as I pieced together my patchwork thoughts. "You know, Grady was the first official to arrive on the scene." I did a lap of pacing in front of the fireplace. "But why would he kill Brenda if they were going to run off together?"

"Lover's remorse? He didn't need her anymore? She knew too much?" Willie threw out a lot of good possibilities. "She was just too damn annoying?"

"Thing is, Willie, it didn't sound like Grady on the phone earlier. And the guy said he wasn't Grady."

"It could have been Grady lying to you and disguising his voice."

Even though I didn't want to think about a murderer in the family tree, I had to admit Willie was right.

Clark and Mom came back downstairs.

Clark dropped a small gym bag at my feet. "There's the money, all two hundred thousand. She had it packed away all over the upstairs like a squirrel with winter nuts. Who knows, probably more where that came from." Mom looked down at the floor as he spoke. "I'm taking Mom to the station. Call me with any news. I'll make sure I answer my phone, no matter what's going on."

Once Clark and Mom were gone, I opened the bag. Inside was a lot of cash, mostly hundreds, neatly wrapped in small bundles, fastened with everything from rubber bands and string to large paper clips. I took a few stacks out. All the bills were old, some wrinkled. They smelled slightly of mildew.

My phone rang. I pulled it out of my shirt pocket, took a deep breath, and answered.

"Got the money?" It was the same voice I'd heard earlier.

Willie got up and came close. He whispered, "Tell him you need more time." I nodded in understanding.

"No, but we're working on it. Should have it soon. I need a few more hours."

"Old lady not talking?"

"You know how difficult she can be."

"Never had the pleasure, but I've heard stories." He chuckled.

"And Clark's been hanging around. You said you didn't want any police involved."

"You'd think the chief would have his hands full, especially with the new murder."

"I want to talk to my husband."

"Not possible."

"I need to know he's still alive."

There was a pause, some scuffling, then heavy breathing.

"Sweetheart?"

My heart leapt out of my chest at the sound of his voice. "Greg! Are you all right?"

"Yes." More scuffling, and he was gone. My heart stopped.

"I'll call back, Mrs. Stevens." It was the voice of the original caller. "You'd better get your hands on that money."

"You sure that was Greg?" Willie asked after I finished the call.

"Yes, but the caller mentioned a new murder. Didn't say anything about Brenda, just that Clark should have his hands full with the *new* murder."

"Could be these guys did Brenda. Could be there's another body we don't know about yet."

"You said *guys.* You definitely think it's more than one?"

Willie shrugged. "Would be too difficult for only one person. Someone had to drive

421

the rental car, and someone would have to guard Greg while they drove. And how did they get here? Unless they walked through those woods behind the house, someone had to drive a car here."

"The guy did reference 'us' when he called earlier."

"There would have to be at least two. One could have subdued Greg, then drove the rental, while the other followed in their vehicle. Three would be best to do a job like this."

I shook my head to clear it. "Geez, even if one is Grady, who in the hell is the other, or others, with Brenda dead? Could one be Clem Brown? He would know about the drug money, but why would he steal from his own business? And how would he know about the fifty thousand in blackmail money unless he was in with Les and/or Grady?"

Willie gave it some thought. "Could be Clem decided to cash in for himself. Steal from the family and make it look like someone from the outside."

There were just too many possibilities. My brain felt like an old piece of luggage that had been stuffed with one too many things and wouldn't close.

Willie's phone rang. We both went on alert. After listening a bit, he asked me,

"Have some paper and pencil handy?"

I dashed into the kitchen and came back with a pen and a piece of paper towel. Willie scribbled something down on the towel, then closed his phone.

"It's show time, little mama."

Thirty-Two

As soon as we got in the car, Willie tried to hand me Clark's gun.

"I don't want that."

"Take it. You might need it."

The last thing I wanted was to hold another gun. Once had been enough. "No."

"If someone's about to shoot Greg and I'm not around, how are you going to stop them? With your good looks?"

I took the gun.

Willie started the engine. Before taking off, he punched some information into the GPS in his dashboard. According to the computer, Greg was only about seven miles away.

"This isn't his exact location," Willie explained, "but it's close enough to hopefully figure it out from there. Pray it's in the middle of nowhere, with few buildings. That will narrow down our hunt."

As the GPS guided us through the town, I

caught sight of a familiar vehicle. It was Tara Brown's minivan parked at a gas station.

"Willie, turn around. That's Tara. I'm sure of it."

"Thought you and Greg already talked to her today."

"We did, and we're both sure she's about to make like a rabbit and run. And you never know — she might have been one of the kidnappers. She's afraid of her husband. He might have coerced her into something."

Willie made a U-turn and headed back. "What's she doing, filling up way over here? Out of her way, isn't it?"

"Not if she's about to get on the interstate."

Willie pulled in front of the minivan, blocking it. Tara had just finished filling her tank and was coming around from the back to the driver's side. Jumping out of the SUV, I met her there. The sight of me made her drop her wallet.

"Taking a trip?" I asked, standing in front of her door.

She bent down to get the wallet. When she stood up, her face was flushed. "No, just getting gas."

"As I recall, there are one or two gas stations closer to the farm. Less expensive ones, too."

She didn't look at me. "I told you all I'm going to."

"No, you haven't. You see, since we last had that chat, someone snatched my husband. Remember him?"

Tara's head snapped up, her eyes full of fear.

"And Brenda Bixby — the woman all cozy with Grady last night at the North Woods — has been found dead."

At this last bit of news, Tara Brown turned so white I thought she'd need a transfusion.

"I'm making a wild stab here, Tara. I'm guessing you're not just running from Clem Brown. I think you know who killed Les Morgan, maybe even Brenda Bixby. Maybe you're afraid you're next."

She looked around like a caged animal. "Please. You don't understand."

"You running off to meet your new man, Tara? Hoping he'll protect you, take you away from all this?"

This time, she went so pale she was nearly transparent. She looked around, scared out of her mind. "It wasn't supposed to happen like this. Please let me go."

"What wasn't supposed to happen, Tara? The killings?"

She went silent.

"Tell me, and I'll let you go."

She studied my face to see if I was telling the truth. I wasn't sure myself.

She cleared her throat. "No one was supposed to die. That's what he told me."

"Who? Clem? Your lover?"

"Clem's not involved. With the drugs, yes, but not with the killing. He knows nothing about it."

"So it was the guy I saw you with at the North Woods?"

She nodded. "He knew we were making the drug exchange that day in the maze. The plan was, after I gave Les the money, Frankie. . . ."

I stopped her. "Frankie? Frankie McKenna?"

Again she nodded, but this time it was served up with a flood of tears. I took her roughly by the arm and guided her around the minivan to the pump side, using the vehicle as a shield from prying eyes on the street.

"He used to do the pickups. We became close." Tara wiped her face with the sleeve of her sweater. "But something happened in Boston. I don't know what, but he said he had to leave. He came here to say goodbye, but instead we decided to go away together. We waited until this week because of the money pickup. We were going to use that to start over."

Willie leaned out of the passenger's window. "Everything okay, Odelia? We need to hurry."

"Hunky dory," I said, not taking my eyes off Tara. I indicated for her to continue and to make it fast.

"The plan was for Frankie to steal the drug money from Les — just knock him out or something like that. He never said anything about killing anyone." Her tears became sobs with hiccup chasers. With my strong urging, she continued. "While Frankie was hidden in the maze, he saw old lady Littlejohn handing money over to Les. Something about blackmail. When he took the drug money from Les, he also took the other money." She looked into my face, willing me to believe her. "The killing was self-defense. Frankie said Les came after him with a knife." But even as she said the words, I could tell she didn't believe them herself.

"So why didn't the two of you just leave? You had both the drug money and the drugs, as well as the fifty grand from Grace Littlejohn."

"I begged him to, but he said if the old lady had cash like that, she'd have more." Again, she ran her sleeve across her face, this time mopping both her eyes and nose. "Last night at the North Woods, I did see Grady's SUV parked at the next cabin. I pointed it out to Frankie and told him that Grady was Grace's son."

She buried her face in her hands. "Today, when Grady went missing, I was worried Frankie did something else."

"You mean *killed* someone else, don't you?"

She started crying harder.

"Do you know where Frankie is right now?"

She shook her head. "I only met him at the North Woods. We were supposed to leave together tomorrow."

"But you're leaving now, without him, right?"

"Please, I beg you. Let me go."

"What does Joan Cummings have to do with this?"

"Joan?" Tara seemed genuinely surprised. "Nothing that I know of."

Back in the SUV, Willie drove like a bat out of hell to make up lost time. Along the way, I reported everything Tara had told me.

"Frankie McKenna, the original corpse." Willie shook his head. "Sounds like he got into hot water in Boston and had to disappear. I'll bet he planted his ID on Les, hoping people would think Les killed him and stole his identity."

After going through Holmsbury, the GPS guided us over rolling roads and past clusters of homes until we were in farmland.

"Isn't this the way to the Blue Lobster?" asked Willie.

The road we were traveling was familiar. "It's also the way to the Brown farm."

Sure enough, soon we reached the busy intersection with the restaurant and Buster's, but according to the GPS we still had a few miles to go.

"That's where the Browns live." I pointed at Farm House Road as we passed it.

After Farm House Road, the road we traveled was unpopulated except for fields on both sides bordered by barbed-wire fencing. I glanced at the GPS — less than two miles more. According to the map on the screen, we were approaching a couple of roads. We were to turn left at the second one — Cold Pond Road. The first road we approached wasn't much more than a gravel drive with trees on either side. A small street sign on a post said it was called Hollow Road. Here, the barbed-wire fence ended.

When the GPS told us to make a left, Willie turned onto a narrow dirt road designated as Cold Pond. Like the previous one, there were thick trees and bushes on either side. Our destination was still up ahead, but not far.

Willie spotted something to the right. It looked like a short drive that was partially overgrown. He drove past it, stopped the SUV, then backed the vehicle into the drive far enough so that it was difficult to see it from the road. The SUV now faced forward, ready for a quick getaway.

"From here, we'll go on foot through the woods," he whispered. "You carry the money. If you have to, use it as a shield or a weapon. And stay behind me. I'll move forward slowly. If the coast is clear, I'll motion for you to follow. Keep your eyes peeled for any sort of building, no matter how small."

Following Willie's example, I got out of the vehicle and gently shut the door, but not all the way. He moved silently from his side to where I stood.

"Put your phone on silent," he continued to direct, "and stick it in your pocket. Put the gun in one hand and keep the other free."

I did as he said, happy to have Willie in charge of this portion of the program. My final act was to sling the bag over my left shoulder.

We moved through the woods slowly and methodically, Willie a few steps ahead, me following behind when he gave me a green light. Each section of travel took us further away from the main road, into thicker growth. I was still sore from my assault and earlier marathon through the woods, and my face hurt like hell. But I kept up, determined to finish the mission or die trying.

At one point, Willie didn't motion for me to follow. Instead, he pointed off to the left. It took a few seconds for me to see it, but there it was, a cabin or shack of some kind. I could just make it out through the trees. I nodded to Willie, letting him know I'd spotted it. Gesturing for me to stay put, he moved closer to it, never leaving my sight. Once he felt it safe, he motioned for me to join him. I scurried over the ground carefully until I reached him. Once there, he pointed again. This time I saw three vehicles. I recognized all three. One was my rental car. One was the truck parked in front of the cabin at the North Woods — McKenna's truck. The third was the old rusty truck that had tried to run me down earlier.

I wanted to rush the cabin. My eagerness to see Greg alive and unharmed fought with my better judgment to wait and follow

Willie's instructions. For a change, my good sense won out.

Willie pointed at the vehicles and mouthed, "Grady?"

I shook my head. I pointed at the old truck and pantomimed someone hitting my face. I pointed to the second truck and mouthed, "McKenna."

We watched the cabin for signs and sounds of movement but saw none. The cabin was at an angle to our view. To the left was a short wall without windows. Next to it was parked the old truck. The other wall was longer and had a high, narrow window much like the cabin at the North Woods. It looked like the main window and door were on the opposite side, facing the other cars. From where we crouched, it was impossible to see who or how many were in there. We waited some more, but no one came out that we could see. Willie could have put an Indian tracker to shame with his stealth and patience.

Willie again gestured for me to stay put. Knowing my tendency to ignore orders, he made the gesture several times to underscore its importance. Then he took off, moving slowly and quietly from tree to tree until he was next to the cabin, directly under the window. I could tell he was listening, trying to pick up any sounds from inside. He held his gun ready.

I watched as Willie started to move around the corner and down the shorter side wall, squishing himself against it. When the old truck obstructed my view of him, I got nervous, allowing myself to breathe only when he once again came into my line of vision. His attention was on the old truck. I watched as he reached inside the back and checked something out. Then he looked my way, again giving me the signal to stay put.

Satisfied that I understood his signal, Willie started back the other way, down the longer wall until he reached the corner and peeked around it. Then he turned the corner, once again disappearing from my sight. Remaining behind a couple of trees, I shifted from foot to foot in a nervous dance.

While Willie was skulking around the far corner, I heard a door open, and a man walked from the cabin to the black truck. It was the guy I'd seen at the North Woods — Tara Brown's lover — Frankie McKenna. In his hand was a plastic grocery bag.

"Just gonna get another pack of cigarettes," he called to someone in the cabin. He went to the truck, opened the passenger's side, and stashed the bag inside. After closing the door, he leaned against the side of the truck, pulled out a pack of cigarettes, and lit one.

I looked again for Willie, but nothing. It drove me nuts not to know what he was up to. I glanced at McKenna, watching him puff away like he was on a coffee break. Once finished, he crushed the butt in the dirt at his feet and headed back towards the cabin. "Let's give the bitch a call," I heard him say, "and see if she's got the money yet. I'm sick and tired of waiting. I want to get out of here."

There was no way Willie didn't hear that, too. It was then I saw him come back around the corner. He motioned to me and I motioned back, letting him know I was retreating. He nodded in agreement.

Knowing my phone was going to ring and I would be expected to answer it, I moved farther away from the cabin, still keeping it in sight. When I thought I was far enough away, I crouched behind some large bushes. Shortly after I arrived, Willie joined me.

"When he calls," Willie whispered, "tell him you have the money and are ready to meet him."

"That's the guy from the motel," I whispered back. "That's Frankie McKenna — and he's probably the guy who chased me."

"The cabin has a small bedroom in the

back. That's where they have Greg."

"Is he okay?" My heart skipped a beat, and I found it hard to keep my voice down.

"Shh, yes, he seems fine. He's tied to the bed. There's just the guy and a woman, I think. No sign of anyone else."

"What did the woman look like?"

"I didn't see her, just heard her voice."

Willie glanced at the cabin. All was still.

"When you get the call, arrange to meet him. I'm hoping he goes alone. In fact, I'm pretty sure he will. With him out of the way, I can take her."

"But how could he deliver Greg if he doesn't take him along?"

Willie glanced at me, then turned back to stare at the cabin.

Understanding sucked the air out of my lungs and turned my world momentarily black. "You don't think they're going to make the exchange, do you?"

Willie turned to look me full in the face. "No, Odelia, I don't. I think they'll take the money and kill Greg. They probably would have killed you, too."

I felt my insides spasm at the realization of what Willie was telling me. "But they said they'd let him go."

Willie moved closer and put his gun-free hand tight over my mouth. Then he whispered in my ear. "Grady's in the back of that old truck. He's alive, but barely."

I screamed in silence against his hand.

"Now here's what we're going to do." Willie kept his hand over my mouth while he whispered. "As soon as that bastard leaves, I'll move around the back and enter through the bedroom window. The screen on it is loose, and the window is open. You will go around the other way and watch the door. If she comes out for any reason, you're to pull the gun on her. Don't even think twice about it, just do it. And if she points a gun at you, shoot her. Got it? Just shoot, don't hesitate."

I nodded. He pulled his hand away.

We waited a few more minutes before my cell phone silently vibrated in my shirt pocket. "Hello," I said, keeping my voice down.

"Why are you whispering?" the caller demanded.

"I don't want anyone to hear me."

"Good. You know where the Blue Lobster is?"

"Yes."

"At the intersection, turn south off the main road. You'll pass behind the restaurant. Follow it for about three miles until you cross a small stone bridge. Just beyond the bridge is a picnic area with tables under the trees. Meet me there in thirty minutes with the money."

"And my husband?"

"You bring the two hundred thousand, I'll bring your husband. But you'd better come alone."

"Yes, of course."

When we hung up, I told Willie about the instructions. Then I leaned against a tree and took several deep breaths while Willie kept watch.

"There he goes," he whispered to me.

I moved forward and watched McKenna climb into his truck and drive off. As Willie had predicted, he did not take Greg along.

"Won't he see your SUV on the way out?"

"Not if we're lucky. Someone coming down the road might, but not someone leaving from this direction. Keep your fingers crossed that this asshole is sloppy and not very observant."

They were crossed. So were my toes inside my sneakers.

"Dial the chief. If you reach him, give me the phone." I did as he instructed, handing it off as soon as Clark came on the line.

"Chief, the killer is not the boy. The real killer is on the move right now." Keeping his voice low, Willie gave him the directions to the meeting and a description and partial plate of the truck. "We're at a cabin at the end of Pond Road. Send an ambulance. Grady's hurt bad."

"Cold Pond Road," I corrected in a whisper, keeping my eyes on the cabin.

"That's Cold Pond Road. We're going in after Greg."

"What did he say?"

"Don't know. Hung up before he could say anything."

A soon as Willie felt it safe, we took off for the cabin, keeping low and quiet. We left the bag of money behind. Willie went towards the back of the house and disappeared around the corner. I pressed myself against the short wall, splitting my attention between the front of the cabin and the road, just in case McKenna came back. I used the old truck as cover. I glanced into the truck bed. Grady was covered in a tarp. I pulled it back and gasped. He looked dead to me, then I heard him moan softly. It wasn't much more than a mew from a newborn kitten. I gently pulled the tarp back so he could get more air.

"Help's coming, Grady," I whispered. "Hang in there."

"If you're the help, he's really in trouble."

THIRTY-THREE

I started to turn but was stopped by the feel of a gun pressed into the middle of my back. "Not so fast," I was told. "Hands in the air where I can see them."

I did as directed. Clark's gun dangled from my right hand. My assailant removed the gun, then told me to turn around. When I did, I was face to face with Joan Cummings. She didn't seem surprised to see my battered face.

"We need to get Grady to a doctor."

Keeping the gun on me, Joan's eyes did a quick scan of the surrounding woods. "Who's with you?"

"No one," I lied. "I'm alone."

"You expect me to believe that?"

"McKenna told me to come alone."

"He also told you to meet him at the picnic area. How'd you even find this place?"

"I tracked it through my phone."

"Couldn't have. We dumped your phone."

"Not my BlackBerry. It was in my tote bag in the car."

"Only emergency personnel can do that." She stared at me with such coldness, the hair on my neck stood and tried to run away. "How many cops are out there?" She jerked her chin towards the woods.

"None." This time I didn't have to lie.

"I don't believe you."

A light wind rustled the branches over-head. Joan tensed. "Let's take this inside." She waved the gun, indicating for me to move towards the front of the cabin.

"But what about Grady?" Although I was concerned for Grady, I also knew the more time we spent outside, the more time I could buy Willie to rescue Greg.

"Grady got what he deserved. Now move!"

Doing as I was told, I shuffled to the front and entered the cabin.

It was a small, rustic building with pine walls and rough plank flooring. Next to the front door was a window looking out to the parking area. A kitchenette was built along the wall to our right. Opposite it was a table with three mismatched chairs and a window looking out at a small clearing. The fourth wall, the one opposite the front door, held two doors on either side of a wood-burning stove that was currently cold. One door was ajar, giving me a view of a tiny bathroom. The other door was almost closed, but not quite. It probably led to the bedroom where they'd stashed Greg. I wasn't sure if the door had been left open by Joan or if Willie had opened it a crack to watch. I would have to make sure my eyes didn't wander to it, looking for signs of Willie and Greg.

Besides the table and chairs, the cabin was sparsely furnished with an old floral-print sofa oozing stuffing and a brown leather recliner with a torn seat. The rips in the recliner's covering had been haphazardly mended with silver duct tape. In a corner was Greg's wheelchair.

"Where's Greg?"

"In the back, trussed like a rodeo calf."

With her free hand, Joan pushed me towards the recliner. When I plopped down, my butt felt the springs in the lumpy seat up close and personal. Joan stood between the front door and window but cautiously out of view from the outside. She kept the gun trained on me. Every few seconds she looked out, totally unaware that the cavalry was already in the cabin, just waiting for a chance to spring without causing bloodshed.

She pulled a cell phone out of her pocket

and punched at it. When no one answered, she scowled. "He must be on his way back. He's not going to like being stood up."

Quick as a bunny, I weighed my options. I could tell her that Frankie McKenna was being met by the police, or I could let her think he was coming back mad as a wet hen. I finally settled on a third option.

"McKenna didn't take Greg to the meeting. He never intended to make an exchange, did he?"

At the mention of McKenna's name, Joan did a double take. "What do *you* know about Frankie?"

"I know he's been seeing Tara Brown on the side. I know he killed Les Morgan and stole the drugs, drug money, *and* the blackmail money that my mother paid Les Morgan."

"Then you know too much, and that's going to cost you when Frankie comes back. I guess one beating wasn't enough. This time he won't be so gentle."

"If he comes back."

When I received another double take, I continued. "He double-crossed me, Joan. He never intended to trade my husband for the money. What makes you think he's not double-crossing *you?* He could have planned to take the money I was bringing and hit the road. Tara Brown was already on the run when I last saw her. In fact, she was gassing up before getting on the interstate."

At that point, it crossed my mind that Tara wasn't running from both Frankie and Clem, but only from Clem. She might have been rendezvousing with McKenna after he took the ransom money. But the white-hot fright I read on her face at the mention of Brenda's death had seemed genuine. If she wasn't afraid of McKenna, she was a damn good actress.

"You don't know what you're talking about." Joan wrapped the comment in a dull sneer.

"No? Then what was in the bag McKenna put in the truck just before he left for our meeting?" I was running my mouth on guesses, but it was better than running on empty.

"He had no bag."

"Right before he left, he went out for a smoke. Correct? He had a plastic bag with him, which he dumped in the truck. Dollars to donuts he's not coming back to the cabin, Joan. I'll bet his plan was to take the money I was bringing and add it to what he took from the cabin. Then *adios,* leaving you holding the bag for the murders and kidnapping."

"Frankie's my cousin. We're close. He'd never do such a thing. Without me, he'd never have gotten this far."

"Were you feeding him information like you were Brenda?" When I received no response, I continued. "I know he worked for the drug supplier from Boston, at least he did until recently. That's how he met Tara."

"I was never involved in his drug business. I hate drugs."

"Ah, yes, your son Marty. Quite the little druggie, isn't he?"

Joan Cummings glared at me in between checking out the window. "You leave my boy out of this."

"But you gave Marty pot the morning of the murder, didn't you? Did Frankie tell you to keep him out of the way?"

"Frankie was looking out for Marty, just as he looks out for me. It was his idea to share the ransom money with me. So see," she said with conviction, "there's no double-cross."

"His idea to share, or his idea to set you up?"

She leveled the gun at my face. "You talk too much."

Guilty as charged.

Sweat soaked my shirt and ran down the small of my back, into my panties. If Willie made a move at that moment, it would be a race to see if Joan's bullet reached me before his bullet reached Joan. So I babbled on, buying time and looking for a split-second opportunity to turn the tables.

"How was Grady involved, Joan? Frankie may be your cousin, but Grady's my brother. I'd like to know."

Joan cackled. "It was Grady who gave clear sailing, as you put it, to Frankie. He was paid well for it, too." She glanced back out the window. "When Les took over the route, he helped him."

"Even though Les was Cathy Morgan's ex-husband?"

"On the take is on the take — doesn't matter to a dirty cop who's paying. And Cathy was just as involved as Grady, make no mistake about that. She was probably the one who pushed him to do it."

An unsavory idea entered my skull. "Les, Grady, and Cathy were working together to get Leland's hidden money, weren't they?" It made sense. Grady knew exactly when to watch Grace gather the money together. Had he not known about the blackmail, he wouldn't have known what she was planning to do with the cash.

Joan shrugged. "I'm not sure how the original blackmail idea got started. We weren't involved in that. After Les turned up dead and the money disappeared, Grady started nosing around. That led him to Frankie."

"And Brenda? What was her role?"

For the first time, Joan Cummings looked genuinely sad when she spoke. "She was just a kid reporter trying to jumpstart her career. She hooked up with Grady to get information. I tried to warn her, but she wouldn't listen. She played him, led him on. In the end, she got in the way when Frankie and Grady came to blows over the money."

"A fight McKenna obviously won."

We went silent for a few moments. It seemed like it was taking Clark forever to find us, but on the other hand, I was worried that the sight of police in the woods would cause Joan to get trigger-happy. I was sure the same thoughts were going through Greg and Willie's minds.

On the small counter in the kitchenette, I spied a messenger bag just like the one Tara had been carrying in the maze. It gave me the idea to return to my original tack. I started to point at it. The movement of my arm caused Joan to go on alert.

"Take it easy, Joan. I'm just pointing." Without lifting my arm too much, I indicated the bag. "That the bag with the money you've stolen so far?"

"You never mind about that bag."

"Check it. I'll bet it's empty now. I'll bet the money is in McKenna's truck."

"You're crazy."

"Am I? Then check it and prove me wrong."

Like termites on wood, I could tell my words, coupled with the lapse of time since McKenna had left, were eating, bit by tiny bit, into Joan's mind. Her eyes darted quickly from me to the bag to the window as she processed the possibility that she'd been had. In the end, she shook it off and made no move towards the bag.

Damn.

Then, after a glance at her watch, she said to me, "Get up and get the bag."

I got out of the recliner and covered the couple of steps towards the counter. My hand reached for the bag.

"Leave it on the counter and turn the opening in my direction," she ordered.

I did what she asked.

"Now slowly open the flap." While I complied, she took a step closer. "A little wider."

I placed one hand around the bag's strap and raised it up, holding the lower portion down with my other hand, until the bag's opening resembled a bigmouth bass.

It was empty.

"That bastard!" Joan cried.

She dashed to the counter to inspect the bag herself. When she did, she let the gun in her hand go slack. It was the chance I'd been waiting for.

With one hand still wrapped around the bag's strap, I swung it upward, catching Joan hard in the chin. As she staggered backward, I barreled into her, taking her to the floor. The gun fell from her hand.

"Willie!" I screamed.

"I'm right here, little mama."

Willie stood over me and Joan, his gun trained on Joan's head.

Thirty-Four

It felt good to be home. The trip to Massachusetts seemed like years ago, instead of just a month ago. As soon as we got home, Dev took Greg and me to dinner and gave us both a sound verbal slapping. Seth and Zee did the same. Steele didn't speak to me for nearly a week, but that was more of a blessing than a punishment. To the horror of our friends and family, we both came off the plane with battered faces.

It also felt good to be loved.

After he'd slipped through the bedroom window, Willie unbound Greg. He was about to spring on Joan when she left the cabin and returned with me marching in front of her. That left Willie waiting for the right moment to make his move.

Following Willie's directions, the state police closed in on McKenna. He put up a fight, turning the peaceful picnic spot into the OK Corral. Thankfully, it wasn't during the summer or on a weekend, so it was empty of visitors. He was killed after wounding a police officer.

Tara Brown was picked up in New Jersey and told the police what she told me. Seems she did have the sense to be frightened of both men in her life. The Brown drug biz was shut down, and Cathy, Clem, and Buster were charged with drug dealing. Buster claimed he knew nothing about it, but his brother and sister threw him under the bus the first chance they had. Sadly, Troy was moved to foster care until everything was sorted out. I couldn't help but think he was the real victim in all of this.

It came out that Joan Cummings had been selling police information to Frankie McKenna and McKenna's previous employer. When McKenna put his plan in motion regarding the drug and blackmail money, he promised her a nice cut if she helped. Originally, they'd gone to my mother's house to shake Grace down, but seeing Greg in the car had given McKenna other ideas. Like Tara, Joan claimed she only thought Frankie was going to rob Les Morgan, not kill him.

When the dust settled, the police unraveled two different schemes with two different sets of schemers — one set out to steal the drug money and the other to blackmail Grace Littlejohn. The two plans had collided that fateful morning in the corn maze, with my mother caught in the middle.

So much for peaceful country living.

Grady Littlejohn died in the back of the rusty pickup truck — the same truck that nearly killed me.

Willie left Tuesday night with Sybil by his side. Somehow he had deftly handled the police questioning, but he wasn't sticking around in case they got curious about him personally. The day of Grady's funeral, Clark asked me about Willie.

"Seems Willie left in a big hurry." The familiar voice came from behind me.

I was on the deck, looking out at the stand of birch trees behind my mother's house. I turned to see Clark dressed in a dark suit, holding a mug of coffee. Behind him in the house, friends of the family were milling about, eating coffee cake and casseroles. The small community was in shock over the string of murders and the drug bust and was doing its best to comfort each other in addition to Grace and Clark.

"He had business in New York. Something he couldn't postpone."

"I heard Sybil Johnson went with him."

"What can I say, it was love at first sight."

I gave Clark a small smile. "They do seem suited to each other."

Clark sidled up to me at the railing. "You know, Odelia, I Googled William Carter, and nothing came up on Greg's cousin. A lot of other William Carters came up, but none of them matched him. Seems odd for a man of his obvious means and talents."

"He keeps a low profile, doesn't like publicity."

"Uh-huh. So it seems." He took a sip of coffee. "Out of curiosity, I ran my gun for fingerprints. I found yours, mine, Joan's, and those that matched one William Proctor. Now *that* name rang a bell."

"I guess the next time you see Willie, you'll have to arrest him."

"Maybe, maybe not. Who knows if I'll be a cop the next time I see him — *if* I see him."

I turned to face Clark. "You retiring?"

"Might not have a choice after this. And even if the people want me to stay, I'm not sure I have the stomach for it anymore."

We heard from Clark last week. He wasn't canned, but he decided to take a leave of absence to sort things out. He said he was going to travel a bit and visit his daughters. Said he might even find his way out to California.

After Grady's death, my mother faded

considerably, though she's still as cantankerous as ever. Greg and I call her every week.
She's moving to a retirement home soon. It
was her choice, and she picked a lovely one
not too far away in New Hampshire. She
told us she didn't want to stay in Holmsbury after what had happened. She also
rounded up more of Leland's money, and
Clark set up a trust for her with it.

I still have mixed feelings about my
mother. I finally have the answer as to why
she left me all those years ago, but there's
still a hunger in my belly — an emptiness
that can't be filled with ice cream and cookies, or even by the love of a wonderful mate.
It's the hollowness of growing up a mother-
less daughter. But I can't change the past,
and Grace isn't emotionally capable of making amends. It's something I will have to
live with. Like a badly patched pothole in
the middle of the street, it jars the car, but
it's no longer a threat to the alignment.

Several weeks after returning from Massachusetts, Greg and I were at our kitchen
table having a lazy Sunday morning breakfast when our doorbell rang. Wainwright
and I answered it to find a somber Enrique
on our doorstep. He was a grown man now
and looked prosperous, reminding me of a
young Jimmy Smits.

After telling Wainwright to settle down, I asked with some worry, "Is Willie all right?"

His serious countenance changed to a wide smile, showing off the crooked teeth I'd remembered so well. *"Hola, mamacita."* His voice was cheery. He handed me an envelope.

"Come in, Enrique, I want you to meet my husband. And, by the way, congratulations on your own marriage." I reached out and gave him a big hug.

"Who's there, sweetheart?" Greg came rolling to the front door.

"This is Enrique, honey."

"Willie's Enrique?"

I introduced the two, and they shook hands.

"I've heard much about you, Greg," Enrique said, smiling. He turned to me. "I apologize, *mamacita,* but I cannot stay. I just came to deliver this." After kissing me on both cheeks, he headed down our walk and hopped into a waiting car.

Even before closing the door, Greg and I opened the envelope. Inside were a couple sheets of paper and a photo of Willie and Sybil dressed in island garb. She held a bouquet. Behind them was a beach at sunset — not just a backdrop but the real thing.

"That looks like a wedding photo, sweet-heart."

"It sure does. That was quick, wasn't it?"

"He knew what he wanted, why wait?"

The letter was short and to the point. They had gotten married and sent their love. He referenced an enclosed letter and told us to watch the news.

The other letter, a copy of one dated the day before and addressed to Anderson Cooper at CNN, said that William Proctor, former CEO of Investanet, was returning all of the millions he'd stolen while at the helm of the Internet investment company. He apologized for any hardship he'd caused and asked that the funds be distributed to the attached list of investors. He'd even enclosed a cashier's check made out to a trust set up to handle the disposition of the monies.

"This is unbelievable, Greg."

"Shows what a good woman can do to a guy." Greg pointed to something on the list of investors. "Looks like something's high-lighted."

On one of the pages of the investors list, one entry had been highlighted: Steven and Cynthia Rielley.

"Oh my gawd, Greg. The Rielleys were among the people who had money in Investanet. Willie stole from them."

"Wow, talk about a small world."

"That explains why he was so solicitous of Mrs. Rielley after he met her. Probably the first time he'd come face to face with the hardship he'd caused everyday folks."

Greg checked out the CNN letter and the list while I continued with Willie's letter. He ended by saying this didn't change his fugitive status, so he didn't know when we'd meet again. And not to worry, he still had plenty of money. The last line made me laugh out loud.

"You never know, little mama, when your conscience will bite you in the ass."

ABOUT THE AUTHOR

Like the character Odelia Grey, **Sue Ann Jaffarian** is a middle-aged, plus-size paralegal. In addition to the Odelia Grey mystery series, she is the author of the new paranormal Ghost of Granny Apples mystery series and the forthcoming vampire mystery series featuring Doug and Dodi Dedham, scheduled for release in September 2010. Sue Ann is also nationally sought after as a motivational and humorous speaker. She lives and works in Los Angeles, California.

Other titles in the Odelia Grey series include *Too Big to Miss* (2006), *The Curse of the Holy Pail* (2007), *Thugs and Kisses* (2008), and *Booby Trap* (2009).

Visit Sue Ann on the Internet at
WWW.SUEANNJAFFARIAN.COM
and
WWW.SUEANNJAFFARIAN.BLOGSPOT.COM

We hope you have enjoyed this Large Print book. Other Thorndike, Wheeler, Kennebec, and Chivers Press Large Print books are available at your library or directly from the publishers.

For information about current and upcoming titles, please call or write, without obligation, to:

Publisher
Thorndike Press
295 Kennedy Memorial Drive
Waterville, ME 04901
Tel. (800) 223-1244

or visit our Web site at:

http://gale.cengage.com/thorndike

OR

Chivers Large Print
published by BBC Audiobooks Ltd
St James House, The Square
Lower Bristol Road
Bath BA2 3SB
England
Tel. +44(0) 800 136919
email: bbcaudiobooks@bbc.co.uk
www.bbcaudiobooks.co.uk

All our Large Print titles are designed for easy reading, and all our books are made to last.